Pilgrim of Death

Felicity Pulman

momentum

First published by Random House Australia in 2008
This edition published in 2015 by Momentum
Pan Macmillan Australia Pty Ltd
1 Market Street, Sydney 2000

A CIP record for this book is available at the National Library of Australia

Pilgrim of Death: The Janna Chronicles 4

EPUB format: 9781760300234
Mobi format: 9781760300241
Print on Demand format: 9781760300296

Cover design by Raewyn Brack
Edited by Kylie Mason
Proofread by Laurie Ormond

Macmillan Digital Australia: www.macmillandigital.com.au

To report a typographical error, please visit momentumbooks.com.au/contact/

Visit www.momentumbooks.com.au to read more about all our books and to buy books online. You will also find features, author interviews and news of any author events.

Felicity Pulman is the award-winning author of numerous novels for children and teenagers, including *A Ring Through Time*, the Shalott trilogy, and *Ghost Boy*, which is now in pre-production for a movie. *I, Morgana* was her first novel for adults, inspired by her early research into Arthurian legend and her journey to the UK and France to "walk in the footsteps of her characters" before writing the Shalott trilogy – something she loves to do. Her interest in crime and history inspired her medieval crime series, The Janna Mysteries, now repackaged as The Janna Chronicles.

Recently awarded the inaugural Di Yerbury writer's fellowship, Felicity will spend several months in the UK in 2015 researching and writing the sequel to *I, Morgana*. She has many years experience talking about researching and writing her novels both in schools and to adults, as well as conducting creative writing workshops in a wide variety of genres. Felicity is married, with two children and six grandchildren, all of whom help to keep her young and technosavvy – sort of! You can find out more about Felicity on her website and blog: www.felicitypulman.com.au or on Facebook.

Also by Felicity Pulman

I, Morgana
Blood Child: The Janna Chronicles 1
Stolen Child: The Janna Chronicles 2
Unholy Murder: The Janna Chronicles 3

Chapter 1

As the small band of pilgrims passed through Wiltune, Janna saw a crowd gathered into a shouting, gesticulating knot outside a cottage ahead. At their center was a cowering wretch who groaned and howled in pain. Those standing close enough kicked out at him or stretched to pull out tufts of his hair. Dogs barked in excitement and pushed past legs to get closer, slavering over the scent of fresh blood.

Ever soft-hearted for someone in trouble, Janna quickened her steps to come to the man's aid, but was stopped by a firm hand on her arm. "Leave him be, lass," a gravelly voice advised. "There's nowt you can do for him now."

"Who is he? What's he done to deserve such treatment?" Janna strained against the pilgrim's grasp. She was angry that he seemed so lacking in compassion, but was even more furious that he had taken it upon himself to tell her what to do.

"'Tis the moneyer." The pilgrim gave a grimace of distaste. "I heard talk among the guests at the abbey about him. He's been issuing base coins, adding lead to silver to make up the weight. But he's been found out and has paid the penalty for his crime." The pilgrim looked from Janna to the fracas. "Punished, aye, but it seems his fellow countrymen will also vent their grievances, for he must have short-changed all of 'em in his time. Leave him be, lass. There's nowt you can do to help him."

Janna nodded in understanding, although she felt helpless in the face of the moneyer's pain. She knew that the penalty for moneyers who shaved coins or made them short-weight was dreadful indeed; knew also that with her knowledge of herbs and healing she might well have been able to ease his hurt. The problem was, she had neither the herbs nor the means to make up any potions or healing salves. She tried to reassure her uneasy conscience with the thought that there were others from whom the moneyer could seek help, like Sister Anne at Wiltune Abbey. The infirmarian was near at hand, and had medicaments already prepared for use.

Janna stopped struggling against the pilgrim's restraint. At once he removed his hand from her arm, and gave her a friendly smile. Like the other pilgrims she was now in company with, he was wearing a broad-brimmed hat with a tin scallop shell pinned to its brim, a sign of their pilgrimage across the ocean to the shrine of St James. He was a goblin of a man, grey-haired and hunch-shouldered under the weight of the pack he carried. She wondered why he struggled with such a burden when most of the pilgrims carried only a light pack and a walking staff.

He in turn was studying her closely. "Allow me to introduce myself properly, mistress. My name is Ulf," he said, and bobbed his head in greeting.

"And my name's Johanna, but I'm usually called Janna." Made somewhat uncomfortable by his intent gaze, Janna turned away. She was not used to being called "mistress," but she realized Ulf had been fooled by the costly gown she wore. It seemed the new apparel given to her by the nuns when she left the abbey had conferred on her a higher status that was unexpected but not necessarily unwelcome.

Ulf hesitated for a moment, as if hoping to engage her in further conversation. But Janna hung back, reluctant to pursue their acquaintance until she'd had time to decide whether or not to reveal her true identity and, with it, her own low place in society. Reason argued against it: she was now a threat to several people who had already taken steps to try to bring about her death. If traveling under the guise of a wealthy young woman could keep her safe, it was certainly worth consideration.

She lagged behind Ulf, hoping he would walk on without her. After a disappointed glance, he strode ahead, giving a series of ear-piercing whistles as he went. A huge, pale hound emerged from among the tight knot of angry townsfolk and loped obediently to its master's side. It had a smooth, short-haired coat, small pricked ears and a long tail. Noting its ferocious expression, Janna resolved to keep well away from it in the future. But Ulf seemed unafraid as he walked on, the dog pacing beside him.

Janna lingered as they moved beyond the confines of Wiltune and out across the downs, looking back for one last glimpse of the town and the abbey that had sheltered her and been her home for the past year. It was almost noon, and the sisters would be sitting down for dinner in the refectory, signing to each other to pass the fish, the salt, the butter, or whatever else was needed. Janna wondered if she'd ever see any of them again. There was great sadness in the thought.

She could no longer hear the bells, even though she strained to catch one last sound. Their constant jangle had dominated her life: the great bell that summoned everyone to prayers during the day and through the night, and the smaller bell that had regulated their lives: waking, eating and sleeping. Janna had thought she'd never get used to their sound, but in time the bells had ceased to disturb her other than as a reminder of where to go and what to do next. In their absence, the silence seemed oppressive.

She quickened her pace to catch up with the pilgrims. They were seven in number, and they all traveled on foot. Just as well, Janna thought, for she would not have been able to keep up with them had they been mounted. But their leader, a bluff and kindly man called Bernard, had welcomed her into the group, along with a girl some years younger, and had warned them that they traveled slowly to accommodate his elderly mother.

Janna hoped they would not take too long about their journey. She was on fire with impatience to reach Ambresberie, for there she would leave the pilgrims and go to the abbey to enquire after Sister Emanuelle, who was once the infirmarian there. Sister Emanuelle, whom Janna had known for most of her life only as her mother Eadgyth, the *wortwyf* who had used her knowledge to heal and care for all who came her way, and who had died because of it.

Turning her back on the life she had once known, Janna whispered a quiet goodbye to those she'd come to know and love during her stay at Wiltune Abbey, and also those outside it, like Godric, and the lord Hugh. She looked down at the fine blue dress she was wearing, and stroked the silky wool with careful fingers before raising her hand to her hair and the gauzy veil that covered it. It amused her to think that, if she met Hugh now, he would think she was a lady and worthy of his respect. She'd read the admiration in his eyes while, dressed as a lay sister, she had tended his injuries at the abbey. She was sure that, if he believed she came from a wealthy family and had a dowry to match, he would have courted her, for his fortune depended on a prestigious marriage. There was no future for him with the daughter of a lowly *wortwyf*.

The scarring memory of the last time she'd seen Godric flashed into Janna's mind. He'd been in the marketplace with Cecily, playing with Hamo. Their laughter had brightened the afternoon, but had struck a deep chill in her heart. She reminded herself once more that Godric was her friend, no more than that. If he'd found happiness with Cecily then she could only wish them a long and happy life together; it was the future that mattered to Janna now, not the past.

"I heard tell you come from Wiltune Abbey, mistress?" A voice at Janna's side dragged her back to the present. She turned to the girl who now kept pace with her.

"Yes, I've been at Wiltune for the past year," Janna confirmed, speaking in the language of the English, for that was how she'd been addressed. She struggled to remember the girl's name from Bernard's introduction. Winifred?

"What's it like, life in the abbey?" She stared at Janna with an intent expression.

"Difficult." Janna considered for a moment, wondering if she'd been unfair. "But not if you have a vocation," she amended.

"I have a vocation." There was no doubt in the girl's voice.

"Then you're going the wrong way for Wiltune."

"I'm not bound for Wiltune. My destiny lies elsewhere." Winifred was silent a moment. "Do you travel all the way to Oxeneford with us, mistress?" She cast a disparaging glance at Janna's blue gown and soft leather slippers.

"No, I go only to Ambresberie."

"To the abbey?"

"Yes. But not to stay."

The girl shot a swift look over her shoulder at the path behind them. She turned back to Janna. "I wish to know all there is about the life of a religious. Will you tell me how it is to live a life devoted to God?"

Intrigued, Janna cocked her head to study her companion more carefully. She was dressed in what Janna felt sure was her best gown, bound at the waist with a shabby cord from which dangled a worn purse made from coarse leather. Her gown was such as a villein might wear, long sleeved and hanging loose; although clean, it was patched and definitely homespun. How could such a girl afford the dowry to give her entry into an abbey? It seemed rude to ask.

"Do you go to an abbey in Oxeneford? Why not stay closer to your home?" she asked.

"There is nothing and no-one to keep me here," Winifred said, and glanced once more over her shoulder.

Janna wondered why she seemed so tense – and also why she'd avoided answering the question. "Which abbey do you go to? Do you have a place saved for you?" she tried again.

"No, I don't." Winifred's lips curved into a sly smile. "But the abbey will welcome me once they see what I have."

"And what is that?" But the girl's lips tightened on her secret, and again she checked the track behind them. Janna wondered if, in spite of her brave words, she was having second thoughts about her chosen path. Or had she run away from home to follow her vocation? Did she now fear pursuit? Having been forced to flee from her own home, Janna felt a spark of fellow feeling for the girl.

"Have you visited Oxeneford in the past? Is that why you wish to go there now?"

"No, I have never traveled beyond my home before. But once I'm accepted into the convent, I intend to stay. Unlike you, mistress. How is it that you have left such an important abbey as Wiltune to take to the road?"

Janna shrugged. She, too, wanted to keep her secrets close to her chest. "I found I had no vocation," she said, sticking to a small truth.

"Then why do you go to Ambresberie?"

Janna debated how best to satisfy the girl's curiosity. "I go to enquire after my mother," she said at last.

"Your mother is at Ambresberie?"

"No." Janna hesitated. "My mother is dead." A sudden rush of misery brought hot, pricking tears. She blinked them away."There is no need to call me 'mistress,'" she said, anxious to change the subject. "My name is Janna, short for Johanna. And you are Winifred?"

"Yes, but not for too much longer. I shall ask to be called Sister Edith once I'm at the abbey." A sudden gleam of humor lit the girl's intense expression and softened the firm line of her jaw. "I'm so glad to find someone young in this company. They're all so *old*! And we walk so *slowly*."

The Sin of Pride? Or was that the Sin of Judgment? Janna couldn't be sure, and wished that Agnes was present to tell her. Agnes was always signaling sins, imaginary or otherwise. She would miss Agnes and her sense of fun. But there was no point in showing disapproval. The nuns would soon discipline Winifred for her lack of charity! She contented herself with saying instead: "You'd walk slowly too, if you'd traveled across land and sea to the shrine of St James at Compostela, and now had to go all the way home again."

"Is that where they've been? All the way to Compostela! Oh, how I would love to make that pilgrimage." Winifred's face was luminous with wonder.

"Did I hear someone mention the shrine of our most beloved saint?" Ulf bobbed up once more. He grinned at Janna. She saw that he was still accompanied by the huge hound, and took several steps away from it, just in case. The animal had something clamped in its mouth. Janna hoped that whatever it guarded so carefully might discourage it from wanting to take a bite out of either her or Winifred.

"Have you visited the saint's shrine? Were you there too?" Winifred peeked out from her refuge behind Janna, glancing nervously at the dog as she did so.

"Indeed I was. We all made the pilgrimage, except for you two young women, of course." The pilgrim sketched a quick bow in Winifred's direction. "My name is Ulf," he introduced himself, and patted his pack. "When next we stop, I shall show you some of the wonders I was fortunate enough to procure while we were there, some of 'em even from our beloved saint himself."

He'd turned to address his last remark to Janna, who was a little confused by his determination to interest her in his wares until she realized that he must think, because of the fine clothes she wore, that he could tempt her into buying something. She tried hard not to smile,

7

lest she encourage him. She had once been duped by a relic seller, but had learned her lesson from it and would not be tricked again. Winifred, however, didn't hesitate.

"Oh, I'd be most honored if you would show me your sacred relics," she breathed eagerly.

Ulf ignored her. "I have a lock of hair from the head of our blessed saint, who was a most beloved disciple of our Lord Jesus Christ," he told Janna. "I even have a scrap of fabric from our Lady's own gown."

Janna nodded, unimpressed.

"Of course, the saint's hand now rests at Wiltune Abbey." Ulf jerked a thumb over his shoulder toward the town they'd just left. "Having been to Compostela to view the shrine of St James, we decided we couldn't return home without visiting his hand as well. 'Tis fortunate we heard of the empress's generous gift to the abbey or we'd have gone on to Radinges in the hope of seeing it there."

"The saint's relic is not a gift, it's a loan, and only until the abbey church at Radinges is completed," Janna corrected Ulf. "With all the unrest in the country, the empress feared for its safety – that's why she brought the hand to Wiltune."

"And I was awestruck at the sight of it," said Ulf, patting his pack again. "But I warrant I have other relics that will astound and amaze you."

"Yet you're prepared to part with them – at a price?"

Ulf had the grace to look slightly abashed. "An offering! They're not for sale," he protested, adding, "and I will suffer sorely to see 'em go."

"I have no coin to make an offering, but I would love to see them," Winifred said eagerly. "Where did you come by such wonders?"

"Oh, here and there, from pilgrims and from...er...merchants." Ulf reddened as he noticed the twinkle in Janna's eye. "They're all absolutely genuine!" he blustered.

"We'll look at them later, when we stop for a rest." Janna meant to keep her promise. Even though she didn't believe a word of it, Ulf seemed a likable rogue and she was interested to see what outlandish objects he might produce.

She surveyed the group that walked ahead, strangers now but in time she would come to know them. As well as those to whom she'd already spoken, there were Morcar and his wife, Golde. Janna wasn't sure if that was her real name or just a description of her reddish-gold hair. She was somewhat younger than her portly husband, closer in age to Janna and Winifred than the rest of the group, although she'd adopted the staid, rather matronly air of the comfortably married. There was also Adam, who seemed to wear a permanent scowl, especially when he brushed up against Bernard. They were talking together now, and although Bernard had his hand on the pilgrim's shoulder, everything about Adam shouted that this show of friendship was unwelcome. Janna wondered what had happened between them to cause such hostility. His pilgrimage seemed to have done little to improve Adam's disposition, but perhaps it was more that he preferred his own company and the long journey in close proximity with others had proved too abrasive and wearying.

Janna studied them all carefully. They were a disparate group. Bernard and Morcar were in their middle-age, while Adam looked somewhat older, as did Ulf. Juliana, Bernard's mother, was by far the oldest and the slowest, but all matched their pace to hers, never walking too far ahead. The fact that they could afford to go on a pilgrimage and that they spoke the language of the Normans suggested they came from a far higher level of society than Winifred, although they, too, were dressed in plain, serviceable garments suitable for a hard life on the road. Where had they slept along the way? What had they eaten? More importantly: where would Janna sleep and what would *she* eat along this journey?

She touched the purse concealed beneath her gown; it contained information salvaged from the burnt wreckage of her home, along with Emma's generous reward for the part Janna had played in saving her betrothed from the gallows. She now had coins enough to pay her way and was grateful for it. The pilgrims had stayed at the guest hall at Wiltune Abbey and she knew they would have made a donation for the privilege. Even though they might try to beg shelter and food along their journey, chances were they would have to pay for it, as would she. Janna hoped they might stop soon; the thought of the nuns at their dinner had set her stomach rumbling with hunger.

She had known hunger and hardship, but not in the abbey. She gave a rueful smile as she recalled her early life with her mother, when everything they grew was either eaten or traded along with her mother's potions and her skill in healing. Even so, they'd often been forced to roam the forest, risking discovery from the king's forester while they hunted for nuts, berries and mushrooms, and the eggs from birds' nests. Small creatures were trapped, and nettles, weeds and the wild seeds from hedgerows were gathered; anything edible to sustain them through the lean and hungry times. Now she might have to get used to that fare all over again.

Grimacing at the thought, Janna hurried to catch up with the others. Winifred matched her steps, seeming determined to keep her company along the way. Janna looked sidelong at her companion, wondering what Winifred could own that she was so sure would guarantee her a place at Oxeneford – or elsewhere perhaps, for Winifred still hadn't answered Janna's question about her destination. Certes she must realize there would be no place for her at any abbey if she had no dowry to offer in return. She must have left – or run away from – her home with something of substance.

From the position of the sun, Janna judged they were walking northeast, following a straight track across the downs. It was scorching hot, she could feel sweat pooling in her armpits, and wished she owned a broad-brimmed hat like the pilgrims. She longed to stop under a shady tree, preferably beside a river, for her throat felt parched and scratchy. Her new shoes were beginning to rub her heels and pinch her toes. Janna debated taking them off and walking barefoot, as once she used to do. But her year in the abbey, wearing either boots or sandals, had softened her feet. She decided to persevere for a little while longer.

Having caught up with the group, she slowed down, letting Winifred walk ahead while she dropped back to keep company with Juliana. Master Bernard's mother appeared to be walking with some difficulty. Janna had observed such a gait before, and knew it was caused by a stiffness of the hips that would become progressively more crippling. But the woman applied her long staff with vigor, using it to support her weight. It seemed a handy aid, and Janna decided to take time out at the next clump of bushes to cut a staff of her own.

"God be with you, my lady," she said. "My name is Johanna, but I am called Janna by all who know me." She spoke once more in the Norman tongue taught to her by her mother.

"I am Dame Juliana." The woman surveyed Janna, taking good note of her appearance. "Those shoes will never take you all the way to Oxeneford," she observed.

"But I go only to the abbey at Ambresberie."

"Just as well." Juliana turned her nose up and gave the air a contemptuous sniff. "A highborn lady traveling with no mount, and only the clothes you stand up in," she muttered. "Why are you keeping company with us? Surely you have your own servants to escort you?"

Janna felt a wry amusement that her clothes had so deceived the pilgrim band. "No, my lady, I have no servants," she answered. "And I value your company for otherwise I would have to make the journey alone."

The old woman gave her a sidelong glance. "Hmph."

"You have come a long way," Janna observed. "Did you find the journey very hard?"

11

Juliana was silent. Janna wondered if she hadn't heard the question. Unless she'd done something to offend the old woman? Her wrinkled face had clamped into a wary suspicion that left no room for friendliness. Janna was about to walk on when Juliana said, "We've been gone many moons, 'tis true, journeying by both land and sea. A merchant ship took us to the shores of Galicia and from there we walked the Camino, following the path of stars with other pilgrims."

"The path of stars?"

Juliana pointed the tip of her staff upward. "The Camino is named for that path of stars that blazes its glittering trail across heaven every night. We followed it, as all pilgrims follow it, for it shows the way to the shrine of St James. 'Santiago' they call him over there, 'Santiago of Compostela.' But the correct name of the place where the saint lies buried is '*campus de la stella*.' It means 'the field of stars.'"

Janna remembered some of her earlier concerns. "Where did you stay along the journey?" she asked. "Did you sleep in fields or find shelter at monasteries?"

"Both." Juliana's mouth twitched into a malicious smile as she surveyed Janna's finery. "If we found a monastery along the route we sought shelter there, but there were many times when we were forced to rest overnight in a barn, a cave, or a field. We have known hunger, thirst and great hardship along the way." She gave Janna a disdainful glance. "It's not a life you are used to, or that you will find comfortable, mistress."

Janna chuckled. "Do not let these fine clothes deceive you," she said. "I have known more hardship than you can ever imagine." She was about to ask the old woman if she considered her pilgrimage had been worthwhile, but decided her question might be considered impertinent. "Was it very wonderful, the shrine of St James?" she asked instead.

"Truly wonderful." Juliana's face glowed in rapturous reminiscence. "A cathedral has been built to house his remains, which lie in the crypt below. Marble steps lead down to his tomb, which is a silver coffer, richly embossed. In truth, I was so crippled by the journey, and so exhausted when first we arrived there, I feared I had no strength left for our return. But I prayed to the saint to make me well, strong enough to undertake our journey home, for I fear that great ill will befall us, befall my son." Juliana paused to cross herself. "We should look to our own souls, and leave justice to God," she said, her voice so low that Janna could scarcely hear her.

Janna frowned in bewilderment. Juliana's words had the ring of prophecy, yet the countryside around seemed utterly peaceful, while the purpose of the pilgrims' journey must surely put them on the side of the angels. Yet Janna had heard enough news from visitors to the abbey to know that peace was an illusion in this year of our Lord, 1141. Following the disastrous battle at Lincoln, England's King Stephen was now incarcerated at Bristou castle. His cousin, the Empress Matilda, had gathered her supporters together and had marched to London to claim his crown, but it was rumored that she'd been put to flight by a horde of angry citizens led by an army of Flemish mercenaries who answered only to Stephen's queen, Matilda of Boulogne. Despite this setback, it was widely thought that the king's cause was hopeless and that this check to the empress's ambition was merely temporary.

"Think you that the civil war is not yet over, my lady?" Janna asked. "Do you fear that more fighting will come our way to upset our journey?"

The old woman shot her a sharp look. "I know naught of that," she muttered. "I listen only to a mother's heart." She bowed her head, looking old, tired, and suddenly vulnerable.

Janna frowned, puzzled by the unexpected change in her companion's demeanor. "Is it not possible for you to travel on horseback so that the journey will pass more quickly and easily?" she ventured.

Juliana pursed her lips, then intoned:
"Stand at the crossroads and look,
Ask for the ancient paths,
Ask where the good way is,
And walk in it,
And you will find rest for your souls."

Janna wondered if the words were her own, or had come from a book of God such as she had seen in the abbey. She didn't like to show her ignorance by asking. It seemed clear that the text had sustained Juliana on her journey, and she wondered what the old woman had done in the past that she needed to find rest for her soul at the cost of such discomfort.

"You look tired. May I help you in some way?" she tried.

Juliana shook her head. Although the woman was looking at her, Janna had the feeling she couldn't see her, for her eyes looked through and beyond her to something far away.

Whatever Juliana saw there did not please her, for her lips thinned into a grim line. "You should not be here," she said, "for death follows you. You, and my son."

"Death?" Alarm sharpened Janna's voice. "What do you mean?" But Juliana bent her head and would not answer.

Janna walked beside her for a while longer, wincing as blisters rubbed deeper, stinging her feet. She became aware that Juliana was observing her once more, watching her limp along in her new shoes. She hoped the old woman didn't think she was mocking her own gait. She quickened her pace, feeling too uncomfortable now to linger in the old lady's presence. She crested a small hill, and caught sight of a thin ribbon of water coiling like a silver snake through green trees below. She swallowed hard over her dry throat, anticipating the pleasures of a long, cool drink.

A sudden shout jerked her to a standstill. It was Bernard, hurrying back to the stragglers and gesturing urgently to one side. Janna noticed that the pilgrims ahead of her had already turned off the path, moving toward the river with its sheltering screen of trees. As Bernard came closer, she understood the reason why.

"Riders ahead," he panted. "Get off the road. Hurry now!" He caught hold of his mother's arm and half dragged, half carried her along, hastily explaining his actions to Janna as she kept pace with them. "We live in uncertain times. Even the barons who are supposed to protect us are known to cut down anyone who stands between them and their lust for new land and castles. And their subjects follow their example, knowing they will not be called to account for their actions. We've heard several tales of travelers robbed and left for dead, so any bands encountered on the road are a source of concern. Come quickly if you value your life."

Catching his alarm, Janna quickened her footsteps. Once safe within their bushy cover, the pilgrims stood motionless, listening to the muted thunder of the horses' hooves and waiting for the danger to pass. At last, when all was quiet, Bernard gave the signal to move on. Janna forged ahead, pushing her way through weeds and reedy grass, keen to slake her thirst as soon as possible.

"You're in a great hurry, Johanna," Bernard observed as he caught up to her.

"I'm hot and thirsty, Master Bernard." Janna quickly wiped a strand of damp hair from her forehead and tucked it under her veil. She remembered then that she was no longer in the abbey and didn't have to hide her hair. In fact, she didn't have to wear a veil at all if she didn't want to, but at least it gave her a small amount of protection from the sun. "Where are we?" she asked.

"We've come off an ancient road that people hereabouts call the *theod herepath*." Janna nodded, understanding that he meant the "people's way." "Ahead of us is the River Avon," Bernard continued. Janna could not see the river now, but she could hear the cool sound of running water in the distance. She licked her dry lips in thirsty anticipation as she listened to Bernard.

"Sarum, that the Normans call Sarisberie, is to the right of us. Once we've had a rest, we'll follow the path of the river until we come to Ambresberie. That's probably the safest way for us to travel now."

"How far is it to Ambresberie?"

"Some days away. My mother tires quickly, and we'll also travel more slowly now that we've left the road." Bernard gave Janna a worried glance. "I fear you are not clad for rough living, mistress. We may have to beg several nights' shelter in a farmer's barn, or even sleep under a hedge if naught else comes our way."

"I have slept in far rougher places, I assure you."

Bernard nodded, although Janna could see he didn't believe her. "We'll make a stop once we come to the river. You can have a drink there, and something to eat." The worried frown came back as he surveyed Janna's empty hands. "You have no pack? And no cloak for protection against the cool of the evening?"

"No. And nothing to eat, either." Janna hoped that, if they did stop at a barn for the night, the farmer might be persuaded to provide them with some bread and ale, or perhaps even some warm milk from a cow.

"The abbey gave us some provisions for the road, and what we have, we share," Bernard promised. He turned to address the pilgrims. "There seems to be a gap in the undergrowth over there," he said, and pointed with his staff. "Wait here while I look for access to the river."

He set off, full of purpose. Janna hurried after him, determined to waste no time in slaking her thirst. She had almost reached the river's edge when she noticed Bernard check abruptly, and stoop down to scrutinize a long, dark log that lay nestled deep in thick grass. He made the sign of a cross and sank to his knees. Intrigued, she came to his side, wondering what it was that smelled so putrid. As Bernard reached out a shaking hand, a swarm of flies buzzed up around his face. With an oath, he swiped them away.

A sickening jolt brought Janna to her knees. It wasn't a fallen log that Bernard was touching so reluctantly. It was the body of a man.

Chapter 2

The man's head was bare, the hood of his black cloak pushed askew from the fall. He had the cropped brown hair of a Norman and lay face down in the grass. It was quite clear that he was dead. Fighting nausea, Janna watched as Bernard gingerly rolled the corpse over. She had seen dead bodies before, from helping both her mother and the infirmarian in the abbey, but she had never seen anything quite like this. Sickness rose from her stomach up into her throat. She swallowed hard against an urgent need to vomit.

The man had been dead for several days, she surmised, as she peered queasily at his corpse. His skin was a greenish color. As soon as his face was bared to the sky, flies buzzed and massed around his eyes, nose and mouth. A seething mass of maggots was already burrowing into the soft cavities of his face. With a heaving stomach, Janna noted that the man's flesh, where exposed, was bitten and torn. He'd been gnawed at by foxes, perhaps, or badgers. The stench of death and his voided bowels was overpowering, and she put a hand over her nose to block out the worst of it while she continued her examination. It seemed important to find out how and why he had died, for the pilgrims might face similar danger.

She knew bodies began to stiffen into rigor mortis after several hours, and that they relaxed once more into softness after a day and a night had passed. Although she was sure that he'd lain here for some time, she stretched out and reluctantly lifted one hand. His arm was limp, his skin cold and clammy to her touch. She dropped the hand in a hurry, and wiped her fingers down her skirt in an instinctive effort to remove all trace of him. A careful survey showed no obvious sign of a fatal wound, or of blood other than what marked the sites of hungry animals.

She stood up to look down on him, noting how his head lay twisted at an unnatural angle from his body. "An accident?" she asked anxiously. "Or could this be murder, think you?"

"Do not fret yourself with morbid fancies, mistress." Bernard patted her hand. "'Tis an accident, no more than that. See? The man's neck is broken." He carefully opened the purse that was bound by a leather thong around the dead man's neck. "There may be something here that will help us identify him." He felt inside, and pulled out a thin strip of parchment folded into a small packet, with a red wax seal on it. Janna looked at it with interest. There was a cross at the top, and some letters in a band around the figure of a man. He wore a crown like a round pot on his head, and carried a staff. Janna peered at the letters imprinted deep in the wax, trying to read them. HENRICUS DEI GRATIA WINTONIENSIS EPISCOPUS. It was Latin, she knew that much. From her time at the abbey she understood that *"dei gratia"* meant "by the grace of God," but she wasn't sure what the other words meant.

Bernard slowly traced the raised edges of the design with his finger. "I've seen something like this before," he said. "I think this is the seal of Henry, Bishop of Winchestre." He stared down at the parchment in his hand. "'Tis said the bishop has changed sides in the war for the crown, that he has swung his support behind the empress now that his brother, the king, languishes in Bristou castle under the guard of Robert, Earl of Gloucestre."

19

Janna nodded. It was common knowledge that the Earl of Gloucestre was the empress's half-brother and most loyal supporter, and that he'd taken the king prisoner during the battle at Lincoln. She looked with new interest at the courier who had met such an unfortunate and untimely death. He was obviously a man of substance, judging from his glossy black cloak, the fine green linen of his tunic, the soft leather of his boots. Janna frowned. Why would he be wearing a cloak in summer, unless it gave him some measure of disguise? There were several jeweled rings on his hand; a gold chain hung around his neck, and a dagger was secreted in a sheath hanging from his waist. Janna crouched down to draw it out. The hilt was silver, and beautifully engraved. It looked expensive. She replaced it carefully and sat back on her heels to sift through her findings. The evidence pointed to an accident, not murder, for if the latter, the man most certainly would have been robbed. So how had he come to break his neck, and in such an unlikely place?

Bernard was still holding the sealed parchment in his hand. "The messenger must have been on his way to Oxeneford, for I believe the empress resides there now after her...ah...unfortunate rout from London," he mused. "I wonder if this message is urgent." He turned the parchment over as if hoping to read something on the other side, but the page was blank, sealed from curious eyes. "We are on our way to Oxeneford ourselves," Bernard continued. As if his course of action had been decided, he thrust the small packet into his own scrip. "I will take it to my brother," he said, by way of explanation. "He will arrange its delivery to the empress."

"You have a brother in Oxeneford?"

"Indeed. Walter is his name, and he is in the service of the empress – in a very minor capacity, of course." In spite of his disclaimer, his face shone with pride. It was easy to see where his loyalties lay, and indeed, after meeting the empress at Wiltune Abbey, Janna shared his sentiments. But she couldn't agree with Bernard's proposed course of action.

"Should you not open the message and read it? This man – " she gestured at the messenger, " – seemed to be traveling light and perhaps in some secrecy. Could the message be urgent, think you?"

"Read a message meant for the empress?" Bernard sounded horrified at the very idea. He shook his head in vigorous denial. "No. My brother will know what to do with it."

"Should you perhaps travel on ahead of us then, Master Bernard, so that the message reaches the empress as soon as possible?"

Bernard stood still for a moment, lost in thought. Then he shook his head once more. "I cannot leave now, Johanna. I undertook to escort our group to Santiago and see them safely home again." His mouth firmed into a grim line for a moment. "It is my responsibility to see that justice is done," he said quietly.

With the echo of his mother's words in her mind, Janna was about to question him further, but he shook his head. "I'll say no more about the matter other than that the empress will have her message just as soon as I come home."

Closing off the conversation, Bernard began to search the man's pack and scrip, looking for anything that might tell who he was. He was busy repacking the man's belongings when the sudden snapping of twigs startled them both. Janna sprang to her feet. A spike of fear set her heart jumping. She looked to Bernard, seeking guidance.

"Stay here!" he commanded, and moved toward the sound, staff held in front of him like a weapon.

Janna was only too glad to do as she was bid. A dead man was one thing, but the thought that they'd misread the signs and that there might be a killer on the loose chilled her blood. The crackles in the undergrowth grew louder. Surely, if the man had been murdered, his killer would be long gone by now? She could hear Bernard's voice. He was talking to someone. She strained her ears to listen, and realized it was not conversation she could hear. It was singing!

The pilgrim emerged from the cover of trees and thick rushes, leading a fine black stallion by its reins and crooning softly into its ear. Their progress was slow for the horse limped badly. "Here's the cause of this poor man's death," he called out when he noticed Janna's anxious expression. "I expect the steed threw its owner at the same time it was lamed." He gave the horse an absent-minded pat on the nose. "Perhaps the creature was affrighted by something. A snake slithering across its path, or a sharp rock jabbed into its hoof? I should say that it stopped without warning and our traveler broke his neck when he fell."

Bernard's words brought Janna a measure of ease. The state of the corpse indicated that Bernard had the truth of the matter. She chided herself for her wild imaginings, and looked with pity at the ravaged body at her feet.

"Come." Bernard still held the reins, and now he took Janna's arm to lead her away. "We must not alarm the others. Let us move upstream a little; we'll stop there instead for our dinner."

Janna resisted the pressure of his hand, and the force of his will. "We can't just leave him here," she protested.

Bernard gave an impatient shrug. "You have seen for yourself that there is nothing anyone can do for him now. I will report our finding at the next hamlet we come to, and make sure that someone brings a horse to transport the corpse back to Sarisberie."

"We have a horse, the man's own mount. Surely we can take him with us to the next hamlet?" Janna hated the idea of leaving the body to the continuing attention of wild creatures and the gathering insect life. She wondered how such a kindly man as Bernard could be so callous.

Her question was answered when he said, "I know not if the message carried by the dead man was important, but we must continue our journey without unnecessary delay. However, your suggestion is good. It may well be quicker to bring the body with us rather than try to describe the site to others, or even have to return in order to show where he lies. Pray you, Johanna, go back to our party. Tell them what's happened, and lead them further upstream. There's no need for anyone else to witness this distressing scene, except for Ulf. Will you ask him to come and help me wrap the dead man in his cloak and lift him onto his mount?"

No need for Bernard to spell out why the body must be concealed from view. "Yes, I will."

Janna was about to hurry off when Bernard stayed her with one final instruction.

"Say nothing of what we have found to anyone," he said. "We live in anxious and difficult times. A man may say one thing to your face and quite another behind your back. That this letter is intended for the empress I have no doubt, but if there are any among us who favor the king's cause there might well be a conflict of interest if it becomes known what I carry in my scrip. I would not risk that for anything, for I have taken it upon myself to ensure that the message is safely delivered. Give me your word that you will say nothing of this, or even that we know this man to have been the bishop's messenger, Johanna. 'Tis better so."

"You have my word," Janna promised, and set out to intercept the pilgrims before they came any closer.

They greeted her news with anxious cries, but Janna quickly reassured them with the story that the horse must have shied in fright and unseated its owner. "An unlucky fall," she told them. She gave an involuntary shiver and turned to Ulf. "Bernard asked that you go down to the river to help with the body." Bernard hadn't mentioned Morcar or Adam, and she noticed that neither of them volunteered their services. Adam stood beside Golde, scowling at everyone. Janna wondered anew why he stayed with the pilgrim band. He appeared to shun all overtures of friendship, although she'd observed that all the pilgrims, at some time or another, had made an effort to walk with him and engage him in conversation.

Morcar and Golde began to walk on. Adam glowered after them but made no move to follow. "Adam?" Morcar stopped, obviously waiting for him to join them. Golde stopped too, and beckoned impatiently. Janna was stunned by the hatred on her face, which quickly smoothed into a smile as she realized that she was being watched.

"Adam," she cooed, soft as a turtledove calling to its mate. The sullen pilgrim shouldered his pack and shambled reluctantly toward them.

Shrugging aside her curiosity, Janna followed the band upriver. The pilgrims lost no time in slaking their thirst at the first suitable site they found. Janna noticed they used their tin badges to scoop up the water, the scallop shells making a more handy cup than bare hands. Having drunk their fill, they unwound their traveling cloaks and spread them onto the grass. Janna's stomach growled in hunger as she watched the party delving into packs and bringing out hunks of bread and cheese. With a sigh of regret, she walked to the river and crouched beside it. She could still feel the touch of the dead man, still smell his decaying flesh on her fingers. She thrust her hands into the cool, rushing water and picked up a handful of river sand. This she rubbed between her palms and through her fingers, scrubbing away all trace of the corpse. She repeated the procedure several times before, finally satisfied, she cupped her hands together to drink her fill.

Shadows flicked and darted in deeper pools; a large trout shot into the sheltering growth of green watercress as Janna reached out to grab it. She muttered a curse under her breath, and instead, plucked a handful of cress, which she chewed while she waited for the trout to show itself once more. But the wily trout stayed hidden. Finally, Janna gave up and rose to her feet. She looked about for somewhere to sit, somewhere clean enough not to soil her pretty blue gown. She was beginning to appreciate the advantages of rough homespun and a stout pair of sandals.

She spotted a fallen tree trunk in the shade, and sat down. Wincing, she eased off her slippers and flexed her toes, noticing that they were already bloodied and blistered. She knew she couldn't bear to put the pretty shoes on again, and resigned herself to walking barefoot after all – like a penitent, a true pilgrim. She didn't feel like a penitent, for she'd done little in her life that she truly regretted. And she'd been long enough in the abbey to hope that God was a merciful and forgiving father; long enough too, to understand that the rules and restrictions the nuns lived under stemmed mostly from the Rule of St Benedict and others like him, and had little to do with the will of God Himself. Or so she believed. So had her mother also believed, Janna thought, as she recalled Eadgyth's words: *"You don't need to go to church when God's great cathedral is all around you."*

With the sound of her mother's voice in her ears, Janna looked about. A beautiful blue demoiselle dragonfly hovered over a bright patch of yellow flag close to the glinting, rushing water. Lusty bulrushes grew in thick clumps at the water's edge, but she could see also creamy meadowsweet and the pale blue flowers of water forget-me-not. Sunlight slanted through the deep green of the trees, casting pebbles of gold upon the grass. A lone cuckoo called. Janna remembered her mother telling her that if she began to run, and counted the cuckoo's cries until she was out of earshot, she would add as many years to her life as she heard the cuckoo call. She smiled at the memory of how eagerly she had run about. If the story was true, she would live to a grand old age indeed! But for now she felt too lazy to move. Instead she leaned back and watched birds swooping about the treetops as they visited their nests and fed their young. On the ground, sparrows hopped ever closer to the pilgrims, keeping a careful watch for stray crumbs.

Janna felt the tension ease from her shoulders, a tension she wasn't aware she carried until it slipped away. She took a deep breath and then another, firming her resolve to leave behind all the cares of her childhood, and move forward with a steady purpose to whatever might await her at Ambresberie. The way to understanding her mother's past had been shown to her. At last she was coming close to unraveling the secret of her father's identity. With his help, she would fulfill her quest to bring him home to Berford to ensure that a killer was brought to justice for her mother's death.

She sat forward and watched Bernard leading the horse toward them, a long bundle tied up in a cloak across its back. Questions raced through Janna's mind. Who was the dead man, and what was in the message he carried? Why was he wearing his cloak when the days were so warm? She sighed with impatience. Bernard was a good man, and a kindly one, but she wished he had a keener sense of curiosity! If she'd been alone and first on the scene, she would have slit the seal and read the message, on the grounds that she needed that information to know how best to proceed. As it was...Janna gave another sigh, acknowledging that she might never know, for she would be leaving the group at Ambresberie, long before Bernard could deliver it into the safe hands of his brother.

"Would you like to share my bread and cheese, mistress?" Janna looked up at the relic seller, admiring his persistence. She was too hungry to refuse his offer, so she accepted a hunk of bread with heartfelt thanks.

"This is Brutus," Ulf said, noticing Janna's involuntary shift backward as his hound flopped down near their feet and began to gnaw on the bone it had been carrying in its mouth.

"Is he a large dog or a small horse?"

"He's an alaunt, a hunting dog. I've had him since he was a puppy. I, er, swapped him for a..."

"An eyelash belonging to some saint? Or a toenail or tooth, perhaps?"

Ulf gave a small huff of amusement. "Nowt so fine. He was the runt of the litter and sickly with it. No-one really wanted him. I must say, I had no idea he was going to grow so big." He spread his cloak on the ground and sat down beside Janna. They ate in companionable silence for a while, although Janna suspected it was only a matter of time before Ulf kept his promise to show her the relics in his pack. He seemed in no hurry to do so, nor did the pilgrims seem in any hurry to move onward, for several had followed Juliana's example and were stretched out upon their cloaks with their eyes closed. Morcar, a rather rotund personage with a bushy beard and moustache, had already begun to snore, fluttering the luxuriant growth on his upper lip with every breath he expelled.

Janna had to admit that she was curious to see what Ulf carried. Coming from so far away as Galicia, there was bound to be something exotic among his treasures. She turned to meet his bright, expectant gaze. "All right, then, you'd better show me what you've got."

He laughed. "I thought curiosity would win over caution," he said. "You'll be amazed, I'm sure, when you see what I have."

"Go on, then. Amaze me."

Needing no second invitation, the pilgrim opened his pack. Juliana stirred into wakefulness, and she and Golde drifted over to see what he was about. Winifred came with them. Wide-eyed, she held a hand to her heart as she waited while Ulf unrolled a linen sheath. Janna longed to sound a warning, but knew she could not. For all she knew, the relics might indeed be genuine, although she doubted it. She reassured herself with the thought that it was unlikely Winifred would have coins enough to exchange for a relic, even if she had the will to do so.

"And what is that?" Janna asked, as a scrap of dirty blue fabric was revealed.

"This is one of my most holy relics." Ulf crossed himself and bent to kiss the fragment of cloth. "This comes from the gown of our Lady Mary, Virgin Mother of our Lord, Jesus Christ."

Janna's eyes widened. There was a startled gasp from Winifred. The other pilgrims pressed closer. "And here." Ulf picked up a lock of dark hair. "This comes from the very head of St James himself. It was given me by one of the guardians of the saint's shrine." Janna leaned closer to see it better. She was willing to wager her life that this, at least, wasn't real, for any hair over a thousand years old would long since have crumbled into dust. Unless it really was…?

No! Janna chided herself for being so gullible. Ulf's glance slanted sideways to Janna's face and read there her mistrust. He rolled up the linen sheath and swiftly produced another to take its place. "A tooth from the head of St John the Baptist," he announced defiantly, scowling at Janna as she gave a gurgle of amusement.

Golde picked up the tooth and inspected it. "How much?" she demanded.

"It's not for sale!" Ulf sounded so shocked that Brutus gave a sharp bark. With a swift word of apology, Golde dropped it on the linen pad and hastily retreated. "But as it's you, and for an offering…?" Ulf amended hurriedly, and held out the sacred object.

Golde shook her husband awake, and muttered in his ear. Looking surly, he heaved himself upright and fumbled in his scrip for a penny. He ventured forward, keeping a cautious eye on Brutus as he did so, and placed the coin in Ulf's hand. Ulf continued to watch him expectantly. With a sigh, the pilgrim extracted a ha'penny. Ulf drew the linen sheath closer to his chest, a slight movement which Golde correctly interpreted. She gave her husband a sharp dig in the ribs. Reluctantly, he pulled out another ha'penny, slapped the coins into Ulf's palm and, in one swift movement, scooped up the linen sheath and rolled the tooth safely into it.

Golde took the small bundle from Morcar and placed it into her own purse. She smiled at Ulf, well pleased with the deal. And Ulf returned her smile, obviously delighted by a transaction that must have exceeded his greatest expectations.

"I've saved the best until last," he said. All the pilgrims were gathered around now, even Adam, although a faint sneer curled his lip as he watched the proceedings. This time Ulf pulled a small, ornately carved box from his scrip. The polished wood shone in the shafts of sunlight, as did the gold clasps that secured the lid.

Curious in spite of her skepticism, Janna leaned forward to peer inside as Ulf opened the lid. The box contained a small and weathered splinter of wood. Janna shot an enquiring glance at Ulf. "Am I amazed yet?" she asked.

He grinned. "You should be. This comes from the Holy Rood, the True Cross of our Lord Jesus Christ, our Savior."

A voice cut in swiftly, before Janna had a chance to express her opinion.

"What pri – offering would you accept in exchange for that?"

Ulf turned to face the bidder. It was Juliana, her wrinkled old face eager as she reached out a hand for the box. Ulf hesitated, then held it out to her. Janna liked him a little more for his reluctance to hoodwink the old lady as he said, "You may give me what you will, my lady, and may God bless you and give strength to your limbs."

"You don't want to believe everything Ulf tells you, Mother." Bernard had come to her side. He tried to take the box from Juliana's grasp, but she hung on fiercely.

"Look to your own affairs," she hissed at him. She tucked the box securely under her armpit, and opened her purse. Bernard's scowled, but he kept silent as his mother extracted several silver coins, which she poured into Ulf's palm. Janna watched the transaction with interest, impressed by the casual way in which Juliana had handed over what amounted to a small fortune. Even Ulf seemed taken aback, although he accepted the coins willingly enough.

So Juliana was not impoverished; she could well have afforded the luxury of a mount to carry her to Compostela and back again. Given how painful walking was for her, this must indeed be a journey of true repentance. Janna wondered what this respectable old lady could have done to warrant such penitence. Could she have been caught dealing in stolen goods? Or running a bawdy house, perhaps? Did she own slaves, which was now against the law? Increasingly bizarre scenarios kept Janna entertained as Ulf secured his pack and put it away. He seemed a little subdued. Janna wondered if he was genuinely fond of the old lady and if there were limits to whom he would cheat.

With the entertainment over, the pilgrims drifted away. Wordlessly, Ulf handed Janna a leather bottle filled with ale, which she declined with thanks, having drunk her fill at the river. "Was that real, that sliver of wood?" she asked.

"Aye. The monk I bought it from swore that it had come from the Holy Rood." Ulf put his bottle away, stretched out along his cloak and closed his eyes. Janna observed him, thinking he was a likeable rogue, but a rogue nevertheless. Her attention moved to Ulf's dog.

"Ho, Brutus," she said carefully, and clicked her fingers. The dog eyed her briefly, but growled as she extended her hand for an experimental pat. Janna hurriedly withdrew, just in case the dog decided it wanted another tasty morsel to chew. It seemed to have finished off whatever it had carried in its mouth, and now it rested its muzzle on its paws, keeping a wary eye on her. Fragments of bone and bits of gristle lay on the grass nearby, bearing witness to the dog's dinner. Janna espied a fragment larger than the others, and frowned. She was almost sure it wasn't a bone from any animal she knew. She picked it up to study it more carefully. It looked more like a human toe, or perhaps part of a finger. She recalled the hand of St James in its reliquary at the abbey. In its great age it had shrunk to skin and bone so that one could almost see the structure underneath. This bone seemed similar. Janna shuddered, and threw the bone away. Had the dog got in among Ulf's relics? She glanced sideways at his pack. Was it full of spare body parts? Was that why it was so heavy?

She sat back with a grimace of distaste, and surveyed her blistered, bloodied feet. She should wash them and find some soothing herbs to heal the broken skin and dull the pain. Yet it seemed almost too much trouble to move. The heat of the day pressed down on her; her senses were dulled by the still, bright afternoon and the heavy silence, which was punctuated only by the splashing river and the languorous hum of bees. A faint sound of snoring came to her ears: Juliana, sprawled out on her cloak once more, resting her tired old bones. Janna felt her own eyes begin to close.

Chapter 3

She wasn't sure how much time had passed when something jolted her awake. What had disturbed her? She looked about at the peaceful scene. The pilgrims were quiet, some resting, some with small books in their hands, some saying the rosary or murmuring quietly to one another.

The sound that had disturbed her was growing louder: the urgent thrum of hoof beats that told of a horseman coming their way, and in a great hurry too. Someone else had also heard the rider's approach. Winifred had leaped to her feet, looking fearful. But Janna recognized the badge of the rider's office even before he dismounted and announced himself to their party.

"I was charged by Abbess Hawise to come after you," he said, scowling at each of them in turn. "Do not think you can hide from her wrath."

"Hide?" Bernard echoed. He spread his hands in bewilderment. "We came this way to escape a band of horsemen on the road, and we stayed to drink from the river and rest. I can assure you, we are not hiding from the abbess."

The guard's stern demeanor told Janna that he did not believe Bernard, nor did he trust any of them. "The hand of our blessed

St James the Apostle was discovered missing from its reliquary this morning," he told them. "It seems you hold the key to the relic's disappearance and you will now submit yourselves to my search. You will travel no further unless and until I give you permission to leave."

"Are you accusing us, a group of devout pilgrims, of this vile and blasphemous deed?" There was an angry gleam in Bernard's eyes as he faced the abbess's messenger.

The guard held his ground. "Yes. But you're not the only group under suspicion," he admitted. "The abbey and those who reside there have all been searched, and the abbess has sent riders after every group that has departed this day. The abbess is wrathful, not least for fear of what the empress will say when she is told of this crime. The lady entrusted the sacred relic to the abbey for safe-keeping. Anyone caught with it in his possession will be severely punished, you may be sure of it."

Janna recalled the fragments of bone on the grass, and felt her stomach lurch in horror. She glanced toward Ulf, who seemed unconcerned by their unexpected pursuer. Did he know what Brutus had done? Moving unobtrusively, Janna edged toward the patch of flattened grass where Brutus, so recently, had eaten his dinner. The scraps of flesh and bone were still visible. She did not dare bend down to examine them but, even scrutinizing them from a distance, she felt fairly sure that they had, indeed, once formed part of a whole hand. She looked from Ulf to the guard, then down at the ground once more, trying to hide her discomfort. Should she say something to the guard? She shook her head; nothing could make the hand whole again. All she would achieve was the imprisonment of Ulf, and she certainly didn't want that on her conscience. And what of the real culprit, who was yet more innocent than his master? She certainly didn't want to take responsibility for a huge, homeless hound! She quickly kicked some loose dirt over the incriminating evidence and joined the party of pilgrims now clustered around the guard.

"Much better to tell me now if you know anything of it, for the abbess may be persuaded to clemency if the sacred relic is returned unharmed and without delay." The guard waited some moments, looking expectantly from one face to the next. But no-one spoke. "Very well," he snapped, his disappointment plain for all to see. "Lay your packs out on the ground. I shall inspect them all, after which I shall search each of you personally, along with the garments you wear." His hard stare moved from pilgrim to pilgrim and came to rest on Janna.

"No!" she cried, outraged at the prospect of having to undress in front of everyone. She looked about for Winifred to join her protest, and her gaze fell on Juliana.

"No," Juliana agreed. "'Tis not seemly for any man to search a woman. However, to serve the abbey's interests, I am prepared to undergo your search. I am no longer of an age where such a thing matters to me. Once you are satisfied that I am innocent, I will undertake to search the women, and their belongings, *in private*." She stressed the last two words, making sure that her meaning was plain.

Janna turned to the guard, hopeful that he would agree to the compromise. To her relief, he said curtly, "Very well then, old woman. I'll make a start with you." He took a step toward her, but was interrupted by Bernard, who belatedly introduced himself as the leader of the pilgrim group.

"This is my mother," he went on, indicating Juliana. "On my honor, I will undertake to watch all the other members of our band while you conduct your search privately, behind that thicket of bushes over there. We shall all watch each other." The guard thought it over for a few moments, before murmuring a reluctant agreement. He walked toward the bushy screen, keeping several paces behind Juliana, who stalked ahead of him.

Winifred materialized beside Janna, breathing hard. "Is he going to search us all?" she whispered.

34

"Yes."

"But I have never undressed before a man! And I will not now."

"You don't have to. Juliana offered to prove her innocence first, and she's going to search all the women afterwards."

"Thanks be to God for that!"

"You should rather thank Juliana for her generosity." Janna already knew the search would prove futile. Not only that, it was going to waste several hours of daylight they could use in walking on to their destination. Should she speak up after all? Another question stopped her: how had Brutus come by the saint's hand in the first place?

She had no pack to dump, but the rest of the group had dutifully set their packs out in a line, and were now busy watching one another. The guard rejoined them and commenced his search, pulling everything out of each pack and exposing it to the view of the pilgrims.

"Careful! There are precious relics in there!" Ulf's shout stopped the guard momentarily. He straightened and scrutinized Ulf. "A relic seller, are you?" He bent to Ulf's unwieldy pack and eagerly began to extract bundles wrapped in linen along with a number of small, wooden boxes. The bundles were unrolled, the boxes opened, and the pilgrims crowded round to view the contents: scraps of fabric, teeth, fingers and other body parts, engraved stone runes, several precious gems. To the obvious disappointment of the guard, there was no hand among them. Ulf growled in protest at seeing his treasures thus exposed, and his dog growled louder, but there was little he could do to prevent the search. The guard, visibly annoyed, moved on, leaving Ulf to secure his precious relics and return them to his pack.

Juliana flounced out from the concealing bushes, red-faced and discomforted. She beckoned Janna to come to her. Once Janna had stripped, Juliana insisted on viewing the contents of the purse she kept hidden under her gown. The old woman's eyes widened as she swiftly calculated the value of the silver coins Janna carried, and grew ever wider as she noticed the brooch, ring and letter also secreted there. She reached out a hand to pick them up for a more careful inspection, but Janna swept them back into her purse, determined that Juliana would not learn her mother's secrets. Instead, she showed her the last treasure from her purse: a small statue of a mother tenderly clasping a child. "Look, I found this out in the forest near where I used to live," she said.

Juliana drew back with a sudden hiss. "Why do you carry a pagan idol?"

"It's the Virgin Mary and baby Jesus," Janna contradicted sharply. She had no way of knowing it was any such thing, but Juliana's ready condemnation annoyed her. She closed her fingers around the small statue and thrust it back into her purse. "And what did you mean when you said that death was following me?" she demanded. "Am I going to die?" She hastily donned her under-tunic, then pulled the silky blue gown over her head.

"We are all going to die. That's the fate that we cannot escape." Juliana turned away. "Send Winifred to me, followed by Golde," she instructed.

Janna thought that Juliana must be lapsing into the senility of old age, yet she couldn't help feeling uneasy. But it was clear the old woman was not going to answer her question, and so she hurried off to fetch Winifred, securing the gauzy veil over her hair as she went.

The search of the packs was over. At Bernard's suggestion, the guard turned his attention to the dead man. Not that Bernard would have left anything incriminating for the guard to find, Janna thought, remembering how thoroughly the pilgrim had searched the body. But she had to admit she couldn't see Bernard covering up something so serious as the theft of the hand of St James. The guard quickly examined the dead man's pack and scrip, wearing an expression of extreme distaste as he did so. Clearly relieved to be done, he shoved everything back where he'd found it and hastily moved away.

Janna wondered what had happened to the piece of parchment. Had Bernard secreted it somewhere about his person? Would he show it to the guard? There was no way of finding out for, taking his cue from Juliana and perhaps mindful of the sensibilities of the other women of the party, the guard now banished them all behind the bushy screen once more, to wait while the men of the party were stripped and searched.

Janna decided to pass the time by fashioning a staff for herself. She began to explore the area, looking for anything that might prove suitable.

"What are you doing?" Winifred bounded up. "What are you looking for?" Her aggrieved expression relaxed somewhat as Janna explained her mission. "The guard's wasting his time – and ours. He's not going to find the hand among a group of pilgrims, is he?" she commented, as she swooped down on a long, straight stick for her own use.

Janna thought of Brutus. "No, I don't think he'll have any success here." She pressed her foot down on a fallen tree and hauled back on a slender branch until it cracked under the pressure.

"I think it was the dead man who stole the hand, and that's why he died." Winifred watched as Janna pulled out her knife and began to trim her new staff.

"No, it wasn't."

"Even if the guard didn't find it on his body, it could be that the man had an accomplice. Maybe he gave it to someone else for safekeeping before he died?"

"He didn't take it. He's been dead far longer than the relic's been missing."

"Then the hand will never be found!" Winifred looked sideways at Janna. She seemed to be plucking up courage to say something. "All those relics in Master Ulf's pack. Do you think they're really what he says they are?"

Janna laughed. "I suspect not. But I couldn't say for sure," she added, wanting to give the rogue the benefit of the doubt.

"But the hand of St James the apostle? That's real, isn't it?"

Janna shrugged. "I was at the abbey when the Empress Matilda visited us and handed it over. There was a special mass said for it. The abbess certainly believes it is a true relic. There wouldn't be all this fuss otherwise."

"That's good. I'm glad about that." Winifred began to pace restlessly among the trees. Janna wondered if she was hoping to catch a glimpse of the pilgrims in a state of undress.

The sun was slanting across the downs from a reddening sky, their figures casting long shadows by the time the guard had finished. As Janna suspected, no unattached hand had come to light. Nothing had been achieved in a wasted afternoon, save that the guard had undertaken to lead the horse and its dead rider back to Wiltune and instigate a search as to the man's identity, so that his family might be notified and the body decently buried.

Master Bernard thanked him heartily for the offer, obviously relieved to be rid of the corpse. But the guard had not quite finished with them. It seemed that what he couldn't achieve with threats he would now try to achieve with bribery. "I am bound by the abbess to tell you that there is a reward for the safe return of this sacred relic," he called out, attracting the attention of the pilgrims, who were now scattered about, repacking their belongings and talking among themselves. The word "reward" galvanized them all. They immediately quietened and came closer to hear what the abbess had in mind. Janna, too, listened with curiosity. Abbess Hawise was notoriously mean and penny-pinching – the guard's offer, probably deliberately withheld until now, spoke tellingly of the measure of her desperation.

"Six silver pennies to anyone with information about the identity of the thief. And a purse of silver to whoever returns the hand of St James to the abbey."

A purse of silver! Janna's next thought was: How big a purse? But no matter how small, it would be a fortune worth thinking about. Janna glanced at Brutus and then at Ulf, who seemed as unconcerned as ever. But he could hardly claim a reward if his dog had already eaten the sacred relic!

The guard stared hard at them all, hoping that someone would break, and tell him what he needed to know. The pilgrims stayed silent. If any of them knew aught of the missing relic, no-one was going to say so. Instead, they looked at each other with calculating eyes, but glanced quickly away rather than meet anyone's gaze. The theft of the hand and the promise of a reward for its return had brought suspicion and greed into hearts that, after a pilgrimage to the tomb of St James, should have been full of love and free from care.

The guard watched them with a hopeful expression, waiting for someone to speak, but nobody did. Finally, with a shrug of resignation, he remounted. Leading the straying horse and its burden beside him, he slowly clip-clopped away in the direction of Wiltune.

Bernard clapped his hands to attract everyone's attention. "We've had the chance to rest for most of this afternoon, so I suggest we make the most of the long twilight. There's maybe time to walk a mile or two before finding somewhere to spend the night." He looked around to see if there were any dissenters. Janna sensed his impatience to push on, and understood what drove him. He must still be in possession of the bishop's message. She wondered how he'd managed to keep it hidden from the guard. Or had he merely told the guard it was his own possession?

"Are you in agreement?" Bernard asked. There were a few murmurs of assent and one or two grumbles before they all bent to pick up their packs once more. Janna noticed Juliana shoulder her burden and limp off behind Bernard. She hesitated a moment, then picked up her shoes and hurried after her.

"Look," she said, hoping to flatter the old woman into explaining her odd prediction. "I have a staff of my own now, just like yours. It's such a help with walking, isn't it?"

Juliana looked from her own fine walking stick to Janna's roughly hewn branch. She gave a grunt, but made no comment.

Janna sighed, and tried again. "Let me carry your pack for you," she offered. "I am younger than you, and I have no pack of my own to carry."

"I carry my own pack." Juliana stumped onward.

Annoyed that her gesture of goodwill had not merited even a word of thanks, Janna was about to give up and walk away when the old woman muttered, "You must go. Leave us. I don't want you here."

"But I have no-one else to travel with. Besides, I need to get to Ambresberie." Janna was determined that Juliana would not get rid of her just because she'd taken against her for some reason.

"Death stalks you." Juliana looked ahead, her eyes glassy and unfocused once more. "And my son." An expression of grief twisted her face. "I fear you will bring us ill-fortune!"

"But I don't wish Master Bernard harm, you have my oath on it." In spite of her protest, Janna was frightened.

Juliana's lips pinched. She made no reply, just hitched her pack a little higher and limped on. Janna watched her go. The woman's words had sent a chill through her, yet they made no sense at all. And in the absence of a sound reason for abandoning the group, she was determined to push on. There was too much at stake for her to leave the pilgrims now. News of her mother awaited her at Ambresberie and, with a bit of luck, what she found out there would lead her, in turn, to her father. She would not be deflected from her purpose by the ramblings of an annoying old woman.

"We'll be there in just a day or two," she muttered to herself. "Juliana will get her wish soon enough." She began to walk behind the pilgrim group, wincing as sharp flints bruised her feet.

When living with her mother at the edge of the forest, Janna had often walked barefoot, for boots were a luxury, hard come by and cherished because of it. Both Janna and Eadgyth had owned a pair of boots, but had carefully preserved them for winter wear or for long journeys to the marketplace. Now, after a year in the abbey, Janna was not used to walking unshod, but she knew her feet would toughen up over time. Until then, she would just have to bear it.

She looked about for Winifred, hoping that her chatter would distract her from the pain of walking, but there was no sign of her. Janna glanced over her shoulder, and was just in time to see the girl emerge from behind a dense clump of holly bushes. Her steps faltered for a moment as she caught Janna's eye. "A call of nature," she said. "Just in time, too! I thought that guard would never leave us in peace."

Janna grinned in sympathetic understanding. "I should have gone too," she said, and looked about for some bushy cover of her own.

Bernard finally called a halt when they reached a smallholding on the outskirts of a hamlet. It was not as grand as the manor farmed by Hugh for his aunt, Dame Alice, but it looked prosperous enough, surrounded as it was by long strips of vegetables and ripening grain in the fields. A sizable number of sheep grazed peacefully on open downland nearby, some accompanied by half-grown lambs. The smell from a pigsty wafted toward them, along with the sound of frenzied grunts and squeals. As they came closer, Janna noticed that a lad had emptied a slop pail into the trough and was watching the swine shouldering one another aside to get their share of the vegetable peelings and other leftovers that made up their daily fare. A flock of geese swooped toward them, hissing a warning, pursued by a young goosegirl, who flapped her hands and shouted "Shoo!" in a vain effort to draw them away.

Bernard stood his ground. "Could you please fetch your master to us?"

She nodded and wheeled about, clicking her fingers for the geese to follow her. As she set off, the geese trundled after her, hostilities apparently in abeyance for the time being.

"I hope we may stay here for the night," Bernard told the group. He bent solicitously over Juliana. "How are you bearing up, Mother?"

"Well enough." She looked up at her tall son. Janna could see the love in her eyes, but could sense also her fear. It was easy to dismiss the old woman as witless yet it was obvious that she imagined the worst. It was also obvious that she believed Janna had some part to play in Bernard's downfall. A frisson ran down Janna's spine.

With an impatient shrug, she shook off her dark thoughts; she would not be with the pilgrim party for too much longer. And yet it was true that there had been a death, albeit of a stranger, and as the result of an accident, if Bernard was to be believed.

Another question cast a deeper chill. Were Bernard's fortunes tied in with the message he had removed from the body? She'd been with him when it was found; perhaps that was what Juliana had sensed? She stood, lost in thought, as Bernard negotiated with the farmer for accommodation and the provision of a meal for them all.

A trestle table was set up in the main room of the farmhouse, with benches for them to sit on. The meal, when it was brought, was plain but plentiful. Janna gladly accepted a bowl of vegetable pottage and a hunk of bread from the farmer's wife. A jug of ale was set before them, along with several leather mugs that had been sealed with pitch to make them watertight. The ale was rather sour, but Janna drank it gratefully for it was a warm evening and she was thirsty after their walk.

The talk around the table began with expressions of shock at the death of the stranger Bernard had found, but quickly gave way to a buzz of speculation as to the fate of the hand of St James. No-one said openly that one of their own party might be responsible for the theft of the relic, but Janna noticed that the pilgrims continued to watch each other carefully. As newcomers to the group, it seemed that she and Winifred were the favored suspects. There had been much whispering that stopped whenever they came close enough to overhear what was being said.

Winifred put Janna's thoughts into words. "They think it was us, either you or me," she said quietly, sounding dispirited. "I can feel it in the way they look at us, and the way they talk about us behind our backs." She took a bite of bread and chewed thoughtfully for a moment, then picked up the mug she shared with Janna and drank some ale.

"It's hardly surprising," Janna said, wondering why Winifred looked so downhearted. "After making such a long journey together, they must all know each other quite well."

"And they don't know us at all." Winifred set the mug back on the table with a sigh. "We have to convince them we're innocent of this crime."

"I don't know how we do that. Telling them won't make them believe us." Unlike Winifred, Janna refused to feel worried about a situation that was not of her making. She looked about for the basket of bread, and was about to sign for it when she remembered she was no longer at the abbey. "Could you pass me some more bread, please, Master Bernard?" she called.

She took a bite of the hard, dark bread, then spooned up a mouthful of pottage to soften it. The bread didn't taste particularly good, but it was filling. Janna thought it had probably been made of rye rather than wheat. She knew, from her own experiences of "the hungry month," that peasants could starve at this time of the year when grain hoards were low but newly growing grain was not yet ready for harvest. She and her mother had often augmented their meager fare with seeds gathered from hedgerows, added to whatever else they could scavenge to fill their hungry bellies. She was grateful that the farmer's wife had found food enough to spare for them. But the pilgrims had paid for the food and also for lodging overnight in the farmer's hall, and that should please their hosts. After some thought, Janna had handed a silver penny to Bernard and asked that it be used as her contribution for any accommodation they might require during the journey, with the promise of another should it be required. It was a pleasure, for once, to be able to pay her way instead of depending on charity.

With the meal over, the table was folded away and the farmer and his wife bade them goodnight. Janna surveyed the rush-covered floor of the hall. By common consent, the men huddled on one side of the room while the women kept together on the other, but indeed the space was so small there was barely enough room for the two groups to stretch out without mingling. A cresset light had been left for the pilgrims to use when seeking the latrine pit outside before they bedded down. Even in its dim glow, Janna could see that the rushes had been laid for some time, and were discolored with dust and dried mud, and strewn with unidentifiable scraps. She looked about for a cleaner patch to lie on, but could not find one. She sighed as, still fully clothed, she settled down. Her fine gown would not stay fine for long, not if this was to be their standard of lodging.

Janna watched Winifred carefully undo her girdle and purse and put them close to one side before wrapping a threadbare cloak around herself. Her hands bore the marks of scratches, some so deep they had drawn blood. Had the girl been mortifying her flesh? Janna had heard talk of mortification in the abbey, how monks, and sometimes also nuns, would flagellate themselves as punishment for sins both real and imaginary. But despite her professions of piety, Winifred was not yet a nun, nor could she possibly have so much on her conscience that she must resort to such a practice. But perhaps it was Winifred's call of nature that had caused the scratches. Janna chuckled quietly to herself, thinking that Winifred must have chosen a particularly prickly spot in an effort to ensure that no-one might observe what she was about. In which case she probably bore painful scratches elsewhere about her person as testimony to her modesty!

With a faint sigh, Winifred settled down beside her. The girl's proximity reminded her, suddenly and sharply, of Agnes, who had shared her straw pallet with Janna on the first night she'd spent at Wiltune Abbey. The lay sister was the first friend Janna had ever known, and she already missed her irreverence, and her sense of humor. Winifred seemed altogether too serious to promise much fun along the journey. But she would not be with the pilgrim group for much longer; not unless there were more dead bodies and missing relics to be encountered along the way.

"God bless you this night and keep you safe, Janna," Winifred said. Janna noticed that her girdle was now looped around her arm, and that she clutched the purse to her chest. It seemed that, just as the pilgrims didn't trust the newcomers to their party, neither did Winifred trust the pilgrims. What was so valuable that she needed to guard it so carefully? Or was the object fragile? Was she afraid she might squash it if she rolled over in her sleep?

"God be with you, Winifred." Janna closed her eyes, hoping that she would be able to fall asleep on the smelly, prickling straw. She told herself that the young girl's secrets were of no concern to her, yet her mind kept throwing up questions. What was in Winifred's purse that she guarded so carefully and kept so private, and was potentially valuable enough to ensure her welcome at any abbey? What was in the message carried by the dead man? And why did the pilgrims seem so out of sorts with one another?

Chapter 4

They made up some of the time they had lost on their second day of travel, although Janna found herself dropping further and further behind, walking slower even than Juliana, as she tried to find a smooth way between the pebbles and flints that strewed their path. No matter how carefully she trod, or how heavily she leaned on her new staff, still she winced with every step. Finally, when she could stand it no longer, she bent and eased on the tight shoes once more, then limped forward to catch up with the others.

It was not as hot as the previous day; gathering clouds spoke of the promise of rain later. Janna sighed at the thought and wished she had a cloak to protect her new gown from the ravages of the journey. As there was little she could do about it, other than hope they found shelter before the rain came, she turned her thoughts away from her gown, and her sore feet, and instead gave herself up to enjoyment of the journey. A riot of twining honeysuckle and wild roses scented the hedgerows. Lacy white elderflowers, privet and creamy meadowsweet added their own fragrance to the air. Tall purple-pink spikes of foxglove and rosebay willow herb and the yellow stars of St John's wort added splashes of color to grassy banks and green weeds. Fat bumblebees nuzzled among pale pink blackberry blossom, while gaudy butterflies and jeweled dragonflies flitted everywhere, busy about their purpose and content just to be.

Janna looked about, automatically noting which plants were of use for healing and which for food, for only a very few were merely decorative. She noticed clusters of red valerian, smelled the spicy scents of wood-sage and fennel. She itched to stop, to pick, to preserve some of them for future use, and smiled to herself, surprised to find how much she missed practicing her healing skills.

The farmer's wife had given them food for the journey, and they stopped to eat it on the path beside the cool, rushing river. Once more Janna found herself in the company of Ulf and Winifred. Her curiosity was fired as she noticed Winifred glance covetously at Ulf's pack. She decided to press the girl a little further.

"So what do you have in your purse that makes you so sure of your welcome when you come to Oxeneford?" she asked, thinking a direct question might catch Winifred off-guard and prompt her to an honest answer.

Winifred stiffened. "Why n – nothing," she stammered, but Janna noticed her hand curve secretively around the purse dangling from her girdle as if to protect whatever was inside. "It's but a – a small thing from my home, something to remind me of my family."

Janna was sure she was lying, yet she appeared somewhat nervous too. A devil of mischief stirred. "You said yourself that they would welcome you when they saw what you carried," she reminded Winifred.

"I – I meant nought but that they would welcome me, mistress, for I am young and healthy, with strong, willing arms and the love of God in my heart." The girl's cry rang out, sincere and passionate, and immediately Janna felt ashamed of her teasing.

"I'm sorry," she said. "I must have misunderstood what you said."

"If you carried a holy relic, lass, you'd be welcome at any abbey." Ulf gestured toward his pack with a sly expression.

Winifred dredged up a shaky smile. "I know you have many fine treasures, Master Ulf, but I have no coin to give you in exchange for even the least of them."

"Perhaps you should search for the hand of St James?" Ulf suggested. "A purse of silver would open any door." Janna shot him a sharp look. Did he not know what his dog had done? Or didn't he care that he was deliberately leading Winifred astray, giving her false hope when there was none?

Her rising opinion of the relic seller dropped several notches. It dropped even further as she noticed color flood Winifred's cheeks, heard the note of hope in her voice as she breathed, "Oh! Do you think, if I found the hand, I might claim a reward for it?"

"We've all been searched and it hasn't been found," Janna said sharply, not wanting to encourage Winifred to hope for such a miracle.

"No reason why it shouldn't be found," Ulf cut in. "Someone must have it, after all. It wouldn't have been too hard to hide such a thing from the guard's view while the search was on. It could have been secreted inside a thick bush, perhaps, or even buried for a time."

"Whoever claimed the reward would first have to find the hand – and how do you do that when the hand wasn't found by the guard when he searched us all? You'd have an awful lot of explaining to do," Janna pointed out.

"Yes. Yes, you're right." Winifred looked thoroughly downcast.

"I wonder why the hand was taken," Janna said thoughtfully, with a pointed glance at Ulf. "For gain, do you think, to be sold on as a holy relic? Or did someone covet it for their own private worship? Or could it have been lost by accident, perhaps?"

"Not an accident, no ways," Ulf said cheerfully, seemingly blind to Janna's unspoken accusation. "I saw the hand at the abbey.

And the reliquary in which it was kept. The hand was open to view while the sacristan was in attendance. And I'll be willing to wager it was kept locked tight in her absence. Whoever took the hand took it by design, and by cunning. And unless the thief intends to keep it forever, for her – or his – private worship, sooner or later it must be returned to Wiltune so that the reward may be claimed, or else sold elsewhere."

Unless the hand had already served as a tasty feed for Brutus! Janna wondered how Ulf could maintain such an innocent expression. Surely he must know what his dog had done, for the hound had carried the thing in his mouth all the way from Wiltune.

"But you are right, mistress." Ulf gave Janna a knowing wink before turning back to Winifred. "Whoever returns the hand will have to answer how it came to be in her possession. She will have need of a very convincing story to escape punishment."

"She?"

It wasn't fair of Ulf to bolster Winifred's hopes in this way, to encourage her to keep looking for the relic in the hope of claiming the reward. Janna shot him a disapproving frown as she puzzled out how to force him to admit the truth. "I saw Brutus eating something yesterday," she said carefully.

"A dog that size, he eats all the time! Pity me having to find the means to feed him," Ulf acknowledged cheerfully, adding, "But of course I encourage him to forage for himself, for he is a hunting dog after all."

"And I saw what he'd hunted yesterday. It looked like he was eating a hand." Janna observed that both Ulf's and Winifred's mouths had fallen open in shock. "I couldn't help but wonder if Brutus was dining on the missing hand of St James?"

Ulf froze into stillness. His gaze slid sideways to Brutus, then to Winifred and, finally, back to her. He looked thoroughly discomfited.

49

"Why didn't you say summat before now? Why didn't you tell the guard what you'd seen?"

Janna shrugged. "If it was the hand of St James, it was far too late to save it. There didn't seem any point in causing trouble."

"That's kind of you, Janna." Ulf hesitated. "And the guard has gone now, so there's no point in stirring things up again. Don't you agree?" It seemed to Janna that he addressed this last remark to Winifred, who nodded eagerly. Janna wondered if Ulf had a plan to get himself out of trouble, and perhaps help Winifred at the same time? Was he planning to find a "hand" somewhere else? Could he and Winifred be conspiring in this together, working out how to share the reward?

Not liking where her thoughts were taking her, Janna rose, brushed the crumbs from her gown, and strode away from the pair. She was ready to scream with frustration. She hated secrets – they had blighted her life from the very beginning. If her mother had only told her the truth, hadn't kept so many things hidden from her, she wouldn't be here now, walking with the pilgrims and hoping for what might prove to be impossible. Instead, she'd be doing...what?

The thought stopped Janna's angry questioning. Her life had changed forever because of her mother's pride, her stubbornness, her secrecy. It was because of her mother that she was on this quest to find her father; because of her mother that she was meeting new people, going to new places and learning so many new things, as she'd always wanted to do, instead of staying at home and marrying Godric, as her mother had wanted her to do.

Godric. He'd stood by her after her mother had died, and after everyone else had turned against her. He'd told her that he loved her. They might well have wed if she hadn't insisted on setting out in search of her father. And she might well have regretted it if she had, Janna reminded herself fiercely. To marry the first man who had shown any interest in her and by doing so never find out the secrets of her family, or gain experience outside the narrow confines of the world she knew...

She shook her head. Far better to be here than there. If she'd married Godric, she would always have wondered what might have been. Yet she couldn't help thinking how sweet life with Godric might be. They might well have had a child by now. She dug her nails hard into her palms in an effort to block the painful recollection of Godric and Cecily together in the market square. That was all in the past, and best forgotten.

Seeking distraction, she glanced back at Ulf and Winifred. If they were concocting a secret plan to defraud the abbess, she wanted no part of it. She bent to pick up her staff and joined the other pilgrims, who were now being roused by Bernard to continue their journey.

*

They made slow time in the afternoon. Clearly, Juliana was in pain, but she brushed away all offers of help. Even Bernard's offer to purchase a donkey for his mother as they passed through a small hamlet was met with a stern refusal. Janna knew what was behind Bernard's offer, and sympathized with it. She couldn't understand why Juliana was so determined to mortify herself. Indeed she might have taken the donkey herself just to save her sore, torn feet if she wasn't keen to hoard her coins.

A small-holding close to the rough track that threaded along the river was their lodging for the night, and the pilgrims were glad to find it, for a steady rain had begun to fall and they were keen to find shelter. But Bernard had to talk hard and fast, for the farmer and his wife were grudging with their hospitality. Perhaps – and more likely – they had little to share. A coin produced some dry, sour bread and a large bowl of thin gruel. Janna noticed that the pilgrims tucked in with good will. Obviously they were used to taking the rough with the smooth.

They were still at their repast when a loud bang on the door arrested their speech. In the silence that fell, they heard the sound of a horse's neigh. There was another loud bang.

The farmer hastened to the door and opened it. A man stepped over the threshold, sweeping a dark green cloak from his shoulders as he came. He flapped it about, sending a shower of raindrops in all directions. He shook his head, reminding Janna of a wet dog trying to dry itself, and swiped his forearm across his face to blot the moisture with his sleeve. That done, he looked about him, registering the presence of the pilgrim group before turning his attention to the farmer, who had closed the door and now stood respectfully beside him.

"Do you have room for one more traveler, good sire?" the stranger asked.

"Yes indeed, my lord." The farmer preened himself, obviously flattered to be so addressed. Janna could understand why, for the farmer and his wife were barefoot and clothed in homespun whereas the stranger wore a red linen tunic that reached to his knees, with embroidery at its hem, neck and sleeves. His breeches were fitted, and were tucked into fine leather boots with pointed toes. He was tall, handsome, and obviously a man of some substance. His bearing and words confirmed it.

"My name is Ralph de Otreburne," he said, and swept the party a low bow.

Bernard bowed in return before introducing himself and the pilgrim band to the stranger. "We are blessed to have shelter on a night like this," he continued, as a sudden gust of wind swept through the hole in the roof, sending smoke billowing around the room.

The man nodded in agreement and turned to the farmer. "I need something to eat and so does my horse. Will you see to it?"

He pulled a silver ha'penny from his purse and tipped it into the farmer's hand.

"Indeed, my lord. I'll see to it straightaway." The farmer's hand closed over the coin. "My wife will find you something to eat," he added, and gave her a meaningful glance.

After a moment's hesitation, Ralph de Otreburne seated himself by the fire to dry, while the farmer stashed the coin into the rough leather pouch at his waist and made a hasty exit. Bernard picked up a dish and ladled into it some of the gruel from the pot still sitting on the table. He handed it to Ralph, who inspected it dubiously before spooning some into his mouth. He pulled a face. Clearly, this was not what he was used to, nor was it to his liking. As he put down the spoon, the farmer's wife placed before him a trencher of bread and a dish of stew thick with chunks of meat.

"'Tis hare, sire, freshly caught only yesterday," she said, with a shy bob of her head.

Ralph took an appreciative sniff. All eyes were on him as he spooned up a huge bite. He noticed their stares. "What is it?" he asked through a mouthful of bread and meat. At once the pilgrims glanced away and began to talk among themselves. But Janna watched as Ralph assessed the remains of the meager meal the pilgrims had shared.

"Mistress!" He summoned the farmer's wife with an imperious crook of the finger. "Some more of this fine stew for my fellow travelers, if you please." And he pulled another ha'penny from his purse and handed it over. The farmer's wife bobbed a curtsy and hurried to do his bidding. Janna felt saliva seep into her mouth at the thought of the treat to come, and smiled appreciatively at their benefactor.

"Mistress Johanna, I believe?" He returned her smile. Janna was flattered that he had remembered her name. She felt a little shy as his eyes roamed from her face down to her silky gown.

Here was someone else who might be gulled by her finery, but she wasn't going to tell him the truth about herself. At least, not yet. She was busy conducting her own inspection, and she liked what she saw very much. Ralph wore his fair hair long, and sported a mustache and a short beard. His eyes were the blue of a summer sky. Something about his expression and demeanor told Janna that this was a man of courage, of daring. He would not be put off once he set his mind to something, even if it took him to the limits of his strength and endurance, even if it led him to the very gates of Hell itself.

She shook her head and told herself not to be so fanciful. Yet the impression lingered as she watched the stranger return to his meal, breaking bread with long, strong fingers and stuffing it into his mouth.

"So you are pilgrims?" he asked the company at large.

"Indeed, sire." Bernard answered for them all. "We have walked the pilgrim path to Santiago de Compostela, and are now on our way home to Oxeneford."

Ralph nodded thoughtfully. "You will have seen many signs and wonders on your travels, I am sure."

"Indeed we have, sire." Bernard stared into the distance. His face took on a dreamy thoughtfulness as he continued, "The Camino is marked in places with a cross, and sometimes the scallop shell sign of the saint, but often it was hard to know which fork in the road to take. Yet always there was a sign, a light perhaps, or a tolling bell, or even a passing traveler to guide us." He took the scallop shell badge from his hat and held it out for Ralph's inspection. "We wear these in honor of St James, who is known as Santiago," he said. "These lines, spread out like a hand, symbolize the work – both charitable and physical – that a pilgrim should undertake. But we were also told another story about the shells."

He paused to focus his thoughts, and to be sure his audience was fully attentive, before resuming. "It's said that, a long time ago, a rich pilgrim coming to the shrine was pursued by bandits. There was a storm, the man's horse was exhausted and could go no faster, and the bandits were closing in on him. He could see the glint of their knives and knew they would show no mercy if they caught him, for he was unarmed.

"He urged on his poor, exhausted horse, knowing his only hope was to outpace the bandits, for there was no turning or possibility of escape. The path he traveled followed the coastline high above the sea, with a steep drop on one side and a high rocky wall on the other. Suddenly the ground gave way, and he and his horse plunged over the cliff into the sea.

"The bandits were sure he could not survive such a fall, and so they turned and left him. Shortly afterward, and still mounted on his horse, the pilgrim emerged safely from the water onto a nearby beach. He was covered in scallop shells! Ever since then, the scallop shell has become a symbol of life and of the Camino and St James.

"But that is only one of the many wondrous tales we heard as we walked the Camino. On another occasion..."

As Bernard told the stories, Janna watched Ralph. She had the feeling that his mind was on other, more pressing matters, for he seemed distracted, only bobbing his head or making some noise in his throat when a comment was called for. She wondered why he was abroad this foul evening. But it was some time before Bernard's travel stories came to an end and she could fit a word in.

"And what is the purpose of your journey, my lord?" she asked respectfully.

He turned his amused gaze upon her. "Why, I am also going to Oxeneford."

"We have our own saint there too, of course," Bernard interposed. "Many pilgrims come to visit St Frideswide's holy well."

"And that is the purpose of my visit," Ralph said. "I am a simple pilgrim, just as you are." He looked to Janna as he answered her question.

"But the lady is not a pilgrim, sire. You mistake her," Bernard observed.

Ralph continued to watch Janna. "Why, then, do you travel with pilgrims, mistress?" he asked softly.

She felt a momentary alarm, until commonsense told her that Robert of Babestoche had no way of knowing her whereabouts, or even that she'd left the abbey. She could feel herself coloring under Ralph's steady regard. "I have my own reasons," she told him, not prepared to divulge either her purpose or her true destination.

Something flitted across Ralph's face, an expression that Janna found hard to interpret. Curiosity? Suspicion? "And it is safer to walk with pilgrims than to take to the road on your own," he said. "I trust you travel in peace and comfort?"

Janna wondered if there was more to his enquiry than mere courtesy. "Not in comfort," she admitted ruefully. She had pulled off her slippers at the earliest opportunity, and now she glanced down at her sore feet before returning her regard to the newcomer.

"Nor in peace! We've encountered nothing but trouble since these two young women joined us," said Bernard, with a wide sweep of his arm that also encompassed Winifred, who sat beside Janna.

"I hope you're not blaming Winifred or me for any of it, Master Bernard," Janna said, not wanting the stranger to get the wrong idea.

"No blame to you at all, mistress," Bernard said hastily.

"Trouble?" The stranger cocked his head and raised an eyebrow.

"The first thing we encountered was a dead man lying close to the river. And his horse grazing nearby, lamed," Bernard explained. "But that wasn't the end of the alarums, not by any means! No sooner had we stumbled across the corpse than we were pursued by a guard from Wiltune Abbey. It seems that a relic was stolen – "

"A dead man?" the stranger interrupted. "But...how did he come to die?"

"Broke his neck when his horse reared and threw him, I suspect," said Bernard.

"But why did his horse rear? Was he attacked? Were there bandits about?"

"On the road, maybe, but none down by the river. I searched the area but all I found was the horse. It was limping. Startled by a snake perhaps, or a sharp stone under its hoof?" Bernard gestured toward Janna. "You were there as witness, mistress. You saw what I saw. Wouldn't you agree that's how it was?"

Janna, thus pressed, had to say that yes, she did agree.

"Could you identify the man? Did you know him?"

"I have never seen him before. None of us knows who he was."

"Surely he carried papers? Something to identify him?"

Bernard shook his head. "We searched his possessions but found nothing to tell us his name." It was no more nor less than the truth, Janna thought. And if Bernard was keeping to his promise of secrecy about the message, then so would she. After all, he had invited her to join their group and had given her a warm welcome. She trusted him, and trusted his judgment.

Ralph turned an enquiring glance on Janna. She shrugged. None of them knew who Ralph supported: the empress or the king. Nor did they know where he'd come from or why he seemed so interested in the dead man. Better, she thought, to keep silent.

But it seemed no more than a casual enquiry after all, for Ralph turned back to Bernard. "I beg your pardon," he said. "I allowed my interest in the fate of an unfortunate traveler to interrupt what you were saying about the theft of a relic?"

Janna admired his courtesy, while acknowledging there was a great deal else to admire about Ralph. He met her gaze once more, and gave her a wicked grin. Janna risked a quick, shy smile before looking away. She felt sure that he suspected they hadn't told him everything, for there was such knowing in his eyes. A man of courage and daring, yes, but perhaps also a man of secrets.

She became aware that Juliana was watching them closely, her face closed tight as a trap. Janna stood up and walked across to the old woman and sat down beside her. Juliana was trembling. Janna reached out a comforting hand.

"What ails you, my lady?" she asked. "Is there aught I can do to help you?"

"There's naught anyone can do, for it has begun." Juliana turned to her and Janna read the fear in her eyes. She gripped Juliana's hand tightly, trying to pour her young strength and courage into the feeble body.

"All will be well," she said. "Pray tell your son of your concern for him. Ask him to take care. Tell him that you watch over him. Tell him we shall all keep watch."

"It's too late for warning. He won't listen to me." Juliana moistened her lips with her tongue. "When I first spoke of my fear for his safety, Bernard told me that our lives are as candles to the breath of God. We may burn bright and steady, sure in our purpose, or we may flicker feebly in the darkness of self-doubt. But our end is always at God's will. And he said that whenever God called him, he would be ready." Her voice sharpened in anguish. "But I will never be ready! I will never be ready to lose my son!"

At a loss for words, Janna sat beside Juliana for the remainder of the meal, and lay down beside her when it was time to take their rest. The small room was stuffy and airless, and reeked of the smell of unwashed bodies and wet clothes, farts and old food, and smoke from the half-doused fire. She itched and scratched, knowing that fleas and lice and probably bedbugs too had found a home in the dirty straw that covered the floor. She turned restlessly, finding it impossible to settle to sleep. Finally, she rose and cautiously threaded her way through the recumbent bodies to the closed door of the farmstead.

She pushed it open and stepped outside, taking a deep and grateful gulp of fresh, cool air. It had stopped raining. The clouds were shifting, showing scatters of stars through their ragged hems. In the faint moonlight she could make out the dark shape of a barn and the humped shadows of animals. She decided to go in search of somewhere quiet and solitary to sleep: a dry patch of grass under a tree, or better still, a bed of hay in the barn.

She was about to close the door behind her when she felt a pressure against her hand. The door opened wider, and the stranger stepped quickly over the threshold. He grinned and put his finger to his lips as he quietly closed the door behind him. Still with his finger to his lips, he took Janna's hand and led her a little way from the hall and the sleepers inside.

"Did you follow me?" Janna demanded, when Ralph came to a stop and released her. He made no answer, but instead leaned a shoulder against the side of the barn, seeming quite at ease in spite of her accusation. She could hardly see his face in the dim light, but thought he might be smiling.

"What do you want? Did you follow me?" she asked again, her tone sharp with underlying fear.

"I could lie and say no, but why should I hide the truth?" he answered quietly. "Yes, mistress, I followed you. Many men would, if given half the chance."

Janna drew a breath, trying to gather her courage. "Then I shall go back inside where there is company and protection, should I need it." She had been ambushed once before, and by a man with murder on his mind. She had avoided harm on that occasion; she might not be so fortunate next time. Were Ralph's words meant as mere flattery or did he, like the assassin before him, desire her death as well as her body? He had taken up a position between her and the farmhouse.

She would have to get past him to reach her fellow travelers. Or she could scream.

"I mean you no harm, Johanna," he said quickly, to reassure her. "My words were meant as a compliment."

"You don't know me well enough to follow me out into the night, or pay me compliments!" Janna retorted, unsure whether or not to believe him.

"All right then, I wanted a chance to talk to you," Ralph admitted. "It's about the dead man. I cannot help wondering if he might be a kinsman of mine. My cousin set out on a journey some time ago, but he seems to have gone missing. I do fear for his safety in these troubled times. Can you tell me what the dead man looked like?"

"His hair was dark, and worn shorter than yours. He was clean-shaven. And his clothes were costly." Janna's sympathy was aroused now, and she was keen to give as accurate an account as she could. As she gave details of his clothing, she was struck by a thought. "If this is your kinsman, he has been dead for several days," she concluded.

"How do you know?"

Janna hesitated, wondering how to phrase her words so as not to cause Ralph undue distress. "His body was...marked. There were...signs that it had lain there for some time." She hoped she'd said enough to satisfy him.

"Signs?"

"Insects. And...and bite marks." She really couldn't tell him that animals had started to eat his cousin.

Fortunately, Ralph had heard enough. "He sounds something like my cousin," he said urgently. "But if so, he would have carried documents with him."

"What sort of documents?" Janna wondered if Ralph's cousin was indeed carrying a message from the bishop to the empress, and if it would be safe to tell what she had seen.

"A letter, or a bill maybe; the sorts of documents any merchant might carry." Ralph was silent for a moment. "One thing I do know is that he carried a letter from his wife to her family, for my cousin intended to visit them along the way. There would have been a red seal on the parchment. Did you see anything like that?"

"Not like that, no." Janna was quite sure now that the bishop's letter could have no connection to Ralph's cousin's wife. She was pleased to be able to set Ralph's mind at rest on that score, while settling her conscience at the same time.

"But you did find something?" He was quick to pick up her slip of the tongue.

"No!" Janna was glad of the dark, for she could feel her face flame with the lie and knew her blushes would give her away. "I am quite sure that the dead man was not your cousin," she added hastily.

Ralph nodded thoughtfully. "I wonder if you and Master Bernard were the first to find him?" he queried. "You say the body may have lain there for several days. Others might have come before you and searched the dead man's scrip, for it seems strange that you found nothing within it. Surely no-one would travel so light?"

"I am sure we were the first to find him, for it was only chance that took us down to the river at that place. There was a party of horsemen on the road and Master Bernard wanted to keep out of their way. Besides, everything about the dead man seemed undisturbed. Any thief would have removed his rings, or the gold chain about his neck, or his silver dagger, but nothing was taken. And any honest man would not have left him just lying there. The dead man's horse grazed nearby; it was an easy enough task to hoist the body onto its back and lead it to the nearest hamlet." She wondered if she'd said enough to put Ralph's mind at ease. "And that's what Master Bernard arranged," she added. "The body was taken to Wiltune by the abbey's guard. He, himself, searched both the dead man and his belongings, and found nothing to say who he was. But he assured us he will pursue enquiries regarding the man's identity and will do his utmost to find his nearest kin. You could ride to Wiltune tomorrow to see the body for yourself, if you wish. It's not far."

Ralph was silent for a moment. Then he said, "It's clear to me that you are clever as well as perceptive, Johanna. If you do know anything about the identity of the dead man, or the papers he carried, you will tell me, won't you? I would make sure you're well rewarded for your trouble."

Pleasure at his flattery was outweighed by anger that he could so misjudge her character. Janna drew herself up to her full height. "We found nothing to suggest that the dead man was your cousin," she said stiffly. "Offering a reward for information will not make me change what I have already told you." She glanced sideways, and caught the gleam of Ralph's eyes reflecting the moonlight. He was regarding her intently.

"Yet it seems to me that you found something, even if it was not exactly what I thought my cousin might have carried on his person?"

Mindful of her promise to Bernard, Janna silently cursed herself for allowing doubt to creep into Ralph's mind. "No," she said firmly, as firmly as her troubled conscience would allow. "We found nothing."

To her relief he accepted her denial. "Thank you for setting my mind at rest, Johanna," he said. "It would seem that my cousin has either been waylaid on his journey or has traveled on ahead. I fear the former, for he ever had an eye for a game of dice and a weakness for ale." He gave a rueful laugh. "Forgive me if I seemed to doubt you. I should have remembered what my cousin is like."

"But will you go to Wiltune to view the body, and make sure?" Janna rather hoped he would not. Now that he'd accepted her word, she thought she might enjoy the company of this agreeable stranger.

"No, you've said enough to convince me it would be a waste of my time." He leaned a little closer in the darkness. Janna felt his warm breath on her cheek as he whispered, "I'll continue my journey along with you, if that's agreeable to your leader. I shall enjoy your company along the way."

Your company? Was he referring to her company alone, or the company of all the pilgrims? Janna shifted uneasily. "And is the purpose of your journey only to visit the shrine of St Frideswide, sire?" She was curious as to why someone, obviously well-born and with a mount to speed his journey, should elect to take the slow way with them.

"Yes, indeed." Ralph sounded somewhat taken aback by her question. "As I said, I am a pilgrim just like you."

"But I am not on a pilgrimage," Janna reminded him. "Besides, my destination is Ambresberie." Not wanting to give him any opportunity to question her further, she hurried on. "Do you have a special reason for visiting St Frideswide? What is that saint's claim to fame?"

"She was a religious. She's wrought many miracles over the years."

Just like every other saint! Janna hid a smile. "And do you need a miracle, my lord?"

"It may be that I do." Ralph sounded unexpectedly serious as he added, "Mayhap we all do."

"And does your cousin also go to Oxeneford? We might meet up with him on our journey?"

"Perhaps." But Ralph didn't sound entirely convinced. Janna wondered if he still harbored secret doubts about the dead man.

"And why do you go to Ambresberie, Johanna?"

Janna hesitated. She didn't want to tell him anything about her family, but after dodging his questions and concealing what she knew about the letter found on the dead man, she felt she owed him something. "I'm bound for the abbey to seek information."

"Oh?" She heard the spark of interest in his voice.

"About my family." To forestall his next question, she added quickly, "I came outside for some fresh air, but I'm tired now.

I'm going inside." Her plan to sleep outdoors was no longer possible, not with Ralph prowling about. Without giving him time to question her further, she scurried past him and returned to the stuffy, malodorous hall.

Chapter 5

"I must talk to you, Janna. I'm so worried, I can't sleep." Winifred shifted closer to Janna as she lay down once more to rest.

"Then you must talk to me here, for we can't go outside."

Ralph had not followed Janna. She wondered what he was up to out there, if he was also finding it hard to sleep in these cramped confines. Or was it worry about his cousin that kept him awake? His curiosity was understandable; she just wished she could tell him that the dead man was the bishop's messenger and so set his mind at rest. But where had Ralph come from this day if not from Wiltune? She frowned at the thought. Yet there was no reason to doubt him, for he could have come from anywhere, traveling as he was on horseback and able to traverse many miles in a day.

Her thoughts moved on to the message itself. While she was fairly sure that Bernard had the truth of the matter, and that the man's death had been an accident, Janna wasn't sure he was right in thinking the message of so little import that it would suffice to carry it to the empress himself, particularly given their slow rate of progress. On the other hand, Ralph had a horse and could travel so much faster than they could; perhaps they should trust him after all.

But whose side was he on in this bitter civil war? There was no way of knowing. Reluctantly, Janna came to the conclusion that Bernard was right. She must say nothing to anyone, nothing at all.

She wriggled about, trying to find a more comfortable position on the prickly straw, and became aware that Winifred was still whispering urgently into her ear.

"...and so I thought I'd borrow it and take it back where it belongs, but after what you and Ulf said earlier, I realize my plan's not going to work. I'm in real trouble, Janna. Please, *please* help me!"

It took a few moments for Janna to realize she had no idea what Winifred was talking about. "What did you borrow?" she asked.

"The hand, of course!"

"The hand?"

"Of St James of Compostela. Haven't you been listening?"

"Yes! No. I'm sorry, you'd better start again. What's all this about the hand of St James?"

"I borrowed it from Wiltune Abbey."

"You *what*?" Janna couldn't believe her ears.

"But Ulf knows I have it. I'm sure he knows. What'll I do if he tells anyone I've got it?"

"Wait. Wait!" Janna shook her head, trying to clear her thoughts. "It was *you* who stole the hand?"

"I didn't *steal* it, I *borrowed* it. Well, not borrowed it exactly, because it doesn't even belong at Wiltune. When I prayed to the saint for guidance, she let me know that my sacred mission is to take the hand back to where it came from. To the abbey at Radinges. You see, if I return it to them, I'm sure the monks will be so glad to have it back again they'll help me realize my heart's dream. I shall ask them to recommend me to an abbey where I can be taken in as a postulant."

"Recommend a thief as a postulant?" Janna was still having trouble coming to grips with Winifred's extraordinary confession.

"I'm not a thief!" Winifred's voice rose high with indignation, and Janna hastily shushed her.

"I didn't take the hand for *me*," Winifred continued more quietly. "I'm going to give it back to its rightful owners: the monks at Radinges. Not Wiltune. Not Oxeneford either. I just said I was going there as an excuse to travel with the pilgrims for part of the way. But Ulf knows I've got it. I could tell by what he said and the way he looked at me. He must have seen me hiding the hand in the holly bush when the abbey guard came to question us."

Janna was silent as several oddities suddenly began to make sense. Winifred's scratched hands, and also her fear when Ulf described what she must have done, almost as if he'd witnessed her behavior. Had he seen her, or was it just a lucky guess on his part? She recalled Ulf's pointed comments, and nodded thoughtfully to herself. Ulf knew all right, and he'd made sure that Winifred understood what he'd seen her do.

"I shouldn't worry about Ulf," she said, trying to reassure the wretched girl. "If he saw you and meant to cause trouble for you, he would have said something to the abbey guard, or gone after him, got word to him somehow." She was silent for a moment. "Are you sure you've still got the relic?" she asked. "Because that dog was chewing on a hand, I know it was. And Ulf looked as guilty as an angel caught dancing with the devil when I said so."

"Whatever Brutus was chewing, it wasn't what I've got." Winifred felt for Janna's hand, and drew it toward the purse she cradled so carefully. "The blessed relic is in here."

Janna's searching fingers touched hard bone through the worn leather of Winifred's purse. "You've got a nerve!" She wasn't sure whether to laugh or be shocked.

"It wasn't my decision. St Edith showed me the way," Winifred insisted. "I was praying at her shrine, asking for guidance as to how I could persuade an abbey to take me in without a dowry. And St Edith answered my prayers! I don't think the sacristan knew I was there, and when she was called away, I was briefly left alone with the precious relics of both St Edith and St James. I'd been thinking how angry and how disappointed the monks at Radinges must feel to have their precious relic snatched from them by the empress, and suddenly here I was with the means to redress that wrong, and at the same time fulfill my purpose in life by serving the Lord! I knew I couldn't shift the reliquary but it was the work of only moments to lift out the hand and shut the lid, and make my escape. I hoped no-one would notice its loss, at least not as quickly as they did."

Janna smiled openly, knowing that Winifred would not see her amusement in the darkness. She'd never yet heard of a thief with the brazen cheek to claim that God – or even a saint – had encouraged their wrongdoing. And yet she knew, of her own experience, how St Edith had intervened in people's lives – including her own. So who was she to say that Winifred's act might not appeal to the saint's sense of humor, or even her determination to bring another soul to God? Who was she to judge the rights or wrongs of the matter?

She remembered the resolute set of Winifred's jaw, and the fire in her voice when she spoke of her calling. The young woman had acted with courage and determination to breathe life into her dreams. No matter how twisted her motives, her action showed plainly how desperately she wanted to retreat from the world and live as a religious. Even if Janna couldn't share Winifred's ambition, she felt some sympathy with anyone who would do something so outrageous to achieve her desire. In fact, she reminded herself, she was hardly in any position to judge Winifred for she, too, was a thief. She had stolen garments *and* set fire to a barn, and had found justification for her actions at the same time.

Janna shifted uncomfortably at the memory of those dark days. She became aware that Winifred was speaking once more. "...and then I realized you were right," she said anxiously. "They'll ask questions about where I found it. They'll suspect that I took it in the first place. And they'll be honor-bound to send it back to Wiltune, so all of this will have been in vain. I was going to call myself Sister Edith, in honor of the saint who helped me. I can't believe she has set me on the wrong path, but I don't know what to do now to make things right. What do you think, Janna? Should I go back and return the hand to the abbey Wiltune?"

"In the hope of receiving a reward large enough to buy your way into the abbey of your choice?"

"No. To confess my misdeed." Winifred sounded utterly miserable. It was clear to Janna that she had given up her dream and was now facing the harsh reality of her actions.

"You'll be severely punished for it, if you do so." Janna felt sorry that such an act of daring should come to naught.

"I'll be punished enough if they just send me home." Winifred's tone was bitter with disgust. "My father will make me wed old Dribblegum and, oh, I would rather be dead than do that!"

"Old Dribblegum?" Janna asked cautiously.

"He's old. He dribbles. And he has no teeth. But he's a free man and he owns a small plot of land, and he will have me for his wife." Winifred shook her head in despair. "And my father has agreed that I will marry him. That's why I ran away, and that's why I prayed to St Edith."

"So your need is to escape, rather than live the life of a religious?"

"No! Well, yes. I needed to escape, but I've always wanted to live in an abbey," Winifred said earnestly. "All that I told you is true, Janna. I don't want to be any man's wife. I *want* to serve God." There was no doubting the passionate sincerity in her voice. Janna sympathized with her predicament.

"Say nothing for the while," she cautioned. "Let's think on this, let's see if we can find some way you may return the hand in safety, and still achieve your heart's desire."

"Is that possible?" Winifred's voice came alive, strong with new hope.

"Shh," Juliana grumbled sleepily.

"I don't know," Janna whispered. "Sleep on it now. Let us hope that St Edith will come to us in our dreams to show us the way."

*

They awoke to a wet and miserable day. Janna shivered in her thin gown as they gathered about the fire for a mug of ale and a hunk of bitter bread to break their fast. Ralph noticed her shiver, and offered her his cloak, which she declined although she longed to protect herself from the rain and cold outside. It would be dreadful out there, she thought, judging from the gusts of wind and spatters of rain that blew down the chimney and set them coughing and choking as smoke billowed from the fire.

"And you walk in bare feet?" Ralph looked down at Janna's toes, which peeped from below her gown, for its former owner, as well as having smaller feet than Janna, had also been slightly shorter.

"My shoes hurt," Janna admitted.

"Then you must ride my horse this day, mistress, and I will walk beside you."

"Thank you, sire, but I do not know how to ride." Janna was touched by his kind gesture. For the sake of her bruised and bleeding feet, she longed to accept, but knew herself to be unequal to the task. It was true she'd been on horseback several times, but as a passenger. Janna felt momentarily faint as memories flooded her mind. She blinked quickly to dispel them.

She noticed that Ralph seemed a little surprised by her admission, and realized that she'd just given herself away. He thought her highborn. She should know how to ride, for she would have been taught. "I'm frightened of horses," she lied, not wanting him to know her true status, wanting to preserve her anonymity.

Ralph nodded in understanding. He produced a penny from his seemingly inexhaustible supply and showed it to the farmer's wife. "This for you if you have a pair of sandals or boots that might fit my friend," he said.

The farmer's wife eyed the coin, greedy for it but unsure about giving up the comfort of a stout pair of boots. The farmer had no such qualms, however, and darted off to fetch them. They were slapped down in front of Ralph almost before he'd finished speaking. Janna felt embarrassed both by Ralph's easy generosity and the thought that he was taking advantage of their hosts. Yet she dreaded the long walk ahead. She picked up a boot and slipped it onto her foot. It fitted easily; in fact, it was slightly too large for her. She looked at the coin in Ralph's hand, and thought of the coins in her own purse now tucked away out of sight and also out of easy reach.

"Thank you. I shall repay you when I can," she told him.

"No need." Ralph held out the silver penny. The farmer's wife glanced at her husband and then, with an air of defiance, snatched it and quickly slipped it up her sleeve. Janna soothed her conscience with the hope that the woman would spend the coin to her own benefit in the marketplace, that it would be enough not only to replace her boots but that she might also be able to afford some small luxury.

True to his stated intention, Ralph accompanied the party of pilgrims. He'd offered his horse also to Juliana but, on her refusal, he now walked beside them all, leading his horse on its rein as they slowly wended their way along the path beside the river. He kept close to Janna, and so did Winifred, which had the fortunate effect of curbing any further questions on his part.

Winifred treated Ralph with a cool shyness, but Janna couldn't help throwing a few coquettish glances his way. He was good company, keeping them entertained with funny stories he'd heard in the course of his travels. More, he proved himself helpful when it came to hacking a way through overgrown brambles, or giving them a hand across the many rough and muddy stretches along the track. Besides, there was no denying he was the sort of man any maiden might swoon over. She shot a quick glance at him from under lowered lashes, and was immensely disconcerted to find he was scrutinizing her just as carefully.

The presence of Ralph meant that she and Winifred were unable to discuss what to do with the hand of St James, for no answers had come to Janna in the night. If St Edith was still on their side she was keeping quiet about it. Today, Bernard walked behind the pilgrims instead of leading the way. He was keeping company with his mother, and Janna watched them talking earnestly. It was clear that he fretted with impatience. Janna could understand why. She wondered if he'd confided their secret to Juliana, for he must surely know where his mother's loyalty lay and whether it was safe to tell her what they'd found in the dead man's purse.

Whether he'd told her or not, they were not happy with each other. Janna watched them at the small tavern where the pilgrims stopped to eat their dinner. Hissed whispers gave way to a strained silence between them as they supped on ale and pies. The other pilgrims ignored the trouble between the pair, instead sharing stories of their travels with another party that had come into the tavern.

Bernard was quick to hurry them outside just as soon as the last morsel had been devoured. He could barely hide his eagerness to move on, although he was gentle with his mother as he helped her outside and took her pack to carry himself. Juliana clung to his arm for a moment before releasing him. Janna saw the shine of tears in her eyes as she turned away, and felt sorry that the old woman traveled with such dread in her heart on what should be a joyous, spiritual adventure.

As they set out along the track once more, she tried to offer some comfort. "Do you feel blessed that you have visited the shrine of St James, my lady?" she asked.

Juliana nodded. She was limping badly, and Janna offered her an arm to lean on. To her surprise, for the old woman had been fiercely independent in the past, Juliana took it and leaned heavily against her. Janna braced herself to take her weight. "Was that your purpose in making this journey? To ask for the saint's blessing?" she ventured.

"Yes. But not – " Juliana broke off abruptly.

"Did you ask the saint to help you walk properly?" Janna knew that Juliana's condition would deteriorate as she aged, and that there was no known cure for it – other than a miracle, if God or his saints were so inclined.

"No, I didn't ask for healing." Juliana's voice was low and fierce as she continued, "I asked for my son's life! I begged the saint to take my life for his. I refused the comfort of riding so that I could walk each painful step of the Camino as a sign of my penitence for past sins, and my willingness to give up my life to save my son! And I pray that it's not too late and that God will hear my prayers, for darkness still walks with me and I fear it!"

Janna was shocked into silence by Juliana's passionate outburst. She had no idea a mother's love could be so powerful, and so strong. But Juliana was not yet done.

"Our safety lies with you, Johanna, I am sure of it. Please, I beg you, *please* leave us. Now, before it is too late."

"Too late for who? For what?"

"For us. For my son." It was the second time Juliana had appealed to her, and still Janna couldn't understand why. What power of life or death did she have over Bernard? It didn't make sense. She wondered if she should talk to Bernard herself, tell him about Juliana's fears, and ask for his opinion as to what she should do. She looked about for the pilgrim, and saw that he was striding ahead with Morcar and Adam. It looked as if they might be arguing, and she wondered anew why Adam kept in their company.

Juliana tugged on Janna's arm, dragging her back to her present predicament. "Please will you leave us? You can travel with someone else. For my son's sake – and for your own."

Troubled, Janna sought for a way to appease the old woman. Could she slow down, walk some way behind the pilgrims, perhaps? She was reluctant to leave their protection altogether, and besides, she didn't think she could find the way to Ambresberie without their guidance, for she had no idea how far it was or even if she should stay on this same path or turn on to another. But if she put enough space between the pilgrims and herself so that she was not really part of their group, she could still keep them in sight and follow them.

After wrestling with her reluctance to walk alone, and even though she believed that Bernard's fate was out of her hands, Janna reluctantly agreed.

"And you'll stay away from my son, and from others in our group?" Juliana pressed her.

What am I, a leper? Janna's impulse was to answer in anger, but in deference to Juliana's age she swallowed her indignation and said, "I shall follow behind you. I'll do my utmost to have no more contact with any of you."

Juliana nodded, and released Janna's arm. "Thank you," she said. "I know I'm making difficulties for you where you see none. I know this is hard for you. And I thank you for being so understanding."

Janna stood still and watched the old woman shuffle off. She was some way behind the rest of the pilgrims, and moving slowly; it would be some time before Janna could safely set off by herself. A fallen log in a sheltered spot attracted her attention, and she sat down on it. Thanks to her new boots, walking was now a lot easier for her, but her feet still stung from the cuts and bruises she'd acquired while walking barefoot, so she was happy to rest for a while. She leaned back and looked up into the nests of the rooks, which nestled between green leaves like great black balls of wool. Caws and screeches melded with the quiet murmuring of the river. It was peaceful just to sit and be quiet. Janna closed her eyes, willing her soul to patience as she waited for the pilgrims to move further along their way.

Her meditation was interrupted by an impatient voice. "What on earth do you think you're doing?"

Janna opened her eyes to find Ralph staring down at her. "I – " She stopped, unwilling to tell Ralph the truth, lest he also think her a pariah. "I'm resting," she said.

"But we could have left you behind! We're not going straight to Ambresberie after all, we're going to visit an ancient circle of standing stones instead. Our fellow travelers were told of it when we stopped for our dinner. It seems miracles and marvels have been wrought there, and now everyone is on fire with enthusiasm to visit the site. It's not far from here, so I believe. There's been quite some argument over it, but Master Bernard eventually yielded to the wishes of the others and they have already set on a path to find the ceremonial passage that will take them to the great henge. I realized you were missing and so I dropped back to find you."

"That is kind of you, but my business is at Ambresberie, and that's where I must go." Had Juliana known of this when she'd urged her to leave them? Janna felt dismay that she would have to make the journey alone after all.

"You cannot travel on your own!" Ralph sounded thoroughly shocked. "'Tis unseemly – and it's not safe."

"Then I shall just have to take my chances." Janna wondered if he'd offer to leave the pilgrim band to accompany her. If so, what should she say? She suspected he had experience and charm to spare when it came to seduction. Even though he seemed honorable, she wasn't so stupid as to stake her life and reputation on wishful thinking. So, if he made an offer, she must refuse it.

"I won't hear of it," Ralph said firmly. "But I can't escort you either, for it would compromise your position in the eyes of your family and your friends." From the bold twinkle in his eyes, and the half-smile lurking about his mouth, Janna knew they'd both been thinking along the same lines. She felt reassured that they'd come to the same conclusion. But that still didn't help her out of her dilemma.

"You must come with us, Johanna, all of us," Ralph continued, when she remained silent. "I cannot, in all conscience, let you travel on alone."

He waited for her answer. Janna wondered what to say. It was all very well for Juliana to tell her to leave the pilgrim band, while Ralph had no power over her to forbid it. So what should she do? The thought of seeing a stone henge and perhaps invoking a miracle – such as finding her father – was greatly tempting, but she'd made a promise, and she should keep it. She sighed, wishing life could be less complicated. All she could think of was a compromise.

"My feet hurt, and I would rest a little longer if I may."

"Or you can ride?" Ralph gestured toward the steed that stood patiently beside him. "I'll sit behind you and hold you safe," he added, forestalling any objection.

Moving fast to catch up with the pilgrims was not what Janna had in mind. "I am happy to rest a while longer," she said. "I am sure we can catch up to the party later." She sensed his impatience to be off and hoped to take his mind off the delay by asking, "Pray, tell me more about this stone circle we are to visit."

"I know only what I learned from the travelers at the tavern. And travelers are ever prone to exaggeration, particularly with a skinfull of ale inside them!" He rolled his eyes in a parody of amazement. "Some said that the henge was built by an ancient people, and that it was used for sacrifices and pagan worship. Others claim that it was some sort of solar or lunar calendar to tell the seasons and the movements of the sun, moon and stars. The story I liked best was that the henge was built by the magician Merlin from giants' stones magically transported from Ireland." He shrugged. "No-one knows the truth of it, other than that it's very, very old; as old as time itself. But the most important thing about it, so far as Mistress Juliana is concerned, is that it was recently the site of a miracle."

"A miracle?" Janna sat forward, wondering if this was what Juliana had been so reluctant to share with her.

"So-called. The travelers witnessed – or were told about – a young boy, crippled since birth, whose legs became miraculously straight and whole after his parents took him to the henge. They washed the stones and the boy bathed in that water, to which some special herbs had also been added, and he was able to walk for the first time in his life. The stones have long been associated with healing, so it is said."

"And Juliana hopes that she, too, will be able to walk in comfort once more if she goes there?"

"No. She seems to have some other purpose in mind, I know not what. She won't talk to me, but gives me dark looks and mutters to herself whenever I cross her path. I don't think she approves of me at all."

Janna looked at Ralph with new interest. She gave a little chuckle of amusement. Juliana must be even more crazed than she'd suspected. The thought assuaged her conscience somewhat for breaking her promise to leave the pilgrims. Thanks to Ralph's intervention, it seemed she would have to continue her journey with them after all.

Now that it was decided, Janna was looking forward to seeing the henge. She could understand, now, the argument she'd witnessed between Bernard and his mother. Juliana would be desperate to invoke a miracle if it would protect her son, but Bernard must chafe at this additional delay. It seemed that he hadn't confided in his mother after all.

"Is it urgent, your business in Ambresberie?" Ralph asked.

"No, it can wait," Janna answered truthfully. She had been ignorant of her mother's past for all of her life. An extra day or two would make no difference to the outcome of her quest, whatever that might be.

"You said you go to the abbey to seek information?" He left the question hanging in the air, clearly expecting an answer.

"About my family." She hesitated over how much to tell, but thought that Ralph seemed genuinely interested. "My mother was once at the abbey there," she said, sticking to the bare facts. "I know little of her life, and I hope to find out more about her, and about my father."

"Who is your father?"

"I know not, other than that his name is John. I am named after him. Johanna. But I am called Janna by my friends." This last was said on impulse, and almost immediately Janna regretted it. How presumptuous she must seem! She waited for Ralph to stride off and leave her now that he'd found out she was bastard-born and of no account, but he did not.

"Not having a father must have made life difficult for you, Janna," he observed.

Janna nodded, feeling warmed by his use of her name and his interest in her family. Pride, and a desire to hold his interest, prompted her to confide in him. "I have some things, keepsakes he sent my mother, which I hope will help to lead me to him."

"What sort of things?"

"A letter."

"A letter?" He leaned forward.

"From my father to my mother. And a ring with some sort of crest on it. A weird animal, like a large cat. I've never seen such a thing before. And a crown. And my father's initial in the center – J, in the shape of a swan."

"Will you show them to me? Mayhap I can help you find your father."

"I cannot." Janna was reluctant to lose such a wonderful opportunity, but it would have meant undressing in front of him.

Ralph frowned. She thought he seemed disappointed. "I keep them in a purse beneath my gown," she said, anxious to explain her refusal. "I can show you later, if you wish, my lord?"

"Ralph." He grinned at her, and her spirits lifted under his regard. He had not thought her presumptuous at all; in fact they could now address each other as equals. She was glad that she had confided in him. Although she tried to dampen her rising spirits, she couldn't help thinking that the description of the ring had meant something to Ralph. Could he help her find her father? Her breath caught at the thought that Ralph might even know him!

He stretched out a hand and drew her to her feet, so close they stood heart to heart. She looked up to find him gazing at her so intently she felt as if she was drowning in his deep blue eyes. She tried to look away, but could not. So had she seen a snake once, with a small field mouse in its thrall. She had stopped, too afraid to venture further, and had watched the snake glide slowly forward until it was within striking distance of its unfortunate prey.

She blinked, and pulled out of Ralph's embrace. He was no snake, nor was she a helpless mouse! She looked about her, suddenly conscious that the pilgrims had vanished from sight. All at once she was filled with an urgent need to go after them, to escape from this man who had placed her heart and mind in such a dangerous whirl.

But escape was not possible. Ralph offered her his linked hands so that she might mount, and then vaulted up behind her. He took up the reins with one hand while his free arm coiled around her waist and pulled her tight against him.

Caught by surprise, Janna gasped.

"Comfortable?" he asked.

"Yes, I thank you." She was glad that he could not see her face. Her body was rigid with embarrassment.

"I have you safe. There's nothing to fear." His breath fell soft against her cheek, while his words brought comfort. She made a conscious effort to relax against him, and felt him shift to accommodate his body to hers. So had she once ridden with Hugh, but that was a long time ago. Hugh was gone now – but Ralph was right here, so vital and alive that the very air seemed to crackle with his presence. Janna smiled to herself. This journey with the pilgrims was turning out to be a whole lot more exciting than she'd expected.

As soon as the group came into view, Janna insisted on dismounting. As usual, Juliana tagged behind the others. She turned to watch their approach, her expression unreadable. Janna felt uncomfortable, but knew she'd done her best to abide by Juliana's wishes, crazed as they were. All the same, she made a private resolution to have nothing further to do with the group if it was at all possible.

Her good intentions went sadly awry when Winifred caught sight of her and turned back. Janna's heart sank. She still had no answer to give the girl. Ulf, too, appeared to have stopped walking. She wondered at her sudden popularity.

"Have you come up with any solution to what we were talking about, Janna?" Winifred whispered, as she fell into place beside her. She flicked a cautious glance at Janna's companion. Her steps slowed to allow him to walk on ahead.

"No, not yet," Janna admitted.

Winifred hardly waited until Ralph was out of earshot before she burst out: "I could hardly sleep last night for worrying about it. And about Ulf. What if he tells the authorities I have it? Will they put me in a dungeon, Janna? Will they lock me away forever?" She was close to tears. "I heard tell of some poor wretch who was kept in chains for so long his feet rotted right away!"

"No, no," Janna soothed her. "That's not going to happen to you. I promise I'll think of something. Try not to worry about it."

"I wish I'd never taken the hand at all!"

"I thought it was St Edith who prompted you to do it? You said it was a sign."

"And so it was! At least, I thought it was. But what if I was mistaken?"

"Mistaken about what?" Ulf had waited until they caught up with him.

Janna's glance flicked down to Brutus, and back again. Here was the means to allay at least one of Winifred's fears. Ulf had something to hide, she was sure of it. Perhaps she had the means to scare him into silence. It was worth a try.

"So, tell me more about the hand that I saw Brutus eating?" she challenged. She tried to read Ulf's reaction to her question. His face was guarded but, somewhat disconcertingly, there was a glint of laughter in his eyes.

"You think it was a sacred relic?"

"No. Yes!" Janna scowled at him, hating the fact that he'd almost tricked her into revealing Winifred's secret.

He raised an eyebrow. "No? Yes? Which is it?"

"You tell me." Janna tilted her chin and stared him down.

"It wasn't the hand of St James." Ulf's eyes rested thoughtfully on Winifred, whose bright blush immediately gave evidence to her guilty conscience.

"If it wasn't the relic, what was it then?" Janna pressed.

Ulf gave a small huff of laughter. "You were right. It was a hand."

"Whose hand?" Janna felt a bit queasy at she recalled the dog slurping and chewing its dinner, and the little fragments of bone and gristle that she'd found scattered on the grass afterwards.

"It belonged to the moneyer."

"The moneyer?"

"At Wiltune. Don't you remember? His hand was cut off as punishment after he was found guilty of adding lead to the coins he made."

Janna gulped down a wave of nausea as she remembered the ugly scene they'd witnessed. "How did your dog get hold of his hand?"

"Brutus must have stolen it," Ulf admitted. "Usually the hand is nailed to the door of the mint, as a sign of the moneyer's crime and as a warning to others. Whether it fell off the door, or Brutus helped it down..." He shook his head. Brutus thumped his tail, and licked his chops, almost as if he knew what they were talking about.

Janna shuddered.

"But I do thank you for not mentioning it to the abbey guard. I'm not sure what the punishment is for stealing hands." Ulf glanced at Winifred once more. "But I suspect it could mean trouble if the theft becomes known."

Janna wondered if he was talking about a sacred relic or Brutus's dinner. She didn't like to ask. Winifred stepped into the breach.

"You know, don't you?"

Ulf gave her a friendly grin. "I suspected, that's all. I saw you dodging away from our group, and I watched you push summat into a patch of holly. Obviously you were desperate to keep whatever it was hidden from the guard. And you didn't leave it behind either, for you've scratched your hands badly retrieving it!"

Winifred quickly thrust her hands behind her back.

"I've also noticed how interested you are in my collection of relics," Ulf continued dryly.

Winifred drew a shaky breath. She looked utterly wretched. "What are you going to do about it?" she whispered. "Will you tell the guard, will you claim the reward?"

"'Tis tempting!"

"You'd have to get hold of it first!" Janna stepped closer to Winifred to protect her, and the hand.

Ulf shrugged. "I'm in the business of relics." He said no more but Janna wondered if he'd go so far as to find something else to take its place and then claim the reward. Either way, she thought Winifred's secret might be safe. He'd had the opportunity to tell the guard but had kept quiet about what he'd seen. For Winifred's sake, she hoped she was right as, together, they walked on in an uncomfortable silence.

Chapter 6

Janna stopped dead, and gasped in wonder as they crested the hill and gazed down. The open plain spread before them, scorched to a pale golden brown in the heat of summer. At the center, and surrounded by a deep ditch and an earthen embankment, stood a great circle of giant stone pillars, with a jumble of larger and smaller stones inside. Although many of the huge monoliths had fallen, breaking the pattern, it was still possible to see that originally they'd formed circles within circles. The outside ring of colossal standing stones was linked in places by lintels that must once have formed a continuous parapet around the top. Janna marveled at how such huge monoliths could ever have been transported, yet their pattern was too ordered to be there by an accident of nature.

"Merlin's magic," Ralph had called it. Although Janna wasn't sure who Merlin was, she felt inclined to agree with him. No human hands could ever have shifted such a vast quantity of stone, and in so mighty a form.

"It's called Stonehenge," said Ulf, as he waved a hand toward the ancient ruins.

Even from a distance, Janna could sense their power and their mystery. She shivered, feeling suddenly cold as the hairs rose on her arms. There were numerous grassy mounds in the vicinity of the towering stones. She had seen such things before and knew them to be ancient burial mounds. It would seem that many people had died here at some time or another.

She began to walk once more, keeping a sharp eye on the stone circle as they approached it, yet it seemed to be as distant as ever. The path they were taking had been trodden flat by other feet, and led in a straight line right into the heart of the stones. Janna had an eerie feeling that she'd become part of a continuum that dated back to the dawn of time, a time of mystery and magic. Delight mingled with dread. Ralph had mentioned pagan worship and sacrifice. She closed her eyes, trying to imagine what the henge might look like on a moonlit night. And suddenly she was there, inside the stones.

A procession of robed people walked with her, carrying smoking torches to illuminate the darkness. They were singing, a strange harmonious chant that sounded like nothing Janna had heard during her year in the abbey but yet seemed profoundly spiritual and full of mystery. A figure at the head of the procession stopped and raised his hands for silence. He was dressed in a long robe and wore a golden band around his head. In his hand he carried a long staff. The ceremony began with what sounded like a prayer, a wailing invocation to the gods. A man was herded out of the stone circle under guard, and dragged to a slab of rock close to the earthen embankment at the entrance. The monolith lay flat along the ground, reminding Janna of an altar. The prisoner was dressed in a long white robe, belted at the waist. The chanting stopped and the assembly gathered around. Janna could sense the anticipation of the crowd in their restive movements, although there was a deep and absolute silence now. She peered more closely at the victim, thinking that he seemed in some way familiar. A hooded guard stepped forward and pushed the prisoner onto the fallen monolith. The other guards held him down. There was a flash of a silver knife. A cry gurgled into silence; blood spilled over stone.

Janna quickly opened her eyes, desperate to dispel the dark scene she'd conjured up. She blinked, taking a few moments to orientate herself once more. The cry of desperation still sounded in her ears, haunting and real, and yet there was no robed figure, and no guards or sacrifice either.

"Something good has happened here, a miracle of healing," she muttered to herself, trying to allay the sense of foreboding that had turned her blood to ice. She forced her thoughts to the lame boy and his family, and the joy they must have felt when he had been made whole. News of the miracle must have spread far and wide, for, while the scene seemed utterly peaceful, they were certainly not the only visitors to the site. Others had arrived at the henge before them; she could see them moving about, tiny as ants next to the huge monoliths.

The stones loomed above them, growing in height as the group came closer. Janna felt awed by their towering shapes, but she could not shake off her apprehension. Why such a feeling of dread? She wished she knew, and told herself she was jumping at shadows caused by her own vivid imagination. She was letting an old woman's rambling get the better of her. So Janna scolded herself as she passed by a couple of standing stones and several fallen monoliths that formed a line down the center of the long avenue. Three huge portal stones stood guard at the end of it.

She crossed the causeway over the deep ditch that enclosed the henge and walked through the long grass between the portal stones. The altar stone lay close beside them, just as she had seen it in her imagination. Janna shivered, and quickly walked on and into the stone circle. Pillars of stone towered above her, casting long, dark shadows in the leaching light of evening. Ravens perched on the lintels, or swooped between the huge monoliths. High above Janna's head a hawk hovered, riding the currents while it searched the grassy downs for a tasty morsel.

Winifred appeared at Janna's side. "Isn't this a truly wondrous place? I know I shouldn't say that about something that looks so...so ungodly, but this is just...just..." She flapped her hands in helpless admiration.

Janna nodded in agreement. The pilgrims had begun to move among the ruins now, exclaiming in astonishment. Still feeling unsettled, Janna stuck close to Winifred as they continued to explore. But before the pilgrims had a chance to spread out too far, Bernard clapped loudly to attract everyone's attention. "My mother wishes to stay here tonight, so I suggest you find what shelter you may."

Janna glanced at Juliana. She didn't need to be told what the old woman was thinking. Protection. Safety. She wondered to whom Juliana would pray this night, for this was not a Christian site; after the scene she'd conjured up from the past, Janna was willing to stake her life on it. Would the gods answer Juliana's prayers and grant safety to her son? For her sake, for everyone's sake, Janna hoped they would.

Bernard seemed about to say something else, but glanced at his mother and stayed silent. Janna knew that he didn't want to be here at all, was impatient to be gone. She was sure he would hurry them away at first light, and so she continued to explore the stone ruins in company with Winifred, determined to make the most of this opportunity to see everything there was to see.

They nodded and smiled at several travelers as they passed by, many of them lame or in some way disfigured. Janna hoped they would all find the cures, or even the miracles, they were seeking. They were stopped by a question from an elderly man dressed in the black robe of a priest, and learned he was part of a larger group of pilgrims who were scattered elsewhere among the ruins. Janna lost interest as the priest and Winifred began to swap travelers' tales, and wandered off. A huddled knot of people attracted her attention. Bernard was talking to a boy scarce grown to manhood. Janna understood his reason for being at the henge when she saw that he was missing an ear. A livid scar marred a face that otherwise would have bordered on handsome. Ralph and Adam stood beside Bernard, who frowned heavily as if listening to unwelcome news. Adam wore a calculating expression that Janna instinctively mistrusted, while Ralph stood slightly aside, observing them all. She wondered what the traveler was saying. Curious, she ventured closer and was in time to hear the boy say, "...an d so 'tis said that the bishop is also at odds with the empress over her refusal to reconfirm the Honor of Boulogne on his nephew, Eustace. King Stephen's son, that is."

Alarmed by what she'd heard, Janna flicked a glance in Bernard's direction.

"The bishop has withdrawn his support for the empress? Is that what you're saying?" It was clear that Bernard had also recognized the problems attendant on this new situation, and that he shared her concerns about the letter found on the dead man's body.

The boy shrugged. "That's what I was told."

"Is there any other information you can give us?" Bernard asked. The boy shook his head and moved onward, clearly more intent on his own salvation than satisfying the curiosity of strangers. Bernard stared after him, his face creased in thought.

"Are you concerned for the empress?" Ralph asked.

Bernard shot him a sharp look. "No!" he said roughly. "Merely curious. And you?"

Ralph laughed. "I have enough to do, worrying about my own soul without worrying about affairs of state."

Bernard grunted, apparently satisfied. Without ado, he grabbed hold of Adam's arm and dragged him off in the direction of his mother, who, Janna saw, was standing with Golde and Morcar. Janna could only guess at the argument that was likely to follow: Bernard would want to leave, move on straightaway. Juliana would want him to stay. And Ralph was still watching them, a witness to everything. Whether he knew it or not, his question had touched a nerve.

Janna understood the reason for Bernard's reaction. She wanted to make sure that Ralph did not.

"It's a great responsibility, trying to please all of the people all of the time, and at the same time steering us all safely to our destination," she said, looking toward Bernard.

"Seemingly one that our leader does not take lightly." Ralph grinned at her. He stepped closer, and cupped his hand around her shoulder. "You were going to show me what you keep in your purse," he said softly. "Is now a good time?"

Janna looked about, and shook her head. "There are too many people here." She gestured toward her waist, where the purse made a small bump through the fabric of her dress. "I have to wait until it's properly dark." She couldn't spell out that she would need to disrobe, but a slow heat suffused her face; she was sure Ralph's thoughts had followed her own.

"I want to explore the henge before it gets too dark to see anything," she said abruptly. "I'll show you my father's ring tomorrow." She hurried off, feeling a mixture of relief and disappointment when Ralph made no effort to follow her.

She was walking quietly among the stones when Bernard found her. He grabbed her by the arm and dragged her out into an open spot where he could be sure they would not be overheard. "No matter what I told Ralph, and in spite of my mother's wishes to the contrary, I've decided I must go to the empress straightaway," he said quietly, for Janna's ears only. "I'll leave tonight, for I suspect, from what that boy told us, that the empress's position might not be quite as secure as she thought. In fact, I fear that the bishop's message might contain an ultimatum." He hesitated a moment, then said, "For your own safety, Johanna, say nothing to anyone of the bishop's messenger and the letter we found on him. Trust no-one."

Janna heard the urgency in Bernard's voice, and sensed his fear on her behalf. She cursed her unguarded tongue as she remembered her conversation with Ralph. He already suspected they'd found a message, although she hadn't told him whose seal it bore. But it was Ralph's concern over his cousin that had prompted his questions, she reminded herself.

"I'll say nothing to anyone," she promised, thinking it would only worry Bernard if she confessed what she'd already given away.

"Good." He gave her an approving smile. "And now I must continue to try to convince my mother that I have no choice but to go on alone. I pray you, mistress, take care of her while I'm gone. She has a morbid fancy that some ill will befall me. Much as I try to reassure her, I cannot console her or change her mind. I won't be gone long, for I intend to buy a horse as soon as I may, and will ride hard to Oxeneford and back again to rejoin you all. After that, whether she will or no, I shall insist that my mother finish our journey on horseback."

"Are you in danger?" Janna could not shake off the memory of her vision; images of blood spilling onto stone haunted her.

Bernard considered the question for a moment. "No. Why should you think so?"

Janna couldn't answer. If he didn't believe in his mother's premonition, he wouldn't believe her either. "Go with God," she said. "And return in safety too."

Bernard gave her a brief smile, but his eyes stayed watchful and wary, belying his reassuring words. "Don't forget what I told you," he said. "Trust no-one."

*

After the scene of worship she'd imagined, with the violent sacrifice at its conclusion, Janna felt uneasy bedding down for the night within the circle of the henge. But Juliana had suggested they all stay together, and Janna wasn't prepared to leave the safety of the pilgrim group to venture anywhere outside on her own. Ulf had lent her a length of homespun, which he'd pulled out of his pack. It was cut unevenly and Janna thought he might use bits of it to wrap up his relics as and when he came by them. Nevertheless, she accepted the homespun gratefully, for it meant she would have something to put between her new dress and the damp grass to sleep on.

She huddled down between Winifred and Juliana in the shelter of a huge monolith. Juliana was now preserving a tight-lipped silence, but Janna could see that she cupped the relic she'd obtained from Ulf reverently in her hands. Her lips moved and Janna knew she was reciting prayers. For Bernard's safety, no doubt. And perhaps also a prayer for her own healing.

Janna closed her eyes against the dark, moonlit landscape that so closely resembled what she'd imagined earlier. She was sure her dreams would be haunted by the ghosts of the henge's past, if she slept at all. But, tired after the day's walk, she fell asleep almost instantly, dropping into a dark and silent void.

Something woke her; she sat up with a jerk. She looked around, but everything seemed still, and quiet. The monoliths towered above her, gigantic ghosts in the moonlight. She told herself to get up and investigate, but found she didn't have the courage for it. What had disturbed her, what had she been dreaming? Nothing came to mind, other than some sort of noise. A cry for help? If so, no-one else had heard it, for her traveling companions lay undisturbed and fast asleep. Or were they? She tried counting them to see if all were present. There were only six when, with the arrival of Ralph, the count should have been nine including herself and Bernard – if he'd decided to delay his departure until dawn. In the darkness, it was impossible to tell who was missing, or even whether some of their band were sleeping elsewhere and she was, in fact, counting strangers. There were others camped here this night, as well as themselves. Morcar and his wife might well have sought more private shelter, while one or other of their party could have gone in search of a convenient bush after swilling down too much ale before bedtime.

A thin scream pierced the silence. Janna tensed, half-expecting to see the pagan band circling among the stones, the condemned man, the flash of the blade, the blood on the altar. She felt sick with fear. And yet there was nothing to see, nor could she sense any movement. She listened intently. All seemed peaceful and still. She glanced upward and there, silhouetted against the silvery moonlight, she saw a dark shape glide silently overhead. A limp body dangled from its talons. A tawny owl. The terrified squeal of its prey must have woken her.

She lay down again, feeling sweaty and tremulous with delayed shock. She was wide awake now, and far too frightened and on edge to go back to sleep. Now that she was fully conscious, the night seemed full of noises. Grunts and snores. A sudden loud fart. The cries of sleepers wrestling with nightmares. The intimate murmur of a couple with loving on their minds.

To take her mind off her wild imaginings, Janna cast her thoughts back to her conversation with Ralph. Just the thought of him warmed her. How kind he was. How thoughtful. In spite of her shamed admission, he still treated her with courtesy and care. She remembered how closely he had held her, how intently he had watched her. Her breathing quickened. She couldn't deny that he made her heart beat a little faster.

Her thoughts ran on. Ralph knew of her humble origins yet, unlike Hugh, he seemed unconcerned that she had no connections, no dowry, no property that she could call her own. More, he had offered to help her find her father. That, in itself, formed a bond between them. At the thought, she cautiously lifted her kirtle and opened her purse. She took out the ring and fitted it onto her thumb. It would be safe enough, just for the short time it took to show Ralph before finding a convenient hiding spot to stow it away once more. If he could help her, if they came closer because of it, might his care and thoughtfulness become the foundation of something infinitely more precious and wonderful? Janna smiled to herself in the darkness. It was an exciting possibility. It was certainly something to dream about – if only she could fall sleep!

*

Once again Janna awoke with a start, but this time the wail of distress was real, for the sound continued after she'd opened her eyes. Her heart thumped with fright as she looked about. She could see nothing but the huge dark shape that loomed above her like a disembodied ghost. She startled back, trembling with fear. At least she was not alone; she could hear voices raised in agitation, while the thin wailing continued like an echo of her dream. Janna blinked, and remembered where she was. She saw that a thick mist had descended, obliterating all trace of the stone circle save for the lonely giant that towered above her.

She stood up and leaned against it, feeling shaky and needing support. The voices grew louder, the wailing continued. Janna extended her arms in front of her and cautiously felt her way toward the source of the noise. Something was terribly wrong. She could not shake the sense that Juliana was at the heart of the trouble, nor could she shake a growing chill of terror.

It was as she'd suspected. She found Juliana weeping and shouting for Bernard. Golde and Winifred stood with their arms around her, begging her to stay calm. As she noticed Janna approach, Juliana quietened for a moment to gather the last shreds of her strength together.

"You should have listened to me!" she cried, her voice tremulous with grief and despair. "You should have gone when I asked you to go!"

"What's happened?" Janna looked about for Bernard to calm his mother, then remembered that he'd probably already left the henge. Her gaze fell on Ulf, and he hastened to explain.

"Adam has disappeared, and Bernard along with him. Mistress Juliana fears for her son's safety."

"Master Bernard told me he had to leave us for a short time. He said there was something he had to do," Janna explained carefully.

"But Adam has also gone. He would never have taken Adam with him!" Juliana choked off a sob. "Something has happened to my son, I know it. I feel it here!" She clapped her hand to her breast.

"Why should Adam's disappearance have anything to do with Master Bernard? They might have left the henge quite separately." Juliana had let her morbid imaginings get the better of her, Janna thought. Bernard had said he was going to deliver the message to the empress, and that he would leave under cover of darkness. He must surely have told his mother the same thing. Really, there was no trouble here.

"You don't understand anything!" Juliana snapped.

"Where did Master Bernard say he was bound? Perhaps we could mount a search, if you are worried about him?" Ralph addressed his question to Janna, who looked to Juliana for guidance. The old woman folded her arms and turned away. Ralph waited for an answer.

"He didn't say where he was going." Janna hated lying, but she'd given her word to Bernard and she couldn't break it now.

"And Adam? What about him?" Ralph asked.

The pilgrims looked at each other, and shuffled their feet. Finally Morcar spoke up. "He would go if he could, but Bernard would have done all in his power to prevent him leaving, as would I. I kept close to both of them in the night, but I heard and saw nothing." He and Juliana exchanged glances.

"It may be that Adam is still here?" Golde said. "If so, we need to find him. I suggest we split up and search the henge and its surrounds before we move on. He may be off exploring, or even sound asleep elsewhere." From her tone, it was clear she didn't think it likely. There was little hope in her voice as she added: "We can't leave without him."

Why not? But Janna didn't like to voice her question.

"Surely he can catch up to us if he still wants to travel in our company?" Ralph objected.

"No!" Morcar said sharply. "Golde's right. We cannot leave until we have found him." Even as he spoke he was moving away through the mist, while Golde stumped off in a different direction.

Bewildered, Janna watched them go. She knew she hadn't imagined the hatred in the glance Golde had given Adam. Why now this insistence on finding him?

Ralph rolled his eyes and heaved a dramatic sigh. "If we are to make this search, which I suspect will prove futile, at least let me have the pleasure of your company, Janna?" he said, and offered her his arm. Janna felt a little flustered as she slipped her hand through the crook of his elbow, and even more so as he pulled her hand close to squeeze it against his side.

"Stay here and rest, my lady," Ulf told Juliana. "Keep Adam with you, and Bernard too if either of 'em comes your way." He cast a dubious glance around the henge. Janna noticed that the mist had begun to lift slightly, burning away in the warmth of the rising sun. The stones and the ground around them were becoming more visible. At least they'd be able to walk about without bumping into anything.

"We'll return as soon as maybe," Ulf continued. "Unless they've already left, I doubt they'll be far away. It won't take us long to search the henge."

Juliana nodded, but her eyes were dull, her expression without hope. "What I most feared has come to pass. It's too late for Bernard, but look for Adam, I pray you. He may be able to tell us what has happened to my son."

Janna wondered anew why everyone was so determined to locate Adam. The pilgrim had done little to befriend them. No-one seemed to like him even though there always seemed to be someone with him. What did it matter if he'd finally left the pilgrim band? The real question was why he'd stuck with them for so long when it was obvious he loathed their company.

One thing seemed clear to Janna: Bernard hadn't managed to convince Juliana that he had to leave. Janna was sure he'd kept to his intention and that it was a waste of time looking for him. But it seemed that Adam was more of a mystery than she'd realized, and she was intrigued to find out more.

"Shall we start in the center and spread outward?" Ralph suggested. Janna nodded. It seemed as good a place to try as any. They picked their way between the monoliths, stubbing toes against smaller stones that had fallen and now lay half obscured in the long grass. They encountered several bodies, still asleep, and circled them carefully, but with not much hope. There was no sign of Adam or Bernard among them.

The full orb of the sun was now above the horizon, bringing light and warmth to the day. Janna gestured toward the embankment that enclosed the henge. "Shall we try over there?"

Ralph nodded, and together they walked between two stone pillars and out beyond the circle. Now that the last tendrils of mist were burning away, Janna noticed that the sun was beaming a path of light down the avenue. It reached right into the very heart of the stone circle. The huge monoliths shone radiant where the sun's rays touched them, and cast long shadows before them on the grass. Other travelers were now rising, packing up and getting ready for departure. Janna noticed a young woman dressed in flowing robes and with a garland of flowers around her neck. She danced among the light and shadows of the stones, her movements slow and graceful, her hands outstretched as if in supplication. It all looked very peaceful, quite different from her feverish imaginings of the day before.

"He seems a man of mystery, your pilgrim leader." Ralph's voice broke into Janna's thoughts.

She nodded, appreciating that it might well look that way to an outsider. Nevertheless, she had already been indiscreet; she would not be drawn again. And so she said nothing.

"He told you he was going away, that he had something to do?"

"Yes." This much Ralph already knew.

"But he didn't say where he was going or what he needed to do?"

"No." Janna made sure her denial was firm enough to convince Ralph.

He clicked his tongue in frustration, but whether it was over her unwillingness to speak, or his impatience over their delayed departure, Janna couldn't say.

"Why didn't he leave earlier if his mission was so urgent? And how does Adam fit into Bernard's plans? Why has he gone missing? Why is everyone so determined to find him?"

"I don't know." Janna was pleased that, for once, she could speak with conviction.

"But you, too, are on a secret mission," Ralph observed, seeming to read her mind. "I see you wear your father's ring on your hand. And you have a letter. Are you going to show them to me?"

"I only have the ring to show you. The letter is private."

"Give it to me then."

Janna slipped her father's ring off her thumb, and handed it over to him. He studied it silently for a few moments, gave Janna a sideways glance, and nodded thoughtfully.

"Do you recognize it, or anything about it?" Janna asked eagerly.

"I may know something about it," he said cautiously. "Tell me about this letter – who is it from? And to whom is it addressed?"

"It's a message from my father to my mother, explaining his absence." Janna hesitated. She wasn't used to sharing information that was so close and so personal. But Ralph had shown an interest, had even offered his help. She owed him the truth in this, at least. "It seems my father was betrothed to someone else. But he was determined to wed my mother, and so he had to travel to Normandy to explain the situation to his own father." Bastard-born she might be, but Ralph should know that her parents had loved each other and had wanted to wed.

"And is that all you carry in your purse?"

"As well as my father's ring, there is also a brooch. And I found a small statue of a mother and child from the forest near where I used to live. There's also..." But no, she wouldn't tell him about Emma's reward, the silver coins she was now using to pay her way in her search for her father. She liked Ralph; she found him exciting – but she hardly knew him. All she had to go on was that he was a man of quality, of importance, a dare-the-devil sort of man, from the look of him and from his manner. But Eadgyth's admonition not to judge people by their appearance had been repeated more than once; the thought brought a wry smile to her lips as she lightly smoothed her hand down her own fine gown.

"Also – what? Do you have other letters, Janna? They can tell us so much more than mere objects, especially if you know what to look for." He handed the ring back into her safe keeping.

"No. I have only the one letter from my father."

"And you say your father's name is John?"

"Yes." Janna hesitated. It was time to ask some questions of her own, she decided. She wanted to know more about this dangerously attractive mystery man who seemed so much more worldly than the pilgrim he called himself. "What about you, Ralph? What secrets do you keep in *your* pack?"

"What do you mean?"

"I mean nothing!" Janna laughed at his wary expression. "You asked me about my family, and now I return the compliment of your interest, that's all."

Ralph looked a little sheepish. "What do you want to know?"

Everything about you! But Janna was wise enough not to voice her thoughts lest she frighten him away. "Where is your home?" seemed a safe enough question.

"Winchestre."

Janna was impressed. She knew that the royal treasury was housed at Winchestre, and that it was an important seat of power. "Do you think my father could be there?" she asked impulsively.

Ralph smiled. "It's possible. Especially if he is who I think he may be. Tell me, Janna, whose side does he support in this battle for the crown between the lord king and his cousin, the empress?"

"How can I know that if I don't know who he is?" Janna countered.

"I thought you might have an opinion on the matter."

"I met the empress when she came to Wiltune Abbey earlier this year." Caution warned Janna not to say more of their meeting or of how she now wholeheartedly supported the empress's bid for the throne.

Ralph stopped and turned Janna to face him. "You have something of her look about you."

Janna was shocked into momentary silence. So, too, had the empress's own tiring woman commented on her appearance, although Janna had been quick to deny any royal connection.

"Only because my hair is fair. It makes my eyes look darker than they really are, as dark as the empress's own," she hurried to explain, all too conscious of his careful scrutiny. "Others have made the same mistake."

Ralph's eyebrow lifted in query. Janna felt uncomfortable, and sought to divert him with the question now burning on her tongue. "So you've also met the Lady of England?"

"I don't know the lady personally but I have seen her, yes."

"I understand her promised coronation came to naught, for the Londoners turned against her and she was forced to flee to Oxeneford.

And from what that young lad was saying yesterday, she is now at odds with the king's brother, the Bishop of Winchestre."

"You are well informed for someone so newly come from an abbey," Ralph commented. "What else do you know?"

"Nothing, other than what I overheard yesterday. But I'm interested in the empress's changing fortune. Will she try again for the crown, think you?"

Ralph lifted his hands and shrugged.

"Do you think she'll ever become queen?"

"It's possible."

Janna thought he could have sounded somewhat more enthusiastic than he did, and felt some indignation on the empress's behalf. "A queen can rule as well as a king, do you not think so?"

Ralph smiled. "We shall see," he said enigmatically.

"She is her father's rightful heir, after all! I understand the barons all swore an oath to King Henry that they would recognize her as their queen after his death."

"I see you have strong opinions on the matter, Janna."

"But isn't it a matter of right and wrong?" she said. "As I see it, King Stephen usurped the throne and, now that he's been captured and imprisoned, perhaps it is time for the rightful heir to claim her crown?"

"So you don't know that King Henry changed his mind about his daughter on his death bed, and released the barons from their vows?"

"No!" Janna was stunned by the news.

Ralph smiled at her innocence. "Hugh Bigod was present to witness the king's change of heart. It was he who informed the Archbishop of Canterberie that Stephen's claim to the throne was legitimate, and the king's coronation proceeded from that. You should remember, Janna, that Stephen is an anointed king and, as such, is recognized by the pope. Can there be a new queen while an anointed king still lives?"

Janna was silenced by his argument. "You know so much of affairs of state," she said at last. "Whose side do you favor in this battle for the crown?"

Ralph laughed, and shook his head. "We live in uncertain times, Janna. You should know that it's dangerous to take sides, and even more dangerous to be seen to be doing so."

"Yet that didn't stop you asking my opinion!"

"I beg your pardon, Janna." He stepped closer, transfixing her with his blue gaze. "I'm interested in you, and everything about you. I'm sorry if you think my curiosity was misplaced."

Janna's heart skipped with excitement. She was about to reassure him that she'd taken no offence when a sudden shout stopped her.

"I've found Bernard! Come quickly! He's over here!"

"Come with me." Ralph grabbed her hand, and hurried her toward Morcar. He was standing beside the monoliths that guarded the entrance to the henge, waving his hands and shouting to attract everyone's attention. Janna ran to keep pace with Ralph. She was filled with a deep foreboding. Something must be terribly wrong, for Bernard would have answered for himself if he could. What had changed his mind, why had he delayed when he'd seemed so anxious to be gone? Her steps faltered, but Ralph dragged her on.

The shout had attracted everyone's attention, and people streamed toward its source. Janna stopped abruptly as the scene she had imagined on their approach to the henge sprang vividly to life. The limp figure of a man lay sprawled across the stone altar, his tunic soaked red with his blood. Blood had spilled over the stone and onto the earth below.

"No!" she gasped, and turned aside, and felt Ralph's arms close around her. He pulled her to him and she burrowed into his chest, shivering with fright.

"Shh," he soothed her. "Don't look. You don't have to look."

But Janna had already looked, and had seen all that she needed to know. Someone had killed Bernard, had slashed his throat and left him to die. Bile rose in her throat, bitter and choking. She swallowed hard, trying not to be sick.

A loud howl rent the air. Juliana. The old woman must have hobbled over as soon as she heard Morcar's call. She had warned Bernard, had warned Janna too, but they hadn't believed her, had made light of her fears. And now it was too late. Too late to make amends. Too late to protect Bernard and keep him safe. The only thought to bring some comfort to Janna was that her presence or otherwise would have made no difference at all to what had happened here.

Ralph set Janna aside, and went to express his condolences to Juliana. She seemed hardly to hear him. Nor was she aware of anyone else, so deep was she in grief. Travelers to the site pushed forward, asking questions and exclaiming in hushed whispers. Morcar and Ulf tried to persuade them to move back, to go away. Bernard had been well-liked and highly regarded by the pilgrims, and deserved their respect now that he lay dead. Golde and Winifred stood close to Juliana, ready to support her if necessary. Janna hesitated, for she was sure Juliana would find something for which to blame her. She stayed back and watched.

"We must inform the authorities of this foul deed, my lady; we must raise the hue and cry. We must also arrange transport for your son's body. Where do you wish to take him for burial?" Ralph had to ask the question twice before Juliana paid attention to him.

Juliana stared up at him with red, tear-filled eyes. "We...we must take him home to Oxeneford."

"In that case we'll need a mount to carry him, or a cart. Some form of transport." It seemed that, in the absence of Bernard, Ralph had become their leader.

"I'll ask around, see what I can find," Ulf offered.

Janna's attention strayed from the problems of transporting Bernard home to an even more pressing question, a question no-one had yet asked. Who had killed Bernard – and why? She looked around the pilgrims, counting them off as she did so. Juliana, of course. Ulf and Ralph. Winifred, looking close to tears. Morcar now had his arm around Golde, protective and reassuring. And Adam was still missing. Was he responsible for this? Or had a common thief taken his chance and caught Bernard unawares?

Janna stood still as something else occurred to her: The message! Bernard had taken it upon himself to deliver it to the empress, believing it had become a matter of urgency. Whoever had killed Bernard might well have stolen it along with everything else he carried. In which case it was probably gone forever. But she owed it to Bernard, and the secret they'd shared, to look for it. And if she found it, Janna resolved to deliver the message herself.

As unobtrusively as possible, she sidled across to the altar stone. Ulf, Ralph and Morcar had gone into a huddle to argue over the best means of transporting Bernard home. They weren't paying any attention to her, but Janna knew that other eyes would see what she was about to do. Nevertheless, she forced herself to inspect Bernard's body.

He lay on his back, his eyes open and staring. She thought his expression was accusing, but told herself not to be so fanciful. She felt his skin. It was cool, and his limbs were starting to become stiff. The body had lain here for some hours then. She glanced about for Bernard's pack and staff, but there was no sign of them. She made a note to look for them later. Next, she patted down his blood-soaked garments, looking for telltale bulges, artifacts sewn into hems, perhaps. But they yielded no secrets. There was no sign of his scrip either.

There was no doubt how Bernard had died – the gaping wound and quantity of blood that had spilled attested to that. Nevertheless, Janna cautiously rolled him onto his side to see what she could find.

Her conscientious examination revealed a contusion on the back of his head, a slight swelling and broken skin, which indicated that he'd suffered a blow some time before he died.

"You seem very interested in Bernard's body," Ralph commented, materializing at Janna's elbow.

Startled, she let go and swung around to confront him. "I – I am a healer by training," she stammered, trying to cover her real interest in Bernard. "Of course I can see that he's dead. No-one could survive a wound such as that. But I wondered how his body came to be here, resting on this particular stone. It seems he also suffered a blow to the head, so I suspect he was probably ambushed and rendered unconscious before the killer brought him here to cut his throat. I just – I can't think why." She turned to Juliana. "You have my deepest sympathy, mistress."

"'Tis just past midsummer," Ralph said. "This is a sacred place for those who practice the dark arts, so I've heard. Could this be a killing to placate the old gods instead, think you?"

"I knew we shouldn't have come here!" Golde wailed. Morcar pulled her close and she pressed her face against his chest.

Ulf brandished a crucifix in the air. "The travelers told us of a recent miracle – but in the past the only tales I ever heard about the henge were of the ancient and evil spirits who dwell here," he said.

"The henge has long been associated with death and sacrifice," Ralph agreed thoughtfully.

"It was at my insistence that we come here!" Juliana wailed.

"If someone wanted a victim to sacrifice, why then steal the victim's scrip?" Janna found she was fast running out of patience with the notion of ritual killings still taking place, even though she herself had imagined just such a vision from the past. "Surely it was Bernard's goods they were after? See, his pack and staff are missing too." She wouldn't mention the bishop's letter, nor her fear that it might be the real reason for the attack on Bernard.

The pilgrims solemnly nodded their heads in agreement. Golde felt sufficiently recovered to remove her head from Morcar's chest and look once more upon the corpse.

"Was there anything in his scrip worth stealing?" Janna asked Juliana, already knowing the answer but interested to hear what the dame had to say.

Juliana looked at her with eyes glazed and red with grief. "He carried coins to pay our passage, and some personal goods too. Worth stealing, especially if you have nothing in your own scrip." She drew herself up and said fiercely: "Adam had nothing! But he had everything to gain by murdering my son and taking his goods. No mystery, then, that he has fled."

No mention of the message that Bernard had decided was so urgent he should leave immediately, even if it meant abandoning his mother and the pilgrims, Janna thought. "*Trust no-one,*" Bernard had said. If he'd followed his own advice, if he'd told no-one of what they'd found on the dead man by the river, then no-one would know about the message and therefore her fears were for nothing. Everything pointed to the probability that Bernard had been killed for the valuables he'd carried. And for some reason, everyone suspected Adam.

"Why should Adam run away? Where's he gone?" she asked.

"He's escaped us, and we must raise the hue and cry after him. He must be made to pay," Juliana insisted.

"What makes you so sure he's behind this foul deed?" Ralph asked. Janna was pleased that Ralph seemed as curious about Adam as she was; perhaps Juliana would answer his question instead.

"He's murdered once before, and now he's killed again so that he can escape his penance and start a new life. All this..." Juliana gestured at the lifeless body of her son. "I believe it's to make us think that this was some sort of sacrificial killing, and nothing to do with him." She began to sob once more, crooking her arm across her face to stifle the sound and blot her tears.

"You already know that Adam is a murderer?" Ralph asked incredulously. "Why, then, is he traveling with you?"

Juliana continued to weep. Eventually Morcar spoke for her. "My father-in-law – Bernard's cousin – was found drowned in a pond early in the spring. He and Adam have long harbored a deep grudge toward each other. It was a matter of the pigs, you see."

Janna was about to ask what he meant, but Morcar continued with his explanation.

"There was a bruise on the back of his head, perhaps a blow hard enough to kill him. For certes, the water was too shallow for him to have fallen in and drowned!"

"My father was murdered, and all know who was responsible," Golde cut in indignantly.

"Adam." Morcar took up the tale once more. "But no-one was willing to speak against him. It was known that my wife's father had consumed a quantity of ale shortly before his death, and the story went about that he was just too drunk to save himself when he fell into the pond."

"He was never so drunk as that! Never, ever," Golde protested fiercely.

Morcar nodded. "The next thing we knew was that Adam suddenly announced he was going to make a pilgrimage to the shrine of St James at Compostela."

"Yes, because the priest made him go as part of his penance!" Golde's voice was thick with rage. "He wouldn't have thought of it else."

"True." Juliana gave a mournful sniff. "We believe he confessed his crime to the priest before the death could be investigated by the shire reeve, and this was his penance: to make a pilgrimage. But Bernard – and Morcar too – insisted Adam be fully punished for his crime. They resolved to accompany Adam, and keep him always in their sight so that he was forced to make the journey and, more importantly, forced to return. Their intention was to bring him back to Oxeneford and insist that he be brought to trial." She mopped her tears on the sleeve of her gown. "I told Bernard, I told him over and over, that he should look to his own soul and leave the dispensing of justice to God," she said, and began to weep once more.

Janna remembered that Juliana had said something of the sort before. She hadn't understood her words then, but she did now. No wonder Juliana had been fearful. Adam had killed once already, if the pilgrims were to be believed, and by a blow to the back of the head before drowning his victim. So, too, had Bernard received a blow to the head before his throat was cut. It seemed that Adam was careful to disable his victims before trying to disguise their deaths as something else. Which meant that he was wily and dangerous, as well as desperate.

"I was against this from the start," Juliana lamented. "I knew in my bones that no good would come from this journey, and so I decided to accompany my son, to keep him safe."

"We know Adam understood our need for revenge, and that he resented being watched all the time," said Morcar. "He hasn't tried before to elude us, but now it seems he has succeeded. He's no stranger to murder, and everything points to his guilt. We must find him. He cannot be allowed to escape justice and punishment a second time."

"Then there's no time to lose in going after him," Ralph said quickly, eager to be of help. He turned to Juliana. "We'll report the death at the next hamlet we come to; we'll raise the hue and cry after Adam. Meantime, my lady, we must come up with a strategy to transport your son's body home. I promise I shall do all in my power to help you in whatever way I can."

Knowing Juliana was in good hands now that Ralph had taken charge, and conscious of her own self-appointed task, Janna hurried back to the place where the pilgrims had lain for the night. Aside from a patch of trampled grass, there was little to see. Most of the pilgrims had shouldered their packs before setting out on their search for Bernard. Janna swiftly searched through those that remained, after first secreting her father's ring safely in her purse once more. There was nothing to find. None of the packs belonged to Bernard, nor was there any sign of his staff.

Frowning thoughtfully, she walked slowly back to the pilgrims. Juliana was seated on the grass, being comforted by Golde and Winifred. There was no sign of Morcar and Ulf or of Ralph. Janna continued her search as unobtrusively as possible, starting from the site of Bernard's body, just in case he was felled where they'd found him. After examining his body, Janna thought it more likely he'd been taken unawares once he'd left the henge, and then dragged back and killed on the slab so as to imitate some ancient sacrificial practice.

Two parallel grooves caught her attention, faint lines that tracked through sand, grass and mud. They led from the henge out to the avenue beyond, and she followed them. Occasionally the tracks faded into nothing, but she discovered she could pick up the telltale signs if she walked on. Sometimes only one line was visible, sometimes two, even if indistinct. To Janna, they looked like the drag marks of boots. Finally, they came to an end some way along the avenue. She cast about for other signs of foul play, but found only a smooth, shallow indentation in the dust – recently made, she thought, or it would have been trodden over and obscured by the passage of visitors to the henge. She closed her eyes, trying to picture what might have happened: Bernard, leaving under cover of darkness, hurrying along the avenue, anxious to reach his destination. Someone had followed him, had hit him on the head and knocked him unconscious. The shallow imprint of his body on the ground told where he had fallen. Janna looked about for signs of blood, but there were none. So her supposition was correct: Bernard had been dragged back to the altar before being killed. Why? To disguise theft as a symbolic sacrifice? Or was the sacrifice real, done to placate the gods, whoever they might be?

Janna shuddered, and looked around her. There were more urgent matters to consider now. Bernard's pack and scrip, and the letter from the bishop. Would the thief have taken everything with him? It seemed unlikely that he'd carry an extra burden of unnecessary goods, particularly if he was escaping on foot. No, not if he could as easily stuff anything of value into his own pack and hide the rest of Bernard's property elsewhere. Janna's gaze settled on a small copse of trees off to the side but no great distance from the causeway. The pilgrims were still searching the stone circles and the ditch for Adam. If there was anything of Bernard's to be found there, she knew they would retrieve it. With a quick glance around to make sure she was unobserved, she hurried toward the grove.

It was the perfect cover – trees and bushes grew in wild profusion, while waist-high weeds thickly covered the ground; they would shroud anything thrown into their depths. Or would they? Janna stopped pushing through the weedy growth and paused to reconnoiter. She noticed the signs that someone had been here before her, his passage marked by bruised and broken stems and bent grasses. In the darkness, whoever it was wouldn't have realized that he was leaving a trail, but in daylight Janna could follow it easily.

Her search was rewarded when she caught sight of a bulky object thrust deep into a thicket of brambles. She forced her hand through, getting mightily scratched in the process, and dragged out a pack. It was stuffed full, clothes and possessions crammed in anyhow as if packed in a hurry – or crammed back into the pack in the dark? Janna pulled everything out, recognizing Bernard's traveling cloak as she did so. She eyed it covetously, and set it aside. Where was his scrip?

She could find no sign of it, but his staff lay close by, almost hidden among a patch of nettles. Stifling a sigh, and this time using her other hand, she carefully extracted it from its stinging nest. That Bernard's possessions had been searched and then hidden seemed beyond a doubt. A casual passer-by would never have noticed them, would not have come near the grove in the first place. Janna's thoughts churned as she carefully searched again the contents of Bernard's pack. She remembered that the guard from Wiltune Abbey had also looked through it, but had found nothing. Had Bernard secreted the message elsewhere, or was there a hidden flap or a pocket, somewhere safe to hide the bishop's message from the guard's eyes?

She ran her hands over the pack, feeling for anything unusual such as an extra seam that might disguise a hiding place. Where could the letter be? Not in this pack, she decided finally, although she patted it down carefully all over again, just to make sure. She rocked back on her heels and thought about it. And came to the reluctant conclusion that the thief, whether Adam or someone else, had stolen something even more valuable than he'd realized when he'd taken the scrip. The question was: Could he read? Would he know the value of what he'd found? Or would he discard the message, leave it blowing in the wind or torn and muddy in a ditch, destined never to reach the eyes of the empress?

How important was the letter anyway? Important enough to change the fortunes of the lady? Or the fortunes of a king?

Chapter 7

Janna was thoughtful as she hoisted Bernard's pack onto her shoulder and picked up his staff. She couldn't shake off a sense of unease as she walked back to join the pilgrim band. True, Adam had disappeared, and everything pointed to his guilt. Yet he'd left the pack behind when some of the things that Janna had noticed inside would surely have brought him a few pence if sold in the marketplace. Perhaps there'd been enough in Bernard's scrip to satisfy his greed? Perhaps he was afraid to take anything that might link him to Bernard?

The missing message hung heavily on Janna's conscience. She shrugged, impatient to free herself from the burden of care, for there was no more she could do to retrieve it. She told herself that her duty now was toward Juliana: she must do all in her power to comfort and bring ease to the grieving woman.

Bernard's staff fitted comfortably into her hand and she leaned on it, relishing its support; it was so much better than the rough stick she'd been using. As she approached the pilgrims, she realized everyone was staring at her. Feeling self-conscious, she held the staff out to Juliana, along with the pack.

"I found these, my lady. I believe they belonged to Master Bernard. I thought you would want them." No need to tell Juliana – or anyone else – where she'd found them. "I couldn't find his scrip," she added.

Juliana accepted the pack, but waved the staff away. "You may keep it. I've said some harsh things, blamed you unfairly. I've misjudged you, and I am sorry for it."

"Thank you, my lady. I shall treasure it always," Janna assured her.

Juliana nodded, and turned to take Ulf's arm. Evidently some heavy bartering had gone on, for a cart stood close by the group, with Ralph's palfrey at its head. Bernard's body had been loaded onto the cart. Juliana now climbed in beside it, helped up by the strong arm of Ulf.

"We must make haste to Ambresberie to report this matter, and raise the hue and cry. There's no time to lose," Ulf explained, as he noted Janna's questioning frown. He swung himself up onto the horse and looked down. "Morcar and Golde will escort you there, along with the lord Ralph and Winifred. We shall wait for you at Ambresberie."

It was good of Ralph to give up his horse, Janna thought; he was a good man, kind and decent. She remembered how she had turned to him for comfort, and how he had tried to shield her from the sight of Bernard's body. A sudden thought sent a flush of heat to her cheeks. Ralph had said he was interested in her, and everything about her. Was that why he'd elected to stay behind rather than accompanying Juliana himself?

The horse and cart set off, bearing the mourners and their sad burden. Morcar and Golde picked up their packs. Their frustrated, angry faces spoke as clearly as Golde's words. "We've searched everywhere," she said. "There's no sign of Adam, may he rot in hell for all eternity."

"I'm ready to leave whenever you are," Janna assured them. They nodded, and set off in the direction that the horse and cart had taken.

Janna followed after them, with Ralph on one side of her and Winifred on the other.

"Wherever did you find Bernard's pack and staff, Janna?" Ralph asked.

"Over there, in that patch of trees." Janna pointed to the spot they were just passing.

"What made you search there for them?"

Janna shrugged. "His pack wasn't where we'd all slept, so I wondered if he'd started on his journey after all, but been attacked by Adam before he could get too far along the way."

"That was very enterprising of you." Amusement danced in Ralph's eyes as he commented, "And you've won a stout staff as a result of your good deed."

Not sure if he was making fun of her or not, Janna didn't reply. Ralph had the alarming capacity to keep her off-balance – she was never quite sure where she stood with him.

"Did you find anything of value among Bernard's belongings?"

Janna shot him a quick glance. "Are you accusing me of theft?"

"Of course not! I just wondered if Adam had left anything behind that might serve to comfort Dame Juliana in her grief?"

Janna shook her head, not answering.

"I believe I'm right in thinking that Master Bernard was in possession of a message carried by the dead man you encountered outside Wiltune. What has happened to it?"

"I know nothing about the message. Ask Adam – if you can find him!" Janna tilted her chin, trying to control her irritation.

"I beg your pardon, Janna. I didn't mean to suggest – that is to say…" He gave her a rueful smile. "It's my cursed curiosity," he explained. "I cannot resist asking questions, even about things that do not concern me in any way whatsoever."

Janna nodded, feeling slightly mollified. She knew how it was to be cursed with curiosity. She herself suffered from the same malady.

Yet Ralph's questions had also pricked her conscience. She hated telling lies, although it seemed she was forever having to conceal the truth from him. Surely she could trust him, especially now that the message had disappeared? She opened her mouth, and suddenly heard Bernard's voice in her ear, sounding as clear as if he was standing right beside her: "*Trust no-one.*"

She clamped her mouth shut. It was probably good advice, she thought, as she recalled Ralph's spirited defense of the king's position. He hadn't been drawn on whose side he supported, but it was too great a risk to presume that he favored the empress just because she did.

Anxious to outpace her uneasy conscience and also to prevent further conversation with Ralph, she quickened her steps. Winifred trotted beside her, keeping pace. "What was that all about?" she asked, once Ralph was safely out of hearing.

Janna shook her head, cursing herself for a fool as she realized that, despite her good intentions, she'd just confirmed Ralph's belief that a message had indeed been found on the corpse.

"It's a shame to quarrel with him, for I think he admires you." Winifred sounded somewhat wistful. Janna wondered if she was having second thoughts about being shut away in an abbey for the rest of her life.

"Have you ever had any admirers, Winifred?" she ventured. "I don't mean Old Dribblegum, I mean someone young and handsome?" She glanced over her shoulder at Ralph. "Did you ever think about becoming a wife and mother instead of dedicating your life to God?"

"No, never." Winifred sounded quite positive about it. "But...but I am so afraid, Janna." She held up her purse. "What am I going to do with this? I can't keep it. But I can't think what else to do with it other than throw it away. And I could never do *that*!"

In all the turmoil, Janna hadn't given Winifred's predicament any further thought. "Probably the best thing is to find some way of getting it safely back to Wiltune Abbey," she said slowly, grappling for ideas, any solution to the problem, no matter how unappealing it might seem.

"I trust you, Janna. Could you take it back for me?"

"Me? You want me to claim the reward for 'finding' it?" Janna gave a snort of laughter. "I don't think so, Winifred! They'll think I took it in the first place."

"No, they won't. They know you. Please, Janna. We could share the reward. You could have something for your trouble, while my share might be enough for a dowry at a lesser abbey. Like the one at Ambresberie, perhaps?"

Janna hadn't suspected Winifred capable of such practical good sense. She was surprised and impressed, but equally determined to have no part in any such enterprise. "Ulf's a relic seller. I'm sure he could come up with an explanation as to how he came by the hand. Ask Ulf to help you."

"No." Winifred hung her head. "I'm too ashamed."

"Have courage," Janna admonished. "Remember, you have St Edith on your side!"

"So I thought. Now, I'm not so sure I understood her meaning correctly."

Neither was Janna, but she believed it would do Winifred no good to start doubting herself now. "You have the relic. It's too late now to wish it away. So, let's rather consider this as an opportunity and make the most of it," she said briskly.

Winifred attempted a small smile. "Please take it back for me, Janna. I'd much rather share the reward with you. Besides, I...I don't know Ulf. I don't know if I can trust him to keep his word."

"I can't go back, Winifred. I must go on to Ambresberie." Janna was sorry not to be able to help the girl, even while she acknowledged that she hated the whole idea of claiming a reward under false pretenses from an abbey that had given her shelter and taught her so much in the year she had stayed there. "Speak to Ulf once we get to Ambresberie," she advised. "If he won't help you, then we'll think of something else. Who knows, we may come up with an even better plan."

She was silent a moment as another idea came to her. She reviewed the contents of her purse, and heaved a reluctant sigh. It might do, if everything else failed. But it would come at a cost, for she knew she would regret it. "I'll come with you to speak to Ulf," she promised Winifred. "If that doesn't work out, I know something else that might."

They walked on. Janna's stomach rumbled with hunger. They'd had nothing to eat the night before, nor had they broken their fast this day. She slowed down to keep pace with Morcar and Golde. "How far is it to Ambresberie?"

"Not too much further." Morcar pointed toward a thicket of trees in the distance. A glint of water ran through them like a silver thread. "There's the abbey." Janna saw a grey stone tower beyond the trees. "We'll be there in an hour or two, mistress."

Ralph fell into step with them all. "What are your plans when you get there, Janna?"

"I shall go to the abbey to make enquiries about my mother."

"Before that, will you let me have another look at the ring you carry in your purse?" Ralph asked. "It may be that I know far more than the good sisters at the abbey can tell you."

Janna looked up at him, unable to disguise the sudden leap of hope his words had given her. From the way Ralph was speaking now, it seemed he might know even more than she'd realized. "That would be kind of you, but I've already put it away."

"I want you to show me everything in your purse. It may be that I recognize something from my time in Winchestre that you cannot know about. I want to do all in my power to help you find your father." There was no doubting the sincerity in Ralph's voice, nor could Janna miss the warm regard in his eyes.

"I thank you," she said, silently chastising herself for being so quick to take offence. True, he had a questioning nature, full of curiosity about things that didn't concern him. But then, so did she. It seemed they were kindred spirits, and well-matched indeed! The thought brought a rosy blush to her cheeks and her smile grew broader.

"You look happier," Ralph observed. "Have you forgiven me then? For I assure you, mistress, I meant no disrespect by my questions. I am only anxious to find out the truth behind this tragic affair."

"As am I," Janna assured him.

"Oh, good," Winifred observed, coming up on Janna's other side and linking arms with her. "You're friends again."

Ralph laughed and so, after a moment, did Janna. "A small misunderstanding," he said cheerfully. "And I guarantee that nothing shall ever come between us again." He hooked his arm through Janna's, and together the three walked on.

As soon as they came to a likely screen of bushes, Janna excused herself and went behind their shelter. Within a few moments she was back, this time with her purse tied to her girdle outside her gown.

"Show me the ring, and whatever else you have in there," Ralph said, as his eyes strayed to the dangling purse. Janna extracted the ring, and held it out for Ralph's inspection once more. She felt light-headed with excitement.

"Whose ring is that?" Winifred asked curiously.

"I think it belonged to my father." Janna watched as Ralph traced the emblems engraved on the ring's surface. "What is that?" She pointed at the cat-like creature.

"It's a lion. And that is a crown. This is the insignia of a king."

"King Henry?"

"Well guessed," Ralph affirmed. "This is not Stephen's insignia."

"My father gave this to my mother before ever Stephen came to the throne." Janna peered at the strange creature that Ralph had called a "lion." She wondered whether such animals really existed. She touched the crown. "Does this mean that my father was the king's loyal supporter?"

"It does indeed. And this…" Ralph traced the initial J with his finger. "This would be the first initial of your father's name. John, I think you said?"

"John." Janna was delighted to have her suspicions confirmed by Ralph. "Is there a John living in Winchestre? Do you know my father, Ralph?"

"I know several men named John. 'Tis a common enough name among the Normans, Janna."

"Oh." Janna's spirits, which had flown to such giddy heights, now collapsed.

"Do not lose heart." Ralph was quick to comfort her. "This ring has given me a good idea of who he is and where we might seek him. Show me his letter. I am sure it will have information we can use."

Janna untied her purse and drew it out. She was about to hand it over, but a sudden scruple made her pause. "It's very private," she said. "My mother kept it hidden all her life, and I shouldn't share it with you now. But I am quite sure there is naught in it to indicate who my father might be, for I have studied it carefully."

"You have read the letter? You can read?" Ralph's tone sharpened with interest, while Winifred's expression reflected awe.

Janna nodded somewhat self-consciously. "I learned how to read and to write at the abbey."

"And this letter?" Ralph queried. "Is it signed 'John fitz Roy?' Or 'John fitz Henry' perhaps?"

"No. It's just signed 'John.'"

"And there is nothing else in the letter about your father, his family, or where he might live?"

Janna shook her head. "He just said that his father had gone to Normandy and that he must follow him there."

"And there are other letters?"

"No." Janna squashed the thought of the missing letter. It had nothing to do with her family. She wished again that she could be wholly truthful with Ralph. A discomforting thought came into her mind: Love and trust belonged together – so how could she think herself half in love with Ralph if she couldn't trust him? She became aware of his steady regard, and was glad that he wasn't able to read her mind. But she'd made a promise. Even though the bishop's letter had likely vanished forever, the truth was still not hers to tell.

"It could be that your father's family has land in Normandy?" Ralph pointed out. "Many barons still hold land over there as well as owning property in England. It's an anxious time for landowners, especially now."

"Why so?" Janna was surprised by the hard edge of anger in Ralph's voice.

"They have to protect their interests from the long and grasping fingers of Geoffrey of Anjou no less than from the Lady of England."

"Isn't Geoffrey the husband of the Empress Matilda?"

"Indeed he is, and he shares his wife's ambition, she for England and he for Normandy and Anjou. Both of them are busy buying support, conferring titles and bestowing land and favors, most especially if the rightful owners are not there to protect their own interests."

Janna looked at him, understanding now where his loyalty lay. She had been right not to tell him about the letter after all. "And do you have land and property at risk?" she asked, feeling her way.

He glanced sideways at her, and gave a grudging nod. "Forgive me if I sound bitter," he said. "These are difficult times for us all."

"Is that why you travel to St Frideswide's shrine? To pray for an end to the misery of this battle for the crown? Is that the miracle you seek?"

"Yes, indeed." Ralph looked a little disconcerted. "But…I have other business to conduct there too."

"Like the land and property you said was at risk?" Janna asked, anxious to understand everything about him.

Ralph hesitated. "Yes, that's right. I can only hope my cousin already has it in hand." He shook himself slightly as if to dismiss his dark thoughts. "But what is on my mind now is your father, Janna," he said briskly. "If he's not in Winchestre, we may have to seek him in Normandy."

Inside, Janna was singing with joy at Ralph's use of the word "we." She would tell Ralph everything, oh yes, she would. She would trust him with the truth just as soon as this was over, when the empress was crowned and none of it mattered any more. "Or he may be in Ambresberie?" she ventured. "That's where he met my mother, so he may own property or have some business there. Once we arrive I intend to question everyone I meet, just in case someone knows something about him."

"Oh, I do hope you find your father, Janna!" Winifred clasped her hands together, her eyes shining with excitement.

"We're going to do our best, aren't we, Janna?" Ralph gave her a conspiratorial wink. "Show me your purse. What else do you have that belonged to him?"

Ignoring his request, Janna extracted the brooch and handed it to him. The silver coins jangled together, reminding her that she had a debt to repay. "This for you," she said, following the brooch with a coin. "For my boots," she added, as he tried to give it back to her. "I will not be in your debt, my lord."

He turned the brooch over and read the inscription. *"Amor vincit omnia.* It means 'love conquers all.'" He smiled at Janna. "Very loving," he commented, "but not very informative."

Janna dropped the brooch back into her purse and drew the string tight against Ralph's curious gaze.

"This is so romantic!" Winifred breathed.

"He must have loved your mother very much," Ralph observed.

Janna nodded, swept by a tide of grief as she remembered how her mother had died with John's name on her lips, while never knowing how much she was loved in return. If only Eadgyth had trusted her lover, she thought. She glanced sideways at Ralph. It all came down to trust.

*

Their first stop, when they arrived in Ambresberie, was the cookshop. Janna's nose twitched at the delicious scent of hot pies, but before she could find a coin to pay for one, Ralph strode up to the counter. He returned with five steaming pasties, and Janna and Winifred stretched out grateful hands to receive their share. Morcar and Golde came into view shortly afterward, and Ralph handed them each a pasty. There was a prolonged silence as everyone ate, for it had been a long time since their last meal.

"That was delicious. Thank you, my lord!" Janna licked her fingers clean of gravy, then washed her hands at the pump. She debated wiping them dry on her gown, as she was wont to do, but decided against it. She could do little to protect the precious fabric against the ravages of the journey, but she certainly wasn't going to compound the problem by adding food or water stains. Winifred and the others had no such qualms, however, and cheerfully swiped their hands down their tunics to dry them.

"I'll escort you to the abbey," Ralph told Janna. He looked at the rest of the pilgrim group. "Pray you, seek out Mistress Juliana and Ulf. We'll come looking for you later."

"No!" Janna said, as a host of problems suddenly presented themselves. She knew what sort of reception she'd get if she arrived at the abbey gates escorted by a man, even someone as personable as Ralph. She was determined to get inside the abbey, perhaps even stay the night if they would have her, for she wanted time to question anyone who might have known her mother. For that, she would have to make the visit alone.

"I thank you for your kind offer, but I must go to the abbey on my own. I know not how long I'll be there," she told him. It was the next complication that bothered Janna; she wasn't quite sure how to address it. She could only speak out, and hope her offer did not work to her disadvantage. She addressed all the pilgrims together. "There is no need for any of you to wait for me, for it was always my intention to leave you once we arrived here in safety. Pray, do not delay your journey to Oxeneford on my account."

"But I have offered to help you search for your father," Ralph protested. "I thought that was what you wanted?"

"You're very kind indeed, sire, but you've told me you have business concerns in Oxeneford. They must surely come first." It almost killed Janna to throw his offer back in his face.

"My affairs can wait," Ralph said airily. "Your quest is important. I know how much it means to you. Share with me what you learn from the sisters at the abbey and, in turn, I may be able to point you in the direction of your father."

"Thank you, Ralph. You're very kind." Janna wanted to throw her arms around his neck in undying gratitude.

"But I – that is, we, still have unfinished business to discuss," Winifred said anxiously, gesturing toward her purse.

Janna nodded. "Speak to Ulf while I'm gone," she advised. "If he can't help you, and you're still here when I come back, then I have another plan for you to consider."

"I'm sure Ulf's time is taken up with Mistress Juliana and arrangements for the transport and burial of Master Bernard," Ralph said. He gazed thoughtfully at Winifred's purse. Janna could imagine the questions he was asking himself as clearly as if he was speaking aloud. She stifled a grin. In his position, she knew she'd have been asking the same questions.

But perhaps Ralph had learned his lesson, for no questions were forthcoming. "I am at leisure while Janna visits the abbey. Perhaps I can help you with your unfinished business, mistress?" he offered instead.

"No!" Janna and Winifred answered together. They exchanged glances. Janna shook her head slightly, a gesture of warning not lost on Ralph, she realized, as she noticed his bemused expression.

"'Tis kind of you, but this is a private matter between Winifred and myself," she said.

"And Ulf?" Ralph observed.

"Perhaps. I'm not sure." Winifred looked uncomfortable at the thought.

"Then let us see if we can find him," Ralph said, and offered his arm to Winifred to escort her. Janna watched them go. She hoped her dismissal hadn't offended Ralph, but acknowledged she would much rather approach the nuns on her own.

The abbey was easily seen: the walls and high spire dominated the small settlement. As she walked toward it, she nervously recited to herself what she might say to gain admission, and what questions she should ask about her mother. And her father. Would the abbess be more generous with her time and information than the abbess at Wiltune? Janna devoutly hoped so, for the abbess at Wiltune was a greedy, grasping woman, with a heart as hard as flint. She just hoped this abbess had been at the abbey long enough to know her mother, and was generous enough to share what she knew.

Sister Emanuelle. She practiced the name silently, trying to reconcile the image of a nun with her memory of Eadgyth, the *wortwyf* who had healed the villagers in return for whatever they were able to give her. Eadgyth, who had offered her daughter little in the way of hugs and kisses but who had loved her nevertheless. Janna understood that now, and understood also that as well as love, Eadgyth had given her the most priceless gift it was in her power to bestow: the knowledge of herbs and healing.

Chapter 8

Janna's heart thumped erratically as she pulled on the bellrope. She heard a loud clanging in the abbey beyond the wall. A young woman opened the stout door. She wore a habit, but it was too long for her, giving her the appearance of a child dressed up in its mother's clothes.

"Yes?" she asked. Her glance moved down to Janna's fine gown, and her features took on a more subservient expression. "How may I help you?"

Janna swallowed hard. "May I speak to your abbess?" she asked, keeping her voice steady with an effort.

"If you have business with our abbey, mayhap you should rather see our sacristan?"

"What age is she?" Janna asked.

"I beg your pardon?"

"Your sacristan. How many years does she have?" Noticing the young woman's blank expression, Janna hastened to explain. "I come seeking information about my mother, who was once infirmarian here. You are too young to know her, certes, but your older sisters in Christ might well remember her. At least, that's what I'm hoping."

The young nun continued to stare blankly at Janna.

"My mother's name was Sister Emanuelle. I'm asking if your sacristan is old enough to remember her?" Janna conceded that perhaps her request was unusual. Nevertheless, she wished the nun would let her go through. Although shaking with nerves, she was also impatient to take the next step to completing her mission.

The young woman shrugged. "Wait here," she said, and closed the door with a bang.

Janna wondered if she was somewhat lacking in wits, then chided herself for being uncharitable. She began to prowl restlessly, keeping an anxious eye on the door. Finally, it opened once more. This time the nun was elderly; even more encouraging, she looked friendly. Janna's impression was confirmed by the nun's first words.

"I believe you're making enquiries about Sister Emanuelle?" She took Janna's arm and drew her inside. "I knew her, as did several of our other sisters, and if you'll wait in the parlor I will bring them to you." She bent her head close to Janna's and whispered, "Do not bother our abbess with your questions. She had little sympathy for Sister Emanuelle's predicament, and time has not softened her opinion."

Janna nodded. So the abbess had known that her mother was with child, and had apparently been as uncharitable about it as the abbess at Wiltune. But her mother might have confided in some of the other sisters and, if this nun's friendly tone was anything to go by, they had not judged her. Janna hoped they'd be prepared to tell her all they knew.

"My name is Sister Amice," the nun said, as she led Janna into the parlor. "May I ask why you are seeking information about Emanuelle?"

"I am her daughter, Johanna." Janna settled onto a stool pushed forward for her use.

Sister Amice's eyes widened. "It's not yet time for Vespers and my sisters will be busy about their various chores, but I'll try to find Sister Marie to talk to you." She bustled out again.

Too on edge to sit still, Janna stood and began to pace the room, imprinting what she could see on her memory. Her mother had been here in this abbey, even in this very room, seeing what she was seeing and sharing her life with those who lived here. Janna had never known Eadgyth to have any friends, but now she was about to speak to those who had lived in close proximity with her, and who might have known her well enough to share her secrets. Now that she was actually here, in this room, Janna felt closer to her mother than she had since the dark days following her death. She was acutely conscious of how much she missed her.

As time went on and Sister Amice did not return, Janna's thoughts turned from her mother to curiosity about the abbey that had once been Eadgyth's home. The candles and their holders were of inferior quality to those that adorned the abbey at Wiltune. There were only a few hangings on the wall, and those somewhat threadbare. But the rushes strewn about the floor were clean and smelled sweet. Someone had taken trouble; someone cared.

She sat down again and tapped her foot restlessly, impatient over the delay. At last the door opened and a woman swept in, garbed in the full regalia of an abbess. She had a nose like a beak and no chin. At once Janna jumped up to greet her. Sister Amice followed behind. As her eyes met Janna's she put a finger to her lips and then made a slicing motion across her throat. Her actions became clear when the abbess stopped and glared at Janna.

"I understand you are enquiring after Sister Emanuelle, who was once our infirmarian?"

"Yes, Mother Abbess." Janna could hardly speak; she felt sick with fright and anticipation.

"And who are you?"

"My name is Johanna, mother. I am Eadgyth's – Sister Emanuelle's daughter."

Sister Amice's eyes rolled up to the heavens. Janna quickly realized her mistake as the abbess's countenance darkened into stern disapproval.

"So you are the offspring of that vile union." She held up a hand to silence Janna, who was about to protest. "You should know that while your mother was under our shelter, and on the very eve of taking her vows, I discovered that she had betrayed our order by consorting with a man. Worse, she left our abbey to live with him!" She glared at Janna as if it was all her fault.

"Of course he deserted her when it transpired that she carried his child, and she returned to the abbey expecting mercy. My predecessor might well have forgiven her had she still been in charge, for she was a lax woman and not fit for her position. But I am not of that ilk, and I thank God for it. Your mother broke her promise to us, she betrayed her sisters. For that, there cannot be forgiveness, and so I told her. It is past, it is done. We do not speak of your mother here."

Janna was stunned by the cold dislike in the abbess's voice. Although she now despaired of hearing anything of her mother's early life, she was determined to speak up in her mother's defense. A voice forestalled her.

"With due respect, Mother Abbess, Sister Emanuelle's position in the abbey was somewhat different from our own."

There was a quiet authority behind the voice, although Janna could not, at first, see where it had come from. Sister Amice moved slightly, and someone else came into view. This nun was tiny, and bent with age. Yet Janna noticed that there was a bright twinkle to her eyes, and compassion on her face as she took Janna's hands into her own.

"You have something of your mother in your looks," she said quietly, "but I do think you more resemble your father."

"You know my father?" The unexpected leap of hope brought sudden tears to Janna's eyes. "Pray, tell me about him, I beg you!" she said. "Please tell me everything you know."

The tiny nun looked at the abbess. Their eyes met and held, and Janna sensed the battle of wills going on between them. She looked from one to the other, hardly daring to hope. If she was to make a wager, her money would have gone on the abbess. But, to her surprise, the abbess gave a slight nod and swept out of the parlor, her face scrunched tight with fury.

A sigh of relief marked her passing. "I am Sister Marie." The tiny nun let go of Janna's hands, and lowered herself onto a stool nearby. "Pray, sit down." She waved her hand toward a bench, and Janna pulled it closer and sat alongside Sister Amice. She leaned forward, eagerly waiting to be told what she so longed to hear.

"Why are you asking us about your father? Why do you not ask your mother what you wish to know?"

"My mother is dead." Janna felt her throat close tight with grief. "Murdered."

"Murdered?" Sister Marie's shock was mirrored on Sister Amice's face.

"She never told me anything about her early life, or about my father," Janna explained. "We argued about it, and finally she promised that she would tell me what I wanted to know. But…but she died before we had a chance to speak of it. We left each other on bad terms, and I didn't get the chance to tell her I was sorry." Janna dashed the tears from her eyes, ashamed of her weakness. "That's why I seek knowledge about my father. I have made a vow that I will find him, for, with his help, I hope to avenge the death of my mother."

"I am so sorry, Johanna. So sorry." Sister Marie shook her head in sympathy. "Tell me what you want to know. I'll do my best to answer your questions."

"I want to know everything you can tell me! Especially about my father."

Sister Marie nodded slowly, as if Janna had confirmed something she'd long suspected. "So he never found you?"

"Found us?"

"Your father. I'm not sure if he knew about you. He came looking for your mother some months after she left the abbey. After she was asked to leave."

"After she was thrown out," said Sister Amice.

"Did anyone tell him that my mother carried his child?"

"I don't know. He was admitted to the abbess and shown the door almost immediately. None of us had a chance to talk to him, I'm afraid."

Janna was silent as she mulled the information over. As she'd suspected, her father hadn't abandoned them. He'd written to explain the delay, but Eadgyth couldn't read what he'd said and had assumed he'd deserted her. Janna felt a great sadness as she imagined how frightened and betrayed her mother must have felt after her meeting with the abbess. It explained so much, and yet things could have turned out so differently if only her mother had trusted her lover, if only she hadn't been so proud. She assembled her thoughts with an effort, and turned to Sister Marie.

"Why did my mother not go to her family to ask for help?"

"She had no family. That was why she came to us, for she was still quite young then, and in need of protection. She told us that she had learned about herbs and healing from her own mother, who was also a healer. A *wortwyf*, she called her. She said that her father had died some years past, and her mother most recently of some pestilence, which also took the life of a younger brother, I believe. Or was it a sister?" The nun's face creased in thought. "I can't remember."

Janna's hopes of locating any members of her mother's family were dashed, although she'd suspected as much from the start. "What else can you tell me?"

Sister Marie sat silent for a moment as she marshaled her thoughts. "As I reminded our abbess, your mother was not bound to the abbey in the same way as we were," she continued. "She came here for protection and offered her services as a healer in return, for she'd heard that our infirmarian had died and that we had no-one to replace her."

Janna nodded. This much she had learned from Sister Anne, the infirmarian at Wiltune.

"So far as I know, she never took any vows, but she dressed as a lay sister and took part in the offices of our daily life. She stayed here of her own free will and worked tirelessly for the comfort and wellbeing of our community while she was here."

"She was renowned as a healer where we lived. Even the infirmarian at Wiltune Abbey knew of her," Janna said proudly.

"Is that where she went? I'm glad she found shelter somewhere. The Abbess of Wiltune is obviously more charitable than our own."

"She wasn't at all!" Janna said hotly. "She gave my mother a derelict cottage, which my mother repaired, and for which she paid dearly for the rest of her life." But Janna didn't want to linger on a past already known to her. "Where did my mother meet my father?" she asked eagerly.

"Right here in the abbey." Sister Marie smiled in reminiscence. "Your father was with a hunting party. He had taken ill with a fever, and his companions brought him here, being the nearest place they could find shelter and healing. And your mother nursed him devotedly."

Unbidden, a scene came into Janna's mind: The abbey at Wiltune; Hugh lying in the infirmary, wounded and bleeding, while she did her best to take care of him. Was her mother's story repeating itself? Was this a sign of some sort?

"We watched your mother fall in love." Sister Marie's gaze was far away as she recounted what had happened. "Your father fell in love too," she said. "I have never seen a couple so devoted. And so, when he'd recovered from his fever and was ready to leave the abbey, your mother said her goodbyes and went with him."

"Where did they go?"

"To Winchestre. I believe your father has property there."

Winchestre! Janna's excitement felt strong and heady as wine. "My father's name was John. Is John. Do you know any more about him than that?"

"He was highborn, I know that much. But he didn't speak of his family, and neither did his companions."

Janna felt in her purse, and produced her father's ring. "Have you ever seen this before?"

"No." Sister Marie took the ring and examined it carefully. "Did this belong to your father?"

"I think so."

"There's a royal crest on it."

"I suppose my father was a loyal subject of King Henry." Something the nun had said was puzzling Janna. "Why, if my mother never took any vows, is the abbess so against her?"

Sister Marie gave a small huff of bitter amusement. "Our abbey gained in prestige while your mother was here. As you see, we are small in number and quite poor. But your mother's skills became known far and wide, and many people flocked here in the hope of a cure."

And brought coins with them to swell the coffers of the abbey! Janna didn't need to be told how the system worked.

"The new abbess was determined that your mother should take her vows. She didn't want to lose her, you see. And Sister Emanuelle may well have made her affirmation if she hadn't met your father. She was sad to leave, I know that. She said her farewells before she left, and expressed her regret that we would be without a healer once more. But she wouldn't – couldn't – let John leave without her. He was the love of her life. So she said, and so we all believed. I don't know what went on between them that she came back to the abbey later, seeking shelter. Especially given her condition, for she was coming near to her time by then. I can't think why your father allowed her to go, or why he didn't come after her straight away. Did they have some argument, perhaps, that should have been patched up before it went too far?"

"No." Janna hesitated, not wanting to share her mother's secret. But the nun had stood up to the abbess in order to tell her the truth, and she felt she owed her the truth in return.

"My father had to go to Normandy, to tell his own father about my mother and ask permission to break his betrothal so they could be wed. He wrote to explain why he was delayed but…but my mother couldn't read the letter. She didn't know how to read. I suspect she thought he had abandoned her. And so she came looking for sanctuary in the only home she knew."

"Oh! Oh, how sad." Sister Marie reached out and took Janna's hand, offering both comfort and her support.

Scalding tears burned Janna's eyes as she recalled the last time she'd seen her mother and the angry words they had exchanged. "My mother would not speak of him to me, I think for shame. But she named me after him. And she died with his name on her lips. She never stopped loving him."

There was a long silence as the nuns contemplated the disastrous end to what had begun with such promise and joy.

Sister Marie broke the silence at last. "Try not to judge our abbess too harshly. Your mother sought shelter at just the wrong time. You see, the bishop was here on a surprise visit. As you might have gathered, our previous abbess was somewhat lax. He came to make sure that we were now scrupulous about obeying the Rule."

"Even if it was at the expense of Christian kindness and charity." Sister Amice observed.

The nun reminded Janna of her friend Agnes, the lay sister whose clear idea of right and wrong had sometimes been at odds with how life was conducted at Wiltune Abbey. They would have got on well together, she thought.

"He certainly did his best to catch us out in wrongdoing or laxness of any sort," Sister Marie agreed. "He was particularly meticulous and careful in his catechizing. Each and every one of us was interrogated separately, and punished severely for even the slightest of misdemeanors or imaginary sins."

"So you can imagine how difficult it would have been for the abbess to explain a pregnant infirmarian in our midst," Sister Amice interrupted once more.

"And so your mother was castigated and sent immediately on her way in disgrace," Sister Marie continued. "If the bishop was impressed by our abbess's strict discipline, we never heard of it, but the rest of us were outraged by the treatment meted out to your mother, and we told the abbess so in no uncertain terms."

"After the bishop had left," Sister Amice interposed.

"By which time your mother had vanished, and it was too late to make amends." Sister Marie pressed Janna's hand. "Now that I've met you, I regret our cowardice even more," she said softly. "After the kind and loving service your mother gave us, we should all have stood behind her and insisted that the abbess offer her shelter, at least until her time was come and you were born." She released Janna's hand and stood up, indicating that their meeting was over. "I shall raise the matter in chapter tomorrow," she promised.

"My mother's dead. Even if you shame the abbess, it's too late, now, to make amends."

"I shall pray for her soul."

"As shall I," said Sister Amice.

"She'll need your prayers," Janna said, her voice suddenly rough with fury. "Our village priest refused to bury her, and so she lies in unhallowed ground in an unmarked grave at Berford."

"But...why unhallowed?"

"After you turned her away, and after the treatment she received from the abbess of Wiltune, she turned her back on the Church."

Let them understand how their lack of kindness had affected Eadgyth, Janna thought angrily. "My mother never lost faith in God, but she lost faith in those who professed to carry out His work here on earth in His name."

A shocked silence followed her explanation. Then Sister Marie said, "And I shall also be speaking of this in chapter tomorrow. I shall do all in my power to have your mother's body disinterred and reburied in hallowed ground. We might even bring her here if the priest proves obdurate. After all, this was her home for a long time, and she served us faithfully. We did her a great disservice in life. At least let us honor her life in death. She deserves no less from us."

"The abbess will never agree to it," Janna pointed out.

Sister Marie gave her a long, cool stare. "You may leave the abbess to me," she said. Janna wondered what power the tiny nun could possibly wield other than her great age. But perhaps that was enough in a place such as this.

She thanked the two sisters, and Sister Amice led her out to the heavy door that closed them off from the world outside. "I am truly sorry for all the hardship that befell your mother, and for our part in making her life so much more difficult than it should have been," she said, as she opened the latch.

Janna could not offer forgiveness, but she could remember the courtesy that Eadgyth had taught her. "Thank you for taking the time to tell me what you know."

She was thoughtful as she walked from the abbey toward the town. She'd learned some interesting facts about her parents, including several things of vital importance. Her mother had never taken her vows. Janna was pleased to have that mystery cleared up, for she'd worried about how her father had so far forgotten himself as to seduce a nun. In truth, she'd found it hard to feel respect for him, yet all had been made clear now. Her mother had never been a nun, and had loved her father as he had loved her. It warmed Janna to think of it.

More important, for her purpose, was Sister Marie's confirmation that her father had property in Winchestre. She had learned all she was likely to learn here in Ambresberie. She would waste no time, now, in setting off for Winchestre.

First, however, there was Winifred's problem to sort out. Janna thought of the figurine she had found in the forest. If Ulf was not prepared to return the sacred relic and share the reward with Winifred, would the figurine be enough of a dowry for the young girl to gain a place at Ambresberie? Janna still wore her purse outside her gown. She untied it, and pulled out the small statue of the mother and her child. She peered at it in the fading light, marveling anew at the sweet expression of the mother and how tenderly she cradled her child. She would be sorry to give up the figurine, for it had brought her great comfort along her journey. But perhaps it had served its purpose. She'd already learned much about her family that she hadn't known before. Perhaps now it was time to pass on its power to heal and bring good fortune to someone else. If the figurine was enough for Winifred to gain acceptance, once she was inside the abbey, she could leave the relic somewhere safe to be found. Janna was sure the abbess would be delighted to claim the reward for the missing hand.

She nodded to herself. It was a good plan. She would share it with Winifred just as soon as she found them all. She thrust the figurine back into her purse and then, conscious of the need to keep everything safe, she ducked behind a bush under the cover of darkness to secure her purse under her gown once more.

There was no sign of the pilgrim band in the streets, although she walked around for some time looking for her fellow travelers. Eventually she spied a bush and a lamp hanging from a post outside a sizable cottage, and turned her steps toward it. Several horses were tethered outside. She thought she recognized Ralph's palfrey among them.

The alehouse was brimming with people, all pushing and shoving to get a seat and a mug of home brew inside them. Janna paused on the threshold, breathing in the smoky air and squinting through the haze to look for the pilgrims. She decided to stop even if she couldn't find them, for she was hungry and thirsty. She walked through the crowd to find an empty seat, and spied the pilgrims huddled at a table at the back. Juliana was not among them.

As soon as Ralph caught sight of her, he shifted over, pushing Winifred further along the bench to leave a space on his other side.

"Did you see anyone useful? Did you find out what you wanted to know?" he asked quietly, once Janna had sat down and greeted them all.

"Yes." She was grateful for his concern. "And you were right! They didn't know much about my father, but he does have property in Winchestre. So that's where I shall go."

Ralph nodded thoughtfully. "It's as I thought."

"And what did you think exactly?"

He smiled enigmatically. "Leave it with me for the moment," he advised. "I don't want to raise your hopes, not until I've made some enquiries."

"My lord! You do try my patience!" Janna gave his arm a playful punch.

He caught her hand and held it. Once more she felt the power of his mesmerizing blue gaze. "Trust me," he said softly. "I'll help you find him, I promise you."

Janna sat quietly, with her hand held tight in his. Her mind was whirling with all she had learned. Her emotions were also in turmoil. Ralph sat close, pressed to her side in the crush of people. She was acutely aware of him, of his regard, of his promise. What could it mean? Excitement distracted her from the hum of conversation around the table, but finally a name caught her attention.

"Juliana?" she repeated, pressing her mouth close to Ralph's ear so that he could hear her above the din. "Where is she?"

"She has accompanied her son's body to Oxeneford."

"What about Ulf?" Janna looked for him down the table. He caught her eye and nodded. She'd never seen him look so careworn before.

"He returned, with my horse. Mistress Juliana made other arrangements to transport Bernard's body."

There was a roar of laughter from a bunch of drunken youths close by. Two of their number came reeling toward them and crashed against their table, bursting into high giggles when they saw what they'd done.

"Watch where you're going!" Ulf shouted, throwing out his hands to try to catch the goblets and trenchers that skidded across the table. The youth in front grinned at him and nudged his companion, who was now busy trying to clear enough space to sit down beside Janna on the end of the bench. Caught off-balance, he lurched sideways.

"Go away!" Janna snatched her hand from Ralph's and pushed him away, just in time to prevent him from collapsing onto her lap. His companion caught his arm, and heaved him back onto his feet. The two of them continued on their merry way, leaving the pilgrims grumbling in protest at the mess on the table. Drinks had spilled, some into their supper so that their trenchers were now soggy with ale. It left an unappetizing mess to be cleaned up, and Ralph jumped up and went off to summon a servant.

Taking advantage of Ralph's absence, Janna leaned over to Winifred. "Did you talk to Ulf?" she whispered. "What did he say?"

Winifred's hand went automatically to her purse. Her face became ashen as she desperately patted down the sides of her gown, looking for it. Her groping hands found her girdle and she untied it and held it up, displaying the neat cut where the purse had once hung. "It's gone!" She ran the girdle through her fingers as if unable to believe the evidence of her own eyes. "My purse!" she wailed. "It's gone."

Janna realized what had happened. "Go after those two young drunkards," she shouted down the table at Ulf. "They've got

Winifred's purse." She knew Ulf would understand the extent of Winifred's loss. "Hurry!" she said urgently, as Ulf hesitated.

He jumped up and pushed his way through the crowd in pursuit of the thieves. Janna turned back to Winifred. "Let's make sure it hasn't fallen under the table," she said, knowing that it was probably hopeless but determined to make sure. She ducked down, already regretting her impulse as she saw what awaited them. The straw under the table was filthy with old bones and scraps of food that added their stink to the smelly boots of the pilgrims. Janna held her breath as she felt about. As she'd feared, there was no sign of the purse at all. She backed out and faced Winifred.

The young woman was rigid with fear, almost beyond thought. "What shall I do, Janna?" she whispered. "Oh God in His mercy, what shall I do?"

"Did you carry valuables in your purse, mistress?" Morcar asked sympathetically.

"No! No, only..." She looked toward Janna, at a loss.

"Only some few things to remind Winifred of her home," Janna said firmly. She glanced about the alehouse, praying for Ulf's success. But it was some time before he returned, and then it was with a rueful expression and a bloody nose.

"They didn't dake kindly to by accusation," he said thickly. "I did by best to search 'em, bud..." He touched his nose, thoroughly sorry for himself.

Winifred shut her eyes, too miserable even to thank him for his trouble.

"Come outside with me." Janna grabbed Ulf's sleeve. "I'll clean that up for you. You come too, Winifred." She knew it would do no good if, in her distress, Winifred confessed her deed to the pilgrims.

"Have you got an old rag of some sort?" she asked Ulf, as they came to a water pump beside a horse trough. He nodded and pulled a small package from his pack, which he carefully unwrapped.

Janna couldn't see what the wrapping concealed, for Ulf was quick to secrete the treasure in his scrip. She took the piece of homespun from him and sluiced it under the spout.

"Have you spoken to Ulf, Winifred?" she asked, as she began to clean the worst of the blood from around Ulf's nose.

"About the hand? Yes, I have, although I had the devil's own difficulty shaking Master Ralph from my side before I could say anything. I didn't want *him* knowing about it too! It was shaming enough just talking to you about it, Ulf." She winced in sympathy as he suddenly shouted, "Ouch!"

"Sorry!" Janna began to dab more gently at Ulf's swollen nose. "So what did you decide?"

"We agreed to take the hand to Ambresberie Abbey together and ask the abbess to return it to Wiltune. Ulf was going to claim the reward for its return, and I was going to ask for a place in the abbey." Winifred began to cry as she realized that the relic was truly gone, and her hopes for the future with it.

Ulf nodded gingerly, wincing as the movement jarred against the cloth in Janna's hand. "Bud I hab sub udder thigs ib by bag."

"What?" Winifred stared at him through her tears.

"In his bag?" Janna indicated Ulf's pack. "I think he's saying he's got some other things in there."

"Relics, you mean? But...I can't afford to give you an offering, Ulf. I've got nothing, don't you understand? I've got nothing to give you in return!"

Ulf shrugged. "There bay be a way – " he began, but Winifred interrupted him.

"I stole the hand from the reliquary, but my sin is doubled for now I have lost a precious relic too! Nothing I do can ever make up for that. I am doomed, damned forever!" she cried. "Those drunken sots! They can have no idea what it is they've stolen. The hand of St James – oh!" She shuddered as she envisaged its fate.

Janna made up her mind. "Don't despair, Winifred. The relic is gone, but I've got something you can have which may be enough to gain your admission into an abbey." She gave Ulf's bloodied nose a last careful wipe. She washed the rag clean under the pump and handed it to him. "Tip your head back and keep this over the bridge of your nose for a little while. It will help to stop the bleeding."

She turned her back and, in the darkness, lifted her skirt and carefully drew the small figurine from her purse. "*A pagan idol,*" Juliana had called it. She must take care not to put any such idea in Winifred's mind.

"This is a precious statue of the Virgin Mary and baby Jesus," she said firmly. Ulf squinted down his nose at her with an expression of disbelief. But he didn't say anything. Winifred stretched out her hand to take the figurine from Janna and took it over to the lamp at the doorway, the better to see it. She turned it around and over, studying the delicate lines of the carving, and the tender expression on the mother's face.

"It's – it's beautiful!" she breathed. "Where did it come from, Janna?"

Janna hesitated. If she confessed to finding it in the forest, its provenance would be forever suspect. Yet her brain stalled, refusing to come up with a convincing explanation. Ulf stepped into the breach.

"Didn't you tell me id was given to you as a parding gift by the Abbess of Wiltune?"

"I…" Janna's mouth opened, then closed. She nodded.

"And you would give it to me?" Winifred's eyes shone with hope. "Oh, Janna, thank you!" Impulsively, she flung her arms around Janna and gave her a hug. "Oh!" She studied the figurine once more, stroking its smooth surface in wonder.

"I hope it will open a door for you." Janna was busy trying to stifle pangs of regret. "Perhaps you could try for admission here at

Ambresberie? The abbey seems quite small, and I don't think it's wealthy. The abbess might be glad of something like this to add to their store of valuables. But don't tell her that I gave this to you. In fact, don't mention my name at all."

"Can we go tonight?" Winifred raised a shining face to Janna, all care seemingly forgotten now that rescue had come her way.

"I am sure there will be a guest house attached to the abbey. We could ask for shelter for the night, and you can look around at the same time and see what you think."

"I must make my farewells to the pilgrims before we go." Winifred danced inside to show off her treasure to the others.

Ulf lingered beside Janna. He breathed in a few cautious breaths in an effort to clear his nose, and gave a loud sniff.

"I'm sorry I don't have a plaster or poultice to ease the pain and swelling," Janna apologized.

"It feels better already," Ulf assured her. "Thank you, lass. You're very kind."

Janna was silent for a moment, feeling regret for the loss of the little statue, and also for the need to tell yet another lie. She turned to Ulf. "You don't believe what I just said about the mother and child, do you?"

"And you don't believe what I just said about the abbess either," he retorted with a grin.

"But – you're a relic seller. Dealer. Whatever you are." Janna couldn't think of the right word to describe Ulf's trade. "Surely you don't tell lies about your relics? You must believe what you tell people."

"Aye. Maybe. You should know that relics, genuine relics, are very few and far between."

"And so you help the process along a little?"

Ulf inclined his head, looking grave. "I don't go so far as some I've met, who resort to such tricks as taking severed heads from pikes and cleaning and drying 'em with spices, and touting 'em as relics. I saw one such, and was told it was the head of St John the Baptist!"

"And did you buy – make an offering for it?"

"I did not, for I know the fellow well by reputation as a charlatan. Others, I am sure, would have been gulled by him – if they did not know that the head already resides in Jerusalem, or in Damascus, or even in Rome – or maybe in all three!"

"So the sliver of wood from the cross of Christ?" Janna didn't know whether to frown or laugh. "Juliana bought it from you in a bid to keep Bernard safe. Is it a genuine relic, even though it obviously didn't work?"

"I have no reason to believe it isn't genuine. Besides, God doesn't always answer our prayers as we would wish." Perhaps Ulf read the skepticism on Janna's face. "Don't be too quick to judge me," he warned. "You say you're a healer so you should know, more than anyone, that the power of prayer, of belief, can sometimes do more than any medicament or treatment to heal an affliction. If someone owns a hand, or a sliver of wood, or a scrap of fabric, and believes that it belongs to a saint or to Christ or the Virgin Mary, their comfort and ease comes from the belief that it will heal 'em, and so it often does."

"Surely their comfort comes from their belief that whoever the relic belonged to will help make things better," Janna corrected him.

"I acquire my relics in good faith. But I sometimes take short cuts for a good cause," Ulf admitted.

"Such as providing the means to help Winifred gain admission to an abbey? Is that why you lied on my behalf?"

"I'm in the business of providing hope," Ulf said. "Without my relics, people would have nowt to comfort or heal 'em, nowt at all."

It was an effective argument, Janna conceded, as they entered the alehouse.

"I believe the figurine that Mistress Winifred is showing everyone once belonged to you?" Ralph questioned, as Janna sat beside him once more. "There seems no end to the treasures you keep in your purse! What else do you have hiding in there, mistress?" There was a teasing twinkle in his eyes, and Janna twinkled back at him.

"I'm sure you'd like to know, my lord, but I am not bound to tell you, for what I carry is my concern alone."

"I'd like to make everything about you my concern, lady," he said gravely.

Janna felt a quick flush of pleasure, until she looked into his laughing eyes and realized he was still teasing her. At a loss, and feeling somewhat discomfited, she raised her hand to beckon a serving wench to order some supper for herself, then quickly lowered it again as she remembered that her purse was hidden beneath her gown.

Her gesture wasn't wasted on Ralph, however. "Would you like something to eat?" he asked and, before Janna could answer, he beckoned an attentive maid and asked for a mug of ale and a bowl of stew to be brought.

"My thanks." Janna pointed in the direction of her purse. "I shall repay you as soon as I can," she promised.

Ralph gave her a cheeky grin. "With what you guard so carefully under your skirt?"

Janna's face heated with embarrassment. But she would not let him see her discomfort; she kept her head bent and said quietly, and with gentle reproof: "What's mine is precious to me. It's not lightly given away, not to anyone, my lord."

"Ah, Janna." He caught her hand. "Forgive me. I don't mean to tease you, only to help you." He came closer, so close that the tavern and everyone in it faded from Janna's sight and she became conscious only of him as he leaned forward and brushed her cheek with his lips. "And you are precious to me," he murmured. "More so, I think, than you realize." He sat back, and reached for his mug of ale.

Janna blinked at him, wondering if it was her own wishful thinking that had conjured up what had just passed between them.

Ralph swallowed some ale, and licked his lips. "If you won't reveal the contents of your purse, tell me instead what you learned from the good sisters in the abbey."

Janna muttered her thanks as a bowl of stew and a spoon were placed before her, along with a brimming cup. The serving wench swung her hips and glanced flirtatiously over her shoulder at Ralph as she walked away. Janna picked up the spoon and, between mouthfuls, began to recount what she'd found out.

"You already know what I've discovered about my father from his letter," she said pointedly, knowing Ralph believed she was still keeping secrets from him. "But I'm finished here in Ambresberie, because my father didn't come from these parts. The sisters told me he was traveling with a hunting party."

Ralph nodded thoughtfully. "How, then, did he meet your mother?"

"He was taken ill. A fever. My mother nursed him back to health at the abbey, and they fell in love." Janna's voice softened as she imagined how it must have been between them. "So it seems I must go on now to make my enquiries in Winchestre, for he took my mother there with him once he was recovered."

"If your father's who I think he is, you may well find that he's living in Normandy now, not Winchestre."

Janna caught her breath in surprise. "So you do know him? You know who he is?"

Ralph smiled at her. "I cannot and will not say any more. Not for the world would I raise your hopes unnecessarily. But I will do all in my power to see you united with him. You may trust me on this."

"Oh, I will," Janna breathed. This was more than she'd dreamed of hearing from Ralph. "And if my father's in Normandy, I shall follow him there too," she announced. "But you are bound for Oxeneford, Ralph, and I am sure your cousin awaits you there. I cannot ask you to go out of your way on my account." It felt like the death of hope to say it, but she felt obliged to make the offer.

"My cousin can act on my behalf, for I have made your quest my own." Ralph caught Janna's hand and, before she realized what he was about, he began to kiss her fingers one by one. She quivered at the touch of his lips, so light against her skin, and so gentle. Yet she sensed the passion in the strength of his grip. She closed her eyes and gave herself to delight, swept away on a sweet flood that yet was wild and strong enough to drown her in its depths.

They sat close together, heart to heart, for some moments before Ralph finally released her hand. He stretched out his long legs and arched his back with a weary sigh. "Janna, let's not leave for Winchestre tonight, I beg you. Tomorrow will be soon enough!"

"Tomorrow," Janna agreed, "for tonight Winifred and I plan to ask for a bed at the abbey's guest hall."

"And I shall come too." Ralph banged on the table and, in the ensuing quiet, made their intentions known. "May I suggest you all come with us? We need a good night's rest after all the troubles and turmoil of this day."

With relief that the day was almost done, for she was beginning to realize how exhausted she was, Janna quickly finished off the remains of the vegetable and marrow stew and left the tavern with the pilgrim party.

Chapter 9

It seemed strange to be sleeping overnight in the abbey that was once her mother's home. Even though Janna was not in the dorter with the nuns, she remembered what offices the sisters kept, and how they were expected to behave. It stretched her imagination to think of her outspoken, courageous mother keeping the great Silence and substitute obeying the Rule. But perhaps, in her youth, Eadgyth had been devout and obedient? She had certainly cared enough, believed enough, to seek shelter here and offer her services as a healer. The nuns had said she dressed as a lay sister, and had kept the offices. This was not the mother that Janna remembered. What had happened to Eadgyth after she'd met Janna's father had changed her forever.

Winifred was hard put to hide her excitement about being in an abbey and coming so close to the life she'd always wanted. She besieged Janna with questions about everything she saw and heard. Together, they attended Mass in the morning. Janna felt a great nostalgia as she smelled once more the spicy fragrance of incense, and heard the chanting that had been part of her mother's life and, briefly, her own. She stood and knelt on cue, and muttered some of the responses, earning Winifred's astonished respect as she did so.

As they filed out of the church, Janna caught a glimpse of a familiar figure. "That's Sister Amice," she said, grabbing Winifred's arm and leading her at a fast trot to the friendly nun. "Speak to her first about coming to the abbey as a postulant. She'll listen to your plea more kindly than the abbess, and I'm sure will give you her support if she believes you are in earnest."

"Come with me!" Winifred clutched on to Janna as they neared Sister Amice.

"No." Janna stood her ground. "This is something you must do alone, Winifred. And don't, whatever you do, don't mention the hand of St James!"

"I won't." Winifred looked stricken at the reminder. "Wish me luck?"

Janna crossed her fingers, and held them up with a smile. "Good luck," she said. "May God go with you, Winifred." Now that the time had come, she felt quite sad to say goodbye – if it was goodbye. She lingered beside the chapel to make sure.

With lifted chin signaling her determination, Winifred marched over to Sister Amice. The nun looked up and caught Janna's eye. She gave her a friendly nod, and then turned to Winifred, who had begun to speak. Janna tried to interpret what was happening. Winifred leaned forward, caught up in the passion of her plea. Sister Amice nodded, smiling. Winifred pulled the figurine from her sleeve and held it out. Sister Amice took it, looking somewhat startled. She seemed to draw back a little, and once more caught Janna's eye. Janna stared at her, willing the nun to accept the gift in the spirit in which it was offered. As if sensing what Janna was thinking, Sister Amice bent her gaze to the figurine. She held it up and turned it around to study it more closely.

She handed it back to Winifred, and Janna's hopes fell in disappointment on Winifred's behalf. But Sister Amice took Winifred's arm and, together, they walked around the corner, Winifred casting one beaming glance behind her before they vanished out of sight. Janna breathed a sigh of relief. It looked as though Winifred had passed the first hurdle on her long spiritual journey. She hurried back to the guest house to collect her staff and find Ralph.

Suddenly she realized just what it was she was proposing to do: set off to Winchestre alone in the company of a dashing and most attractive man! Her heart gave a double skip of excitement, before doubt crept in to spoil everything.

You know so little about him, she reminded herself. *What if he has something else on his mind, and is using lies about your father to entrap you?*

"He is honorable! That's why he insisted that we keep company with the pilgrims for the sake of my reputation."

So why isn't he putting forward the same argument this time?

"Oh, shush!" Janna tried to dismiss her unease, but she was quaking with nerves as she approached Ralph. He was waiting for her among a small group of other travelers, who stood beside their horse and cart ready for departure.

"Janna!" he said, indicating the group with a sweep of his hand. "This is Master Thomas and his band of jongleurs. They are bound for Winchestre, and he has invited us to travel with them. I have accepted his kind offer, for it is more seemly for us to travel in the company of others. I hope you don't mind?"

"No! No, not at all." Janna beamed her relief at Ralph, then turned her smile on the jongleur. "Master Thomas," she said gravely. "I thank you."

Master Thomas took her hand and kissed it with an elaborate flourish. "The pleasure is ours, mistress," he said gallantly in the language of the Normans. He released her hand with obvious reluctance. Beside him, his wife bristled with displeasure. Janna noticed Ulf standing close by with Golde and Morcar, and went across to say her farewells while Ralph fetched his palfrey from the stable.

"Are you not coming on with us, Janna?" Ulf asked.

"No." In spite of her doubts about the relic seller, she found herself sorry to say goodbye to him. "I came to Ambresberie to seek information about my family and I must go on, now, to Winchestre. The jongleurs and...and Master Ralph have suggested I accompany them." She felt her face grow hot under Ulf's penetrating gaze. "I suspect you've also lost Winifred, for she is staying on here at the abbey," she continued quickly. She hoped, for Winifred's sake, that she would prove correct. She recalled the determined tilt to Winifred's jaw, and smiled to herself. There was really no doubt in her mind about Winifred's future. The young woman's determination had carried her thus far, and would see her through to the end.

"You've lost us too, for we've decided to stay on here a few days more in case there's news of Adam," Golde announced, with a sideways glance at Morcar.

"And we'll continue the search for that devil spawn," Morcar added grimly.

"So that leaves just me!" Ulf hoisted his pack on his shoulders and whistled for Brutus. "I think I shall try my luck with you, Janna," he said cheerfully. "I'm sure the good people of Winchestre will be interested to see the treasures I carry."

Without ado, he bade Morcar and Golde a brisk farewell, and led Janna toward the jongleurs. "My name is Ulf," he introduced himself, and bobbed his head to Master Thomas. "I deal in relics and I'm sure I shall be an asset to your company if you will allow me to travel along with you?"

"You are welcome, Ulf, so long as you can pay your own way." Master Thomas's dubious expression gave the lie to his greeting. And he looked positively frightened when he realized that Brutus would also be joining them.

"I have many wonders in my pack that I guarantee will open doors along our journey," Ulf said with a bright smile, apparently not perturbed by Master Thomas's lack of enthusiasm. "Once I attract the good folks' interest, you may dance or sing, or whatever it is you do. I feel sure we shall all be made most welcome."

Master Thomas looked even more skeptical. Somewhat reluctantly, he began to introduce the rest of his troupe – his wife Elanor, young son Faldo, and troupe members Nicholas and Jocelin. Elanor's mouth pursed as she looked them over, but Nicholas and Jocelin beamed a welcome. They threw back their shoulders and sucked in their stomachs and tried altogether to make of themselves something more than they were.

Janna was flattered by their efforts on her behalf, and hoped that Ralph had noticed. He, however, was scowling at Ulf, not at all pleased that the relic seller had elected to join their party.

"Why's he coming with us?" he mouthed at Janna, jerking a thumb in Ulf's direction.

Janna shook her head. It was a good question, but one to which she had no answer.

Ralph's question stayed in her mind as they followed the jongleurs past the abbey walls and out onto the track that would lead them to Winchestre. Was Ulf really so free he could alter direction at a whim, or was there some other purpose to his journey? With an effort, she set aside her misgivings and, instead, thought of their destination. For the first time since she'd set out, she was confident that she would find her father, be it in Winchestre or in Normandy. She wondered how far it was to Winchestre. How long before she stood before him and told him of her existence?

She smiled to herself as she imagined his surprise. Would he welcome her – or would she be an embarrassment to him? This question was quickly followed by others, quenching her excitement as effectively as a bucket of water thrown over a fire. Did he already have a wife? And children?

She would make him welcome her, she decided, determined to recapture her sense of happy anticipation. She would make her father love her, just as she was prepared to love him.

"What do you know of Master Ralph?" Ulf's voice broke into Janna's musing.

"Why, as much as you do, I suspect," Janna said, surprised by the question. She glanced at Ralph, who was striding ahead with Master Thomas. They seemed to be sharing a joke, for they were both laughing heartily. Ralph looked content; full of energy and purpose.

"Mistress Juliana and I had a long talk after Bernard's death, while I was escorting her to Ambresberie," Ulf went on. "A *long* talk."

Janna wasn't quite sure what he was hinting at. "A long talk about Adam?"

"About Ralph, among other things. How far do you trust him, Janna?" Ulf's voice was unusually serious.

"Why should I not trust him?" Janna countered. "Do you know something about him that I don't?"

"I know nowt for certain. What interests me is why he told us he was bound for Oxeneford, but now comes with you to Winchestre."

"Why should you question his motives when you're doing exactly the same thing yourself?" Janna said hotly, embarrassed that Ulf might imagine the worst about her and Ralph.

Ulf opened his mouth, but Janna didn't give him a chance to reply. "Are you not anxious to get home to your family, Ulf? You have been away for so long."

"I have no home and no family."

"I thought you lived in Oxeneford?"

"No. I met the pilgrims at the tomb of St James. I decided their presence would lend me an air of respectability." He cast a worried glance at Janna. "So you see, I am free to go where my fancy takes me – and my fancy takes me now to Winchestre. Besides, I promised Mistress Juliana that I would do my best to look after you, for she claims – "

"I know what she claims!" Janna said harshly. A vision of Bernard's blood-stained body flashed before her eyes. She blinked quickly to dismiss it.

"She was right to be worried."

Janna wondered if Ulf's advice was as kindly meant as it sounded. "It's not what you think about me and Ralph," she muttered, annoyed at having to explain herself. "I'm looking for my father and Ralph thinks he knows where he may be found. He's kindly offered to come with me to Winchestre to help me look for him. That's all."

A skeptical expression crossed Ulf's face. "If you're sure there's nowt else to it but that?"

Actually, there was a great deal more to it than that! But Janna didn't want to share with Ulf her hope that Ralph's real purpose in traveling with them was to be close to her just as she longed to become closer to him. He had shown himself kind. Honorable. In truth, when she was with him he stirred her senses till she burned as if with a fever. But she would not share those thoughts with anyone, least of all Ulf.

"Is there any news of Adam?" she asked, anxious to talk about something else.

"Nay, not yet, but the cry has gone out for him." Ulf was silent for a moment. "Juliana told me about the message Bernard found on the dead man. Do you know what became of it, Janna?"

Janna froze. All her doubts about Ulf came flooding back. "I know nothing about it," she said tightly. Anxious to put him off, she continued: "Master Bernard's scrip is still missing. If there was anything of value inside, then Adam will have it."

"If Adam was the culprit."

Why should Ulf doubt Adam unless he knew something she did not? Janna was about to ask him when Ulf continued: "I noticed that you searched Master Bernard's body very carefully when you thought no-one was looking. I wondered if you'd located the bishop's message."

"If I'd found it, what would you expect me to do with it?" she challenged, hoping to force him to show his hand.

"I'd expect you to take it to the empress, as Bernard intended. But you're going the wrong way."

"Is that why you're following me?"

"No. I've already explained my reasons for accompanying you and the jongleurs."

Janna wished she could believe him. "Who do you support in this battle for the crown?" She waited anxiously for Ulf's answer.

He hesitated. "Being always on the road as I am, I have found it safer not to have an opinion or take sides," he said at last.

Which meant she couldn't trust him. Nor could she trust his explanation for traveling with them. He might well want to keep watch over her but not because Dame Juliana had asked him to do so.

"I looked for the bishop's message, but I didn't find it," she said curtly. "So you can go your own way, Ulf. There's no need for you to follow me around."

Ulf was about to answer when one of the party, a youth, fell into step beside them. "My name's Faldo," he introduced himself, even though Master Thomas had already made the round of introductions. Faldo had long hair, unusually long for a youth, and a merry smile. He was some eight years younger than her, perhaps ten or eleven summers.

"And I am Janna, and this is Ulf." She smiled at the youth, glad of the interruption. Ulf's words had left her feeling deeply uneasy. "Pray tell me, for I have never met a jongleur before. What is it that you do, exactly?" she asked.

She caught the flash of surprise in his eyes, and knew that she was once again in danger of betraying her humble origins. Then he smiled. "I sing for my supper at the castles and manors of lords, mistress," he said. "So do we all."

"Sing?"

"And tell stories of noble warriors and heroic deeds." He grinned sideways at her. "What *chanson de geste* would you hear me recite? Something from *The Song of Roland*? Or we have heard a new story about an old king of Britain called Arthur, who has many fierce battles against giants and creatures from the Otherworld. But his greatest battle is against his ambitious nephew, who seizes the crown and wins the love of Guenevere, Arthur's wife. When Arthur and Medraut meet in a battle for crown and queen, Arthur gives Medraut the death blow and is himself mortally wounded. Would you like to hear some of it?"

"That sounds…interesting," Janna said cautiously, thinking quite the opposite. What a bloody tale of treachery and horror!

Faldo clasped his hand to his heart, struck a pose, and began to recite:

"Shoulder to shoulder
Heart to heart
Arthur and Medraut, united
In hatred.
Deadly enemies sworn
For love of crown
And Guenevere the Fair.
Each draws his sword.
Each suffers the death blow
In the mud and blood at Camlann."

He looked at Janna and Ulf expectantly.

Not quite sure what was expected of her, Janna clapped her hands together. "Well done," she cried.

Ulf patted Faldo on his shoulder. "It sounds like a fine tale, lad. I'll look forward to hearing you recite more of it," he said, immediately giving the lie to his words by whistling for Brutus and striding on ahead.

Janna knew that she had offended Ulf, and hoped that Faldo didn't mind his seeming indifference to his recital. She wondered if there was more to come, hoping for something happy about love and lords and ladies this time, but Faldo began to walk on once more. She fell into step beside him.

"That's not the end of the story," he said modestly, clearly pleased by her applause. "Everyone believes that Arthur still lives, and that one day he will return again to save England. There are also marvelous tales about Merlin and his prophecies."

"Merlin?" The name seemed familiar, and now Janna remembered why. "It's said that he magicked giant standing stones from Ireland and put them in a huge stone circle," she told Faldo. "It's near here. Have you seen it?"

"Indeed, I have," the youth said enthusiastically. "It's all part of the stories about him. The Giants' Dance, it's called. But that's only one of many magical deeds that Merlin performed. There's a tale of how he found dragons sleeping below Vortigern's tower. By telling Vortigern why his tower kept falling down, he saved himself from being put to death. Another story tells how he transformed Arthur's father into the likeness of Gorlois, the Duke of Cornwall, so that Uther Pendragon could lie with the duke's wife. Uther was Arthur's father, you see. That's how Arthur came to be born, through trickery and deceit."

Janna listened with interest, thinking that a journey with jongleurs was bound to be far more entertaining than traveling with pilgrims. "And what do you sing when you're not reciting about battles and things?"

"Love songs mostly," Faldo said with deep hatred. "And I'm learning tricks and juggling too," he added. "My father, Master Thomas, is our leader. He recites the deeds of kings and nobles to entertain the houses that take us in. I've been learning these stories all my life and, soon enough, my turn will come." He drew himself up and struck a noble pose. "When I am of age and too old to play the parts of ladies!"

"You'll do it very well, I'm sure." But Janna was more interested in hearing a love song. "Will you sing something for me?"

Faldo thought for a moment. "I know a good song in the language of the English," he said. "Have you heard this one, mistress?

"Sumer is icumen in
Lhude sing cuccu,
Groweth seed and bloweth mead,
And springs the wood anew.
Sing cuccu."

It was a cheerful and infectious song, and Janna's head bobbed in time to the beat as they walked along.

"Now it's your turn. You sing me something," Faldo commanded.

"I...I don't know any songs," Janna admitted.

The youth stared at her with pity in his eyes. "No songs?" he repeated incredulously.

"I've spent the past year in an abbey," she said by way of explanation.

"An abbey is full of singing, so I've heard. My father told me that sometimes the songs we sing began as a chant in the abbey, but sometimes it's the other way around. Always with different words, of course!" he added hastily. "Will you sing a chant for me, mistress, and see if I know it as a song by another name?"

"I can't." Janna felt miserable as she made the admission. It was perfectly true. There had been no singing in her life with Eadgyth, although her mother had sometimes hummed a sacred chant when she'd thought she was alone. Janna had asked about it once. Eadgyth had been angry with her, and so she'd come to think there was something wrong, something sinful, about singing. It was only when she came to live in the abbey that she realized what it was that Eadgyth sang, and why she was so dismissive when Janna questioned her.

But the lesson had already been learned. To Janna's chagrin, when she'd opened her own mouth to take part in the services, she'd found that she'd been unable to join in.

"You can't sing?" Faldo looked even more astonished.

"What's all this about 'can't sing?'" Ralph questioned. Janna hadn't noticed his approach, and jumped at the sound of his voice. He put out a hand to steady her. "Is that can't, or won't?"

"Can't." It cost Janna a great deal to admit it.

"Everyone can sing," Faldo asserted. "Everyone. Listen, mistress: *Sumer is icumen in, lhude sing cuccu.*"

"*Summer is icumen in, lhude sing cuccu,*" Ralph copied him.

"Now it's your turn," said Faldo. They both looked expectantly at Janna.

She felt her throat grow dry and tight. "I can't," she whispered.

"You can," Ralph assured her. "Sing along with both of us." He glanced at Faldo. "Come on." And they both sang the first two lines in unison.

Janna stayed silent.

They sang the lines again.

Still Janna stayed silent.

"We're going to keep on singing this until you either join in with us or die of boredom," Ralph warned. There was a wicked gleam in his eye as he issued the challenge.

"*Sumer is icumen in, lhude sing cuccu, Sumer is...*"

"*...icumen in, lhude sing cuccu.*" Janna's voice was thin, scratchy with terror, but she felt a certain sense of accomplishment as Faldo beamed at her, and Ralph gave her a congratulatory pat on the back. By now the other jongleurs had gathered around, looking from one to the other to see what was going on.

"*Sumer is icumen in, lhude sing cuccu...*" This time Faldo kept on singing while, one by one, the others joined in, so that each sang a line behind the one before, and their voices contributed to a harmonious whole. Janna felt her face burst into a smile with the joy of the sound they made.

"I shall teach you all of it, and you shall sing the song with us wherever we stop for the night," Faldo promised.

"You expect me to sing for my supper too?" Janna didn't know whether to be amused or alarmed by the prospect. "We'll be out with the pigs if you leave me to do it!"

"Not you, mistress," Faldo said cheerfully, "but we're expected to pay for our board and lodging by entertaining the owners of the manors where we stop. With luck we'll find plenty of work and shelter in Winchestre, enough to tide us through the bitter months of winter. If not, we'll have to journey on to London."

Janna gazed at him in wonder. She had no idea that some people earned their living in this way. She looked around the small band. All were men save for Master Thomas's wife, whom Janna thought of as her chaperone. She wondered where the other jongleurs' womenfolk were, or even if they were married and had families. Not Faldo, of course; he was too young. But what of Nicholas and Jocelin? It must be a hard life, and a lonely one.

"Now, sing along with me," said Faldo, getting back to business. *"Sumer is icumen in, lhude sing cuccu."*

Ralph was still walking with them, and he repeated the line, smiling sideways at Janna as he did so, daring her to try again.

Heaving a resigned sigh, she joined in with them both as, once more, they began to sing about summer and the cuckoo. "Do I sing it in tune? Do I sound all right?" she asked anxiously at the end of it.

"You sound very well," Faldo assured her.

"Like a nightingale!" Ralph added. But the glint in his eye warned Janna that he was teasing her once more.

*

Days passed as they slowly made their way to Winchestre. Faldo hadn't exaggerated when he told Janna that they sang for their supper. What Janna hadn't realized was that they would stop at every likely-looking manor or farm house to ask for a night's lodging in return for giving entertainment. They didn't always find shelter for the night; sometimes they had to take their rest in barn or hedgerow, or even under the cart if it was raining, but they always stayed as long as they could wherever shelter and employment was offered to them.

Although Janna sometimes became impatient with their slow journey, she enjoyed the company of the jongleurs and the fun they had as they walked. Nicholas taught Faldo magic tricks and tried out new ones of his own. Janna always watched carefully, but she could never tell how the white dove got into a hat, or a ribbon up a sleeve, or a silver coin behind an ear, even though they always invited her to inspect everything before they started, just as Nicholas invited members of each audience to do the same thing.

When not engaged in practicing magic, Nicholas accompanied the players on his fluting pipe, or kept everyone in time to the beat of his small drum. Master Thomas's wife, Elanor, played both the harp and the rebec, and occasionally Jocelin took a turn on the hurdy gurdy, but he was also a skilled juggler and fiery sword swallower. Janna couldn't work out how he was able to do such things, but marveled every time she saw them. She could tell, as she watched Faldo practicing under Jocelin's keen eye, that it took confidence and skill. And patience, she thought, as Faldo dropped a ball and vented his annoyance by swearing at it.

As Faldo had said, Master Thomas was their leader, and the noble deeds of kings were his to tell. But between them, Nicholas and Jocelin had devised some funny routines: a block-headed husband and a pushy wife; a deceitful merchant and a dissatisfied customer; a peasant triumphing over an evil baron, or vice versa depending on their audience. These re-enactments were accompanied by jokes, quips and insulting repartee and provided some light entertainment between the more uplifting tales of heroes and battles.

Janna enjoyed the company of the irreverent pair, their tricks and jokes and great enjoyment of life. They, in turn, had danced attention on her until Ralph's proprietary air cautioned them to discretion. Janna didn't know whether to be pleased that Ralph was so attentive, or annoyed that he was taking it upon himself to sanction her friendships. Yet every day saw her falling deeper under his spell.

Sometimes, when they stopped in a market square, one or other of the jongleurs would bring out an instrument and play a carol. The rest of the band would link hands and dance in a ring, while encouraging the crowds to join them. After watching a few times, Janna ventured to take part, delighted to be learning a new skill. The touch of Ralph's hand set her senses on fire with delight. In her imagination, they became a great lord and lady, dancing in courtship, dancing in love.

While Ralph had no qualms about paying his way along their journey and being independent, Janna preferred to save her coins in case of hard times ahead and, instead, contributed time and labor to the jongleurs' cause whenever she could. Her chores kept her busy, but Ralph claimed her time when she was at leisure. His attentions aroused curiosity on the part of the jongleurs, and even some ribald speculation, which she did her best to ignore. But the question was always in her mind: what were Ralph's intentions toward her? On one occasion, when she overheard Elanor asking Ralph why he traveled with the jongleurs, she crept closer to listen in the hope that his reply might settle some of her own doubts.

"It is for my own pleasure, lady," he replied. "I have taken it upon myself to help Janna search for her missing father. But I confess, my interest goes deeper than that." He swung around, so suddenly that Janna was afraid that he would notice her. She shrank further behind the cart, and was relieved when he started speaking again.

"I would have her for my wife, but she is innocent of the ways of the world," Ralph continued. "I plan to give her a chance to know me better, and to trust me, for at present she is alone in the world, with no-one to guide her or speak for her."

Janna missed Elanor's low-voiced reply, but by then she'd stopped listening, so overwhelmed was she by Ralph's words. She clasped her hands to her breast, suffused with delight and savoring the moment. This was all and more than she had hoped to hear.

Caution kept her hidden until the pair had moved away. Not for anything would she reveal to Ralph that she'd overheard his declaration of love. At last, when she was quite sure they had gone, she crept out of her hiding place and continued with her task, which, today, was to cut fodder in a nearby field for the jongleur's carthorse. But her heart was singing with joy and the task passed as lightly as her thoughts.

On Janna's conscience was the continuing coolness between her and Ulf. Sometimes he joined the company for their evening meal but often he went missing. Janna wondered if he was scouring streets and rubbish dumps looking for new "relics" or whether he had some other purpose altogether. She didn't question him. She didn't quite know how to heal the breach between them. Worse, she still wasn't sure whether or not she could trust him.

They retraced their steps for some time until, finally, they came through a sprawling settlement and up to an old walled hill fort that Master Thomas told her was called Sorviodunum in ancient times, although the Normans referred to it as Sarisberie or Sarum.

They crossed the drawbridge over a deep moat and there had to wait while Master Thomas spoke to the gatekeeper. After some persuasion and what looked like a coin exchanging hands, they were at last given access to the outer bailey.

Janna's gaze was immediately drawn to the gleaming chalk ramparts that dominated the inner bailey at the center of the large hill fort.

They were topped by a timber palisade, and surrounded by a deep and seemingly impregnable ditch. The white chalk was so dazzlingly bright in the sunlight that she had to squint her eyes against the glare. A wooden drawbridge over the ditch gave access to the gatehouse, a strong and imposing building that towered above their heads. The jongleurs wasted no time looking around the small settlement that spread out to one side of the outer bailey, instead forging ahead to the gatehouse.

"We'll try our luck on the way out," Faldo explained as they walked past the houses and the shops of craftsmen and traders, all those who were useful to the castle and who might have been expected to welcome the prospect of entertainment from the jongleurs.

Janna was wide-eyed with excitement, for she'd never been near a royal castle before. She waited impatiently while Master Thomas crossed the drawbridge to seek permission to enter from the constable of the castle. She was fearful they'd be denied entry, but Faldo laughed at her misgivings. "We have been here before, mistress, and have always been welcome in the past," he explained. "It's not often the castle's inhabitants get the chance to watch such marvelous entertainment as we provide!"

To Janna's relief, his words proved true. The first thing she saw, as they passed through the gate into the inner bailey, was the full extent of the castle keep. It rose before her, a huge tower with bright, whitewashed stone walls. Faldo explained to her that this was where everyone would take shelter if the castle came under siege and, by chance, the enemy managed to storm the outer defenses.

"But surely that's impossible!" Janna exclaimed, thinking of all the ditches and ramparts and gates and walls that would have to be breached.

Beside her, Ralph chuckled. "There are other ways to bring about surrender than siege engines and armed combat," he said. "Time. Thirst. Starvation," he added as he noticed Janna's puzzled expression.

Janna looked up at the windows of the keep. They were long, vertical slits, wide enough for archers to take aim at enemies outside but too narrow for enemy fire to penetrate. The keep was topped by flat ramparts, where a flag hung limp in the hot and airless afternoon. Soldiers might go up there, she thought, and fire arrows at their enemies, or cast stones or pour boiling oil down upon them, for she had heard the jongleurs discussing some of the battles they'd witnessed on their travels, as the king fought his cousin and the barons fought each other for possession of castles and land. This castle was well set up for warfare – but not, perhaps, for food. Nor water either, she thought, for there was no sign of a stream or any running water up here.

The royal palace abutted the keep. It wasn't quite so high, but was built of the same stone, painted a dazzling white, and topped with red-tiled roofs. There was a covered well outside where women stood and chattered as they drew their buckets up and down. All conversation stopped at the jongleurs' approach. They were subjected to scrutiny as they walked on past, threading their way through the clutter and clamor of the courtyard. It was crowded with merchants and traders, horses and carts, soldiers mounted and on foot, visitors and castle servants, all busy about their own purpose.

Janna gazed around, drinking in every detail as they were shown up to the great hall in the palace where the jongleurs had been instructed to perform. She had thought the manor house at Babestoche very grand, and the abbess's quarters at Wiltune the very height of luxury, but she'd never seen anything like this before. Awestruck, she stood and stared. The walls were painted with various scenes. One depicted a hunt, with men on horseback in pursuit of a deer. The artist had captured perfectly the eager expression of the hunters as well as the terror of the deer as it fled for its life. Janna felt uncomfortable as memories stirred. She knew how it felt to run for your life. She hoped that, on this occasion at least, the deer had outpaced its pursuers.

She drew in a breath as she came to another painted wall. Flowers, trees, birds and butterflies formed a colorful backdrop to a courting couple. Although only their hands touched, their ardent yearning for each other was evident in their expressions and in every line of their bodies. Janna imagined herself and Ralph standing just so, and knew how they felt. She, too, longed for Ralph's touch, the warmth of his regard, a word of love. Without meaning to, she looked around to find him. But he seemed to have disappeared on some errand of his own. She realized then that the jongleurs had also withdrawn to make preperations for the coming entertainment.

Servants rushed about, setting up trestle tables and benches for the meal to come. The hall was soon overflowing with people, from the castellan and his family and other notables who sat at the high table to the lowliest of the king's subjects, who sat some distance away. There was a loud buzz of conversation, everyone shouting above his or her neighbor to be heard over the general din. After the quietness of their meals at the abbey, the noise seemed deafening to Janna.

She stood to one side, feeling awkward and useless as Master Thomas recited *lais* from *The Song of Roland*, after which the rest of the group played their musical instruments, juggled, sang and generally played the fool. She wondered if there'd be any dancing and, if there was, whether she would be allowed to take part. But the castle occupants ate their dinner, laughed and talked, and for the most part paid little heed to the entertainment provided by the jongleurs.

Later, in the kitchen where they were given something to eat, Faldo explained that they were used to being ignored. "But it matters little to us what they pay in attention so long as they pay us good silver." He gave a sudden snigger. "Barons are always a'frighted we'll spread stories of how stingy they are. It's enough to open their purses wide. They feed us well too, and for the same reason."

"Mmm," Janna agreed through a mouthful of leftover goose. She smacked her lips and turned her attention to a dish of frumenty.

Her mother had taught her how to make it, but this looked somewhat different, she thought, as she spooned some into her mouth. It tasted different too, for eggs and almond milk had been added to the wheat, as well as saffron to turn it a rich, yellow color. Janna drained her bowl, and took another helping, before finishing her meal with a portion of cream custard pie. Her stomach strained tight against her gown at the end of it, and she sat back with a sigh, well contented. Beside her, Faldo gave a loud burp, grinned, and heaped some more slices of beef onto his trencher. He shoveled it down hungrily, for he was of an age where he was growing rapidly. Meals like this seldom came his way and he was clearly making the most of it.

Keen to know more of how the nobility lived, Janna struck up a conversation with one of the serving wenches as she helped clear the tables in the Great Hall. Her name was Goda, she told Janna, and she proved to be a fount of information once Janna started asking questions.

"The king's chamber is through there at the back," she said, pointing to show Janna where she meant. "And his privy chambers are on the other side of the courtyard. It's like three sides of a square, see. But of course there's no king now, and no bishop either," she added thoughtfully.

"Will the empress be welcome here, if she comes?" Janna asked, hoping that the empress would visit the castle while the jongleurs were still there.

Goda gave a fleeting grin. "Yes, I think she would be welcome after what's happened."

"What's happened?" Janna asked, eager to hear more.

"This castle was once occupied by Bishop Roger. He was the old king's justiciar and he rebuilt and refurbished the castle. After Stephen became king, he captured our bishop and imprisoned him in an old cowshed. It was a great scandal! The king also captured the bishop's son, who was the chancellor, and two of his nephews, but one of them managed to get away. They were bishops too, and one of them was also the old king's treasurer. In one ill-judged swoop, the king got rid of his wisest and most experienced advisers."

"How do you know all this?" Janna asked, impressed and intrigued.

Goda shrugged. "People talk, and I listen. I'm just a serving wench, so no-one pays me any mind." A smile crossed her face, with just a hint of calculation in it. Janna wondered if Goda sometimes profited from the information she was able to pass on, or perhaps was convinced to withhold. She looked at her with wary respect.

It seemed Goda was quite willing to share her knowledge now, for she continued to tell Janna all she knew. "Bishop Roger died soon after his arrest, and the king would not appoint anyone in his place. He took possession of this castle and all the property and wealth belonging to the bishop and his family, and glad he was to get his hands on it, so 'tis said, for he'd emptied his own coffers buying the loyalty of the barons. The king is much hated and feared because of what he did. Indeed, some say that what happened at the Battle of Lincoln was God's punishment for this crime."

Goda lowered her voice, and Janna leaned closer to hear her. "The lord William, brother of Patrick, Earl of Sarisberie, is both governor and castellan here and 'tis said he favors the empress's cause. So yes, I think she would be very welcome here." Goda took Janna's arm and pointed across the courtyard. "That would be the lady's chamber, if she came to visit us. There's a private chapel there too, the chapel of St Nicholas. And there's always a candle of wax burning there, day and night, whether the castellan is in residence or no!" It was clear from Goda's tone that she considered this a huge extravagance.

"There's a chapel below, too, for the soldiers and the castle servants. We sleep here in the hall and the soldiers sleep in the Great Tower next to the palace," Goda continued. "Back there is a kitchen and garderobes." She held her rough, chapped hands in front of Janna for inspection. "I work hard and long," she said, "and see, my hands bear the marks of it." She wrinkled her nose. "But at least I don't have to clear out the cesspits below. We have gong-fermors for that."

Janna had never heard of gong-fermors, but she understood well enough what Goda meant, and shared the servant's pity for those unfortunates whose lot it was to clean the waste from the cesspits. She knew that the task wouldn't end there, for the waste would then have to be carted out to the fields and spread about to enrich the soil for the crops to come. It had been Janna's least favorite task when she lived with her mother, but she'd done it because their livelihood depended on what they could grow for food and medicaments. Imagining the size of the castle and the number of its occupants, Janna's pity increased. A dreadful task indeed.

Goda was also a great source of gossip about the castle's occupants, Janna discovered, as she spent more time with her and gradually won the girl's confidence. It seemed there was a prison in the castle keep where several wretches were held captive, either awaiting punishment or serving time. It was only when Goda began to name them that Janna remembered, with a jolt of alarm, that this was where Mus had been sent after he'd attacked her. Dame Alice had insisted that he be kept imprisoned, although her husband might well have secured the wretch's release by now.

"Do you know of a man called Mus? Or Alan? That's his real name," she interrupted anxiously.

"Mus?" A slight smile tugged the corner of the girl's mouth. "He tried to sweet talk me once when I took a message to his jailer. Not that it did him any good, fettered as he was. But no, mistress. His lord purchased his freedom some moons ago, and took him back to his manor under warrant for his good behavior in the future."

A shiver of fright ran through Janna. Mus was free! But after what had happened, surely the abbess would not tell either Robert or Mus where she had gone, nor would anyone from the abbey know anything of her present whereabouts. The thought was reassuring; nevertheless, she resolved to keep an eye open for the villain, for she knew well that he wished her dead and would pursue her if he could, as would the lord Robert.

The girl had named someone else, but it had passed her by in the horror of the news about Mus. "Did you say someone called Adam is imprisoned here?" she asked now.

"Indeed, mistress. The sergeant brought him in only yesterday. He is accused of murdering a pilgrim, and of theft, and of breaking his pledge to visit the shrine of Compostela and return to his home. The pilgrim's mother has been sent for, from Oxeneford, to hear his answer to the charge. But he is already saying he's guilty of nothing but breaking his pledge."

Adam would say that, of course, Janna thought. Nevertheless, and in spite of the coolness between them, she wasted no time in passing on the news to Ulf.

The relic seller's face became unusually serious as he listened. "I'll ask if I may see him," he said.

"Goda told me that Dame Juliana has been sent for, to hear Adam answer the charge against him."

"Do you think Adam speaks the truth when he says that he is innocent of Bernard's murder?"

"If not Adam, then who?" Janna was interested to hear Ulf's thoughts on the matter.

"I suppose it could have been someone unknown to us? Someone who saw that Bernard was the leader of our band, and would expect him to be carrying a pile of coins to pay for our passage. Bernard's scrip went missing, after all. Easy enough to disguise coins as your own; not so easy to disguise someone else's pack and walking staff. Nor is it necessary to take 'em, if you already have your own. So it could be that Adam tells the truth. I have to see him, Janna. I want to hear what he has to say for himself."

"I want to come with you."

"Nay, lass!"

Janna was about to argue, but Ulf spoke over her. "I promise I will report everything that Adam says to me, if that's what's on your mind. But don't you come. Indeed, I doubt you'd be given permission, for a prison is no place for a woman."

*

"It's as you were told," Ulf reported, some time later. "Adam denies the charge most vehemently. He also denies all knowledge of any letter. His scrip and pack have been stolen, he says, so we have no way of telling whether or no he speaks the truth. He claims that at first he had no intention of breaking his pledge, for the priest had given his word that he would receive absolution on his return from Compostela. Which in itself is an admission of guilt, even if Adam doesn't realize it. But he said that, when he woke in the night at Stonehenge and saw that Bernard was gone, the temptation to escape was too great to ignore, and so he made a run for it. He also says he regrets it now; that it was a stupid thing to do, for he encountered nowt but trouble on the road. He was severely beaten and robbed by bandits, and suffered great hunger and thirst and discomfort all the while. Not that his dungeon is an improvement!" Ulf shuddered at the memory. "It stinks, but that's hardly surprising. The straw is filthy with human waste, and there are all manner of creatures down there, including rats and blood-sucking insects."

Janna felt her skin crawl. "Do you believe Adam?"

Ulf nodded slowly. "In this, aye, I do. But indirectly he's admitted that he was responsible for Golde's father's death, so he is guilty of one murder at least. After I'd spoken to him, I questioned the guard about his belongings and about the letter, but the guard claims he knows nowt about any of it. There's nothing more we can do, I'm afraid."

Was Ulf telling her the truth about the letter? Janna resolved to keep close watch on the relic seller, just in case he'd managed to get hold of it. But if he believed in Adam's innocence regarding Bernard's murder, that surely indicated that he, too, must be innocent otherwise he wouldn't have hesitated to implicate the villain.

So who was responsible for Bernard's death? Had he been murdered for his belongings, as everyone supposed? Or was the letter at the heart of everything that had happened? Janna hoped that the truth would come out once the shire reeve questioned Adam in Juliana's presence. But even if he wasn't responsible for Bernard's death, she knew Adam would be held until such time as someone else was apprehended. And that was unlikely to happen, not while a suspect was already under guard.

Chapter 10

In her free time – when not keeping costumes and props in good repair, or helping with other chores – Janna went exploring. The jongleurs were housed in the outer bailey. They shared a shed with their horse and cart, along with the cage of white doves and other props used in their performances. Also in the outer bailey were the barns, sheds, workrooms and dwellings of the craftsmen, artisans and others who served both the castle and the cathedral. The huge stone cathedral stood on the far side of the outer bailey, its high tower dwarfing even the castle keep. The bishop's palace was set close by, along with the houses of the clergy. Janna soon became known to the gatekeeper and passed freely between the outer and inner baileys. She enjoyed her solitary rambles and her glimpses into lives entirely different from anything she'd ever known.

One afternoon, the jongleurs were invited to the steps of the cathedral to entertain the resident canons and other clerics after their dinner. Janna was amused to notice that there were some changes to the repertoire. Master Thomas recited some lais from *The Song of Roland*, which were well received. The death of Roland was particularly poignant, to such a degree that several clerics were seen to surreptitiously wipe tears from their eyes afterward. On this occasion, there were no songs of cuckoos and summer or of love lost and found. Instead, Faldo's high, clear voice rang out in a chant that Janna hadn't heard before. The tune was familiar but the last time she'd heard it, the song had told of a faithless mistress and a vengeful lover. She couldn't understand what Faldo sang now, but his quiet reverence and formal stance told her that the song had been adapted for its new audience.

"*Stella maris, semper clara,*
Rosa munde, res miranda,
Misterium mirabile."

Unlike the castle audience, a solemn silence prevailed during their performance, although one of the clerics kept humming under his breath, providing a somewhat tuneless accompaniment to the jongleurs.

The cathedral was almost as sumptuous as the castle, Janna thought, as she walked into the nave after the performance was over. Huge stone pillars were set at intervals down the aisles, soaring up to a shining ceiling high above her head. The walls were decorated with red porphyry and green marble while the floor was fashioned of alternate slabs of white and green stone. Gold and silver chalices, candlesticks and other precious objects adorned the altar, gleaming in the light that streamed through the delicate stone tracery of the numerous windows. She bowed her head and made a reverence, feeling nostalgic as she recalled the abbey at Wiltune and the sisters who had both befriended her and shared their knowledge so freely.

A sudden barking cough broke the silence and she looked about for its source. It was Ulf, with streaming nose and bleary eyes that spoke of his discomfort. Horehound and licorice, Janna thought, automatically naming the herbs most useful for such a malady. But she had no herbs, nor the means to make up any remedy. It irked her to feel so useless. Nevertheless, she spoke to Goda when they returned to the castle precinct, and a farthing changed hands. If she couldn't make up a nostrum herself, she could at least make use of the healer at the castle.

When the potion was placed in her hands, she took a cautious sniff and then a small sip, for she was interested to find out what was in it. She pulled a face, surprised how bitter it tasted. It was not made up to a recipe she would have used, but she thought it would serve well enough. She went off to find Ulf, pleased that she'd found something to give him by way of a peace offering. She'd watched him carefully since she'd told him to go his own way and leave her alone, noting that while his attitude toward her was more stiffly polite, his courtesy and care of her remained unchanged. It made her feel uncomfortable about her continuing suspicion. She hoped that the gift might help to soothe her uneasy conscience.

"For you," she said, and pressed the leather flask into his hands.

"Me?" His eyebrows lifted in surprise.

"For the rheum that troubles you. And the cough. Take a sip now and another before you sleep tonight."

"That's kind of you, lass. Very kind." Ulf took a hearty swallow, and pulled a wry face. Janna grimaced in sympathy. No licorice and not enough honey.

"It would have tasted better if I'd made it," she told him.

"You know summat about such things?" Ulf looked at her with sharpened interest.

Janna nodded. "My mother trained me, but I also used to help the infirmarian at Wiltune Abbey," she said. "And I find now that I miss not being able to use my knowledge."

"It is a gift indeed," Ulf agreed, "and one that will stand you in good stead, whatever life and fortune may have in store for you."

*

Having finally exhausted all opportunities at Sarisberie, the jongleurs set off on the old Roman road that led to Winchestre. Janna's spirits rose – she was at last coming close to achieving her quest.

True to his word, Ulf's relics sometimes opened doors that otherwise would have remained closed to them. Several of their hosts made generous donations in return for the various precious objects he pulled out of his bag. Janna wondered what he'd do once his supplies ran out. Recalling his frequent absences at night, she realized that the possibility was unlikely.

She enjoyed the long days of walking, for they gave her time to talk to Ralph, time for them to forge an ever closer bond. Their time together was mostly spent under Ulf's watchful eye or with Faldo, who was always a lively companion. But on one occasion Ralph had followed her out into the dark, and had put his arms around her and kissed her until she felt as if her bones had melted, so weak was she with wanting. He had pulled her down with him, so that they lay together. His hand had stroked her breast, while she shivered with delight. But then his hand had crept downward, and under her skirt, and had then commenced a cautious exploration upward. Coming to her senses with a jolt, Janna had jerked away and jumped to her feet, wrapping the folds of her skirt close around her. Ralph had stayed where he was, his expression too hard to read in the dark. But his voice was languid as he whispered: "Come to me, my pretty, for I am hard with wanting you. In truth, I cannot resist you a moment longer."

Torn between desire and the shrill alarum sounding in her mind, Janna had hesitated for a few long moments. It was only the memory of Cecily's downfall, and her mother's fate, that cooled her ardor and gave her the strength to walk away. She had immediately sought the company of the pilgrims, knowing that if she delayed any longer she would weaken, for she longed to explore further the delights that men and women shared within the marriage bed.

Ralph had approached her the next day, shame-faced and full of apologies, and with the promise that he would not let his feelings run away with him again. And she had accepted his word, and they had continued as before. Janna was content to let love bloom slowly, determining that she would be wed before she allowed Ralph, or any other man, to take liberties with her body. But with that thought came the memory of Godric. And Cecily. And the pain was as acute as if she was witnessing their happiness together all over again.

She reminded herself that it was the future that mattered now: a future that held the possibility of finding her father as well as making her life with Ralph. To that end, she set herself to find out more about him and his family. And while she kept her own counsel regarding her support of the empress, she couldn't resist questioning him about the doings of the royal court and the wealthy noblemen who were part of it, for he seemed remarkably well informed, while his astute observations and pithy comments brought to life a world completely unknown to her.

"How do you know so much about all these people?" she asked him one day.

He laughed. "In Winchestre, everyone knows everything – and what they don't know, they invent! I found things were no different at Sarisberie."

"So what you're telling me isn't necessarily the truth?"

Ralph looked a little taken aback. "I thought you liked hearing about the courtiers, whether the stories are true or not?" He grinned at her. "For instance, I hear the empress has not given up her fight for the crown. It seems her chief supporter, the Earl of Gloucestre, has come from Oxeneford to Winchestre to see the bishop."

"Does the Earl of Gloucestre hope to get the bishop back on side with the empress?"

"Why do you ask that?" Ralph looked suddenly serious.

Janna cautioned herself to be careful lest she reveal where her loyalty lay. "Don't you remember what that young boy told us at the henge?"

"Of course. But he was talking of a mere difference of opinion, no more than that. The bishop has pledged his loyalty to the empress, remember."

"So why should the earl need to visit him then?"

Ralph gave a small chuckle of amusement. "The empress alienated many of her subjects when she came to London. She made promises which she has broken. Worse, she imposed a large tax on the Londoners, and would not hear their pleas when they told her they were unable to pay. And she has dealt harshly with some of her supporters, who might well have expected more preferential treatment from her. I suspect the Earl of Gloucestre is worried that she has lost some of her key supporters. Certes, she's in a less favorable position now than she was before ever she came to London."

Janna tried to conceal her alarm at his words. "And where does the bishop stand in all this?"

"He knows the Londoners, and can advise the earl."

"So Robert of Gloucestre comes to discuss with him how to ensure that the empress will secure the throne?" Janna asked carefully.

"Yes." Ralph gave a wolfish grin. "I expect that's exactly why he has come." There was a dangerous glint in his eyes that Janna found exciting. Yet Ralph's words had disturbed her too, for she sensed in them some unnamed threat toward the empress.

"So," Ralph continued, "what do you think the outcome of their talks will be?"

"It's not safe to have an opinion, remember? You taught me that!"

"In truth, it's good advice." He nodded gently. "If you won't give me your opinion on affairs of state, tell me some more about yourself instead." He tucked Janna's arm through his and they walked on.

They stopped for a rest several miles beyond a small hamlet. Ralph's palfrey had thrown a shoe and, after some conversation with Master Thomas, he decided to walk it back to the hamlet where there was known to be a blacksmith, rather than taking his chances further on. The jongleur assured Ralph that they would await his return before moving on. Faldo unhitched the cart horse to roam free in search of fodder, while the jongleurs untied the sack of food they'd cadged from their hosts of the night before, and sat down to make a hearty dinner.

As they all drowsed in the heat of the day, Janna dreamily recalled what she'd learned about Ralph. He'd told her that his father was dead, but that his mother lived in a hamlet north of Winchestre, along with his two sisters. Both of them were wed, and he was uncle to a little boy and two little girls. There had been great love in his voice as he spoke of his family, as he described to her the games he played with his nieces and nephew. It thrilled Janna to think that he could show so much care for his own. And he'd shown his care for her too, she thought, remembering how he'd tried to shield her from the sight of Bernard's body. How close he had held her, how protective he'd been. The memory of how he'd kissed her in the night, and the strength with which he'd held her, sent a ripple of wanting through her body, combined with a spiraling hope that indeed their relationship might grow into a love that would last through time.

A prickle of unease touched Janna momentarily as she recalled that Ralph had not said exactly what it was that he did for a living, if living he needed to find. Nor had he said anything more of his reason for visiting Oxeneford, the property he thought might be at risk and that perhaps was the basis of his livelihood.

Not that he'd said very much about himself at all. Indeed he always seemed far more interested in finding out everything about her. Janna had described their cottage close to the forest and how she'd learned from her mother about herbs and healing. She hadn't told him all the circumstances of her mother's death, instead making him laugh with her tales of life at Wiltune Abbey: the irreverence of her friend, Agnes, and the pet-keeping habits of the nuns that had led to so much upset and trouble. There seemed no end to Ralph's curiosity, and she reveled in it. They were becoming closer every day, with many stolen kisses to seal their relationship even though these were often interrupted by either Ulf or Faldo.

She lay back on the grass, her mind full of Ralph and of the future. She'd never met anyone like him before. The twinkle in his eyes promised secrets, if only she could find the key to them. She longed to hear him speak of what was in his heart and make his pledge to her, yet she feared his wrath once he found out what she had concealed from him. It hung heavy on her conscience that she'd never told him about the bishop's letter, even though it was now lost. But she couldn't forget her promise to Bernard to keep it secret.

If there was love, surely there should also be trust? Should she trust Ralph with the truth? But she was sure he did not share her sympathy with the empress's cause, and didn't want to risk causing a rift between them, at least not until the empress was safely on the throne and it no longer mattered whose side he was on. The fact that Bernard had recognized the bishop's seal on the letter strengthened her resolve. There could be no possible connection between the dead man and Ralph's cousin, whom he now never mentioned at all. It occurred to Janna that, in fact, she need never tell him about the message they'd found, for it no longer mattered what the bishop had written to the empress. The Earl of Gloucestre had come to Winchestre, and so the bishop could tell him in person whatever it was that he'd wanted the empress to know.

Sunlight slanted through the trees, touching the treetops with gold and encompassing grass, flowers and the reclining bodies of the jongleurs in its warm glow. Bernard's staff lay close beside her, illuminated in its own pool of light. Janna picked it up, feeling a pang of regret for the untimely death of the kind pilgrim. Was an unknown thief responsible for his death? The idea did not sit easy in Janna's mind. A stranger would have knocked Bernard unconscious and made his escape with the spoils. There was no need to kill him – unless he was known, unless Bernard could identify him.

All the evidence pointed to Adam, who was already paying penance for one murder. Why shouldn't he kill again in order to escape? It also made sense that Adam would take the trouble to stage an elaborate sacrifice in order to disguise his motivation. Yet Ulf believed in Adam's innocence, for this death at least. Was that because Ulf himself knew differently?

Janna gazed thoughtfully at Bernard's staff, wishing it could tell her what she wanted to know. She turned it around in her hands, and saw a fine line just under the handle. The crack ran right around the wooden shaft. She hadn't noticed it before, it was only because the sunlight illuminated the length of the staff save for that small, telltale shadow.

She examined it more closely, hoping that the crack wasn't as bad as she feared, and that the staff would be strong enough to support her until she reached Winchestre. She gripped the handle with one hand and gave the shaft a twist, testing its strength. To her surprise, the handle turned slightly. She gave another tentative twist and it turned further. Suddenly apprehensive, she glanced around. The jongleurs were either dozing or chatting among themselves. No-one seemed to be paying her any attention. Nevertheless, she turned her back on the group and continued to unscrew the handle of Bernard's staff.

It was hollow inside. Janna's heart bumped erratically as she noticed the small packet of parchment carefully concealed within the handle. Knowing already what she would find, she carefully drew it out and studied the bishop's seal. So this was how Bernard had managed to secrete the parchment from the eyes of the abbey guard

– and from anyone else who might have an interest in the letter. Was this why he was killed? Janna gave a shudder of unease, knowing that any supporter of Stephen's might think it worth taking a life to intercept a message from the bishop to the queen-in-waiting.

Ralph supported the king!

She tried to banish the thought but it lay uneasy in her mind. Ralph was no killer, she told herself, but what about Ulf? Was his guise as a relic seller designed to cover a deeper and darker purpose? She turned the letter over in her hands, and studied the seal. The Earl of Gloucestre was now with the bishop. Ralph had said so. This letter, therefore, was no longer important.

Succumbing to curiosity, she slit the seal to read its contents.

To my lord liege and brother, greetings. I bid you be of good cheer, for a blow has been struck from which the empress cannot recover. While she was preparing for her coronation, and on my advice, your queen brought her army from Kent to the south bank of the Thames. Under the command of William of Ypres, they caused great havoc and destruction along the way. By that action, your queen has warned the Londoners of what will befall them should they lend their support to the empress, for they know now that the empress is powerless to stop the queen's army.

On the eve of Matilda's coronation, the bells of London were rung as a call to arms. The Londoners rose in revolt and stormed the palace of Westminster. Matilda was forced to flee back to Oxeneford, along with those who still support her claim. Knowing our cousin, I doubt this setback will stop her misguided attempt to claim your crown. However, she continues to make herself extremely unpopular with everyone, the Londoners in particular. They resent her high-handed attitude and, even more, the large tax she has imposed on them which, I suspect, was punishment for their previous support of you.

Have courage. Your queen's troops remain armed and ready. We shall continue to oppose and thwart the empress's ambition at every turn. God willing, she will soon fall into our hands and we shall then have the means to set you free.

Your brother in name and in Christ,

Henry, Bishop of Winchestre.

Janna read the letter swiftly. She feared she'd misread it, for it didn't make sense. She read it again. This time she read slowly and with care, for it was written in Norman French and she needed to think about some of the words. But the letter still didn't say what she thought it should. She read it through once more, thinking beyond the words to their meaning. And, at last, she came to comprehend the full extent of the bishop's treachery, and the grave importance of what she'd found.

Her hands trembled as she swiftly folded the parchment and returned it to its hiding place. After a quick glance around to make sure that no-one was watching, she twisted the handle into the shaft of the walking stick to conceal the evidence. Her senses were reeling with the enormity of her discovery. She closed her eyes, the better to think through the implications.

Had Bernard died for this? Or had Adam killed him to make his getaway, not knowing what the pilgrim had concealed in his staff? And what of Bishop Henry, now entertaining the empress's envoy with lying smiles and flattery, and treachery in his heart? Did he know his letter had never reached his brother, the king? Had he taken steps to retrieve it, knowing his treachery would be revealed if it fell into the wrong hands?

Janna gave an involuntary shudder. No-one knew of this letter other than herself, Bernard and Ulf. Bernard was dead. That left Ulf. What did she really know about the relic seller? He'd been with the pilgrim band for a long time, even if not from the start.

He'd won Juliana's trust enough to accompany her to Ambresberie and to persuade her to confide in him. But had Ulf known about the message before that?

Janna was fairly sure that Bernard supported the empress, and that he'd taken the letter in good faith that it was meant for her eyes. If he'd confided in Ulf his real reason for leaving the pilgrim band, then it could be that Ulf was responsible for his murder. She remembered that she'd once questioned him about where his loyalty lay: with the empress or the king, and that he wouldn't answer her. Could he have killed Bernard to get the message and prevent him from taking it to the empress? And was he now traveling with the jongleurs because he believed Janna had it in her possession?

What frightened Janna most was the thought that, if Ulf had killed once to get at the letter, he would not hesitate to kill again. She took a shuddering breath, and struggled for calm. The more urgent question was: What should she do now? The empress must see this letter without delay. Her half-brother, Robert of Gloucestre, might have walked into the bishop's trap already. Who could she turn to for help with this? Ralph? He had his own steed. He could travel far more quickly than she could. Could she trust him with the truth, knowing that he almost certainly supported the king rather than the empress?

Janna buried her face in her hands in an agony of indecision. With all her heart she wanted to confide in Ralph, and pass the responsibility for action on to him.

Ralph! Janna froze as she recalled how he had come to the farmhouse on a stormy night, and had then stayed on and made the pilgrims' journey his own. Why? She'd flattered herself that his interest was in her – but had his purpose been to locate the bishop's message all along?

She felt ashamed of her doubts when she remembered his kindness, but found she could not dismiss them, for they were marching through her mind in battalions now, and trampling all over her dreams.

Where had Ralph come from that he should find them in such an out-of-the-way place – unless he'd seen the dead messenger at Wiltune, and recognized the peril if the message was found? It seemed clear that he supported the king's cause, as did the bishop. Could he even be the bishop's spy, paid by Henry to track them down and retrieve the message?

Janna remembered his questions about the contents of her purse – and the hand beneath her skirt that might have been probing for something other than her maidenhood! Sickened, she sprang to her feet and began to pace, but she could not outrun her thoughts. Ralph's missing cousin. Did he really exist – or was this just an excuse to find out what the pilgrims knew of the contents of the dead man's scrip?

Janna's mind was in turmoil as she tried to reason her way through to an answer. The thought that Ralph might have been lying to her all along was appalling – but she could not discount it, nor the fact that she might be mistaken, for there were others who may have been responsible for Bernard's murder.

One thing was clear so far as Ralph was concerned. She must not let him suspect what she knew: not if she wanted his help with finding her father. And so she would keep her suspicions to herself until she had proof either way – and at the same time pray that she was wrong.

But a greater problem now was what to do with this knowledge that had come, so unexpectedly, into her keeping. Janna trembled as the question repeated itself endlessly in her mind. She knew she had to do something – and quickly. The empress was in danger, and so was her envoy. They must be warned of the bishop's treachery and betrayal. The Earl of Gloucestre had come to negotiate with the bishop in good faith. He was already in Winchestre, where the jongleurs were bound. Should she continue to travel with them and give him the letter on their arrival, which might take days, or should she flee to Oxeneford to warn the empress? Surely the latter, for speed was of the essence. But she had only her two feet to walk upon – unless she could beg or steal a mount from somewhere?

Impatient for action, but unsure how to act for the best outcome, Janna continued to pace as other considerations came into her mind. True, the empress was in Oxeneford, but she would be surrounded and protected by her supporters there. The earl was nearer at hand; he was also alone and unsuspecting in the enemy's camp. As the empress's chief supporter, the leader of her army, he was the one most at risk. So she should take the letter to him and she should leave at once, for further delay would put his life in ever greater danger.

But first, she would have to make her farewells to Master Thomas and to Ulf. Before that, she needed to come up with a good reason for leaving their company so abruptly, both to explain her haste to get to Winchestre but, more important, to allay any suspicions they – and most particularly Ralph – might have about her going. But she couldn't think of a single thing, nothing that sounded in the least convincing.

She wondered what Ralph would do when he found her gone. Would he continue his journey to Winchestre with the pilgrims, would he fulfill his promise to help her find her father once the party arrived? Was she jeopardizing Ralph's goodwill by going on without him? Janna went cold at the thought. If only she could forget her suspicions, and trust him.

"*Trust no-one.*" Bernard's words came back to her. It was good advice, Janna thought, remembering that her mother, too, had trusted no-one: not her daughter with the truth, nor even the man whom she'd loved for all her life. Janna had thought her wrong, and had blamed Eadgyth for the hard life they'd lived because of her pride and lack of trust. But perhaps her mother had taught her the most valuable lesson of all, a lesson to live by: Trust no-one.

Chapter 11

Janna picked up the staff, realizing that it was important to treat it as just that – a staff, something of no importance. She used it to support her weight as she approached Master Thomas. He was declaiming the description of the Battle of Roncevaux to Faldo. The boy listened intently, getting the sense of it even though he would never learn it all by heart, for the *chanson* was far too long. But he obviously relished the challenge as he wielded the props that were transported in the cart, mimicking his father's gestures while Master Thomas declared at full voice:

"Distraught was Roland with wrath and pain;
Distraught were the twelve of Charlemagne,
With deadly strokes the Franks have striven,
And the Saracen horde to the slaughter given..."

Faldo puffed and sweated as he swung his trusty sword Durendal against imaginary Saracen hordes, and finally blew a mighty blast on his horn, Olifant, to summon, too late, the Emperor Charlemagne to come to his aid.

Unfortunately Brutus seemed intent on ruining the dramatic effect by barking and snarling and trying to snap at Master Thomas's feet, which – every now and then – aimed a kick in the dog's direction.

"For the Lord Christ's sake, Ulf, get your dog out of the way," Master Thomas shouted at last, exasperated beyond bearing.

Muttering apologies, Ulf produced a length of twine and looped it around the animal's neck. It became an act of strength, Ulf against Brutus, as he tried to drag the huge dog away. Janna's attention was divided between their tug of war and Master Thomas, who began now to declaim the stanzas dealing with the death of Roland.

Janna dawdled beside them, still trying to find an excuse for leaving the jongleurs in such haste. "I'm not feeling well. I need to see a *wortwyf*. Or a doctor." Who would believe her? No-one.

"I've had word that my father is about to leave Winchestre, and I must see him before he goes." But who could have brought word to her without everyone seeing it?

She looked about, praying for inspiration. A movement caught her eye and she started in surprise. A man was watching them from along the track. How long had he been there? Could he have seen her unscrewing the staff and extracting the parchment? No! She tried to quieten her racing heart. She'd been sitting with her back to the pilgrims, but how much would he have seen? Her gaze moved to the spot, trying to gauge angles and direction. If he was innocent, then she would also seem innocent, no matter what he'd observed.

He was riding toward them now; fearful, she waited to find out his purpose in accosting them.

"God be with you," he greeted Master Thomas, and dismounted. "I am Walter of Eglesham." A chorus of greetings came his way as the other jongleurs realized they had company and roused themselves. Janna stayed silent, watching him. She wondered if she'd seen him before. There was something familiar about him, although she couldn't quite name what it was. His face? Clothes and build? His hair was dark and worn quite long. A yellow cloak was tucked carelessly into the pack on his saddle; part of it was hanging out on view. As Master Thomas made the introductions, Walter looked around the company. It seemed to Janna that his gaze fixed on her and on the staff she carried.

"Ulf?" Walter's eyes flickered as he registered the presence of the relic seller, who had stopped wrestling with his dog and was now watching him with cautious, calculating eyes.

"And this is Johanna," Master Thomas continued with his introductions. Janna gripped the staff, then made a conscious effort to relax her fingers.

With the introductions over, Walter spoke. "This is a happy chance, meeting you here, Johanna." His glance rested on Janna and lingered there. Coloring under his scrutiny, she turned her head and looked away.

"Do you travel to Winchestre?" Walter asked. Janna wasn't sure if the question was directed at her, but Master Thomas answered in her stead.

"Aye, but our journey is interrupted. We're waiting for one of our party whose horse cast a shoe. He has taken it back to the hamlet we've just passed."

"That gives me time to talk to the daughter of an old friend," Walter said, and moved to Janna's side. At once she stepped away, but was stopped by a firm hand on her arm. "A word with you, mistress," he said softly.

Fighting panic, Janna stayed still. Despite her good intentions, she began to tremble. She took a couple of long breaths to calm herself.

"You have no reason to fear me," Walter said, and drew her away so that no-one could overhear their conversation. "Am I right in thinking you traveled with a group of pilgrims from Wiltune to Ambresberie?"

Janna gave a reluctant nod. The man's familiarity bothered her. Where had she met him before? She summoned up all her courage and looked into his eyes, trying to settle the mystery. She read there a deep and weary sadness. Instinctively she began to relax her guard.

"You knew my mother, Juliana, and my brother, Bernard, I believe?"

Janna stifled a gasp, understanding now why Walter seemed familiar. He was shorter, stouter than his brother, but he had something of the same visage as well as Bernard's air of quiet competence.

"You carry my brother's staff," Walter continued. "My mother gave it to you, I know, thinking you had a good use for it. But I've come to ask you, mistress, if you'd mind returning it to me, for she's had a change of heart. She has nothing to remember my brother by, and she craves some memento."

As Walter spoke, Janna's hand tightened on the staff. Frightened, she stared at him. If he'd come just a little earlier, she would have given it to him, and willingly. But she knew now that he hadn't chased all these miles after her just to reclaim a memento. This was no casual request. Walter knew the importance of the message secreted there, even if Bernard had not.

Trust no-one. Not even Walter? Bernard had told her that he was in the employ of the empress. But so was the bishop, or so everyone had thought. No matter that Ralph had told her that the empress had no right to rule, Janna still had no doubt in her mind as to whom she was supporting in this fight for the crown. But what about Walter? She had no way of telling whose side he was on now, not when allegiances constantly shifted with the changing fortunes of the principal players and the promises of land, property and titles to sweeten a betrayal. What had Walter been promised? Whom did he now support?

"I cannot give you the staff," she whispered, knowing that he was quite capable of taking it by force, if necessary. She glanced around, taking comfort from the close proximity of the jongleurs. They would surely help her to protect her property, if it came to it. Except it wasn't her property. Ulf knew that the staff had belonged to Bernard, and so Walter had every right to claim it. "I need the staff to walk to Winchestre," she said firmly.

"And you may keep it, if that is your wish, mistress," he assured her. "But I know there is a secret compartment inside the handle, for Bernard and I instructed the craftsman to make up identical staffs to our specification. I know that there is something secreted inside, a small memento which I may take to my mother. Surely you cannot begrudge us such a thing?"

Stricken, Janna stared at him. She could not give the letter into his keeping, for she knew not what he would do with it. Supporting the empress's cause as she did, she was desperate to warn the earl of the bishop's treachery. But without the letter as proof, no-one would take her warning seriously. If Walter was in the pay of the bishop, and destroyed the evidence, then the earl was doomed. And so was the empress. She couldn't give the staff to Walter, not if her life depended on it.

He was waiting for her answer. "No!" she said desperately, hugging the staff close to her chest. "Your mother gave this to me. I'm sorry, but I cannot let you have it." Their voices had begun to attract attention. Ulf looked at them, as did Faldo. The boy winked at Janna. He balled his hands into fists and boxed the air a couple of times. She felt comforted by this small show of support. It gave her the courage to face Walter.

"I beg you, mistress, do not make a scene," Walter said quietly, abandoning any pretense that his was merely an idle request. "It is not safe for anyone to know what's hidden inside the staff." He glanced over his shoulder to make sure they could not be overheard. "You've found the secret hiding place, haven't you?"

After a moment's hesitation, Janna nodded. It seemed pointless to pretend any longer.

"Is there a letter inside?"

"No!" Janna hoped she might yet talk her way out of this trap.

Walter's gaze sharpened. "May I look for myself?"

Janna clutched the staff tighter to her chest in a futile gesture of defiance.

Walter sighed. "I don't want to arouse suspicion, nor do I want to take the staff from you by force," he said, his voice a low mutter so that Janna had to lean closer to hear him. "It's too dangerous, both for you and for me, to draw any more attention to ourselves than we already have. Let me, instead, tell you what I know of the letter my brother found on the dead body of the bishop's messenger. The letter bore the seal of the Bishop of Winchestre. I know you saw it too, for Bernard told my mother all about it. Although my brother didn't read the bishop's letter, he told my mother that it was important it should go to the empress as soon as possible. My mother argued against it for several reasons, not least of which was that he must stay to guard Adam. But Bernard insisted on it. He told her of a conversation he'd had with a young lad at the henge: that the empress and the bishop had argued over several broken promises. My brother was fearful there might be forces plotting against the empress, and thought she should be warned as a matter of urgency."

"But your brother's death had naught to do with the letter!" Janna said, desperately hoping to deflect Walter's purpose with the promise of vengeance. "Adam has been captured and is held at the castle at Sarisberie. He has killed once before and tried to disguise his deed by making it look like an accidental drowning. In the same fashion, your brother was also hit on the back of his head and, while still alive, dragged to the site where he was found. His death was disguised to look like a blood sacrifice." Janna remembered her vision. "Such things have happened before at the henge. I know it! I've seen it!"

In spite of her misgivings about Adam's guilt or otherwise, she was determined to convince Walter; anything to take his attention off the staff and what it contained. "If it's justice you seek, you'll find Adam at Sarisberie," she urged.

"My mother has gone to Sarisberie to see Adam," Walter said grimly. "But first she told me all she knew about the letter, for she knows I am in the empress's employ. What she didn't know was where the message was hidden, and whether or not my brother's killer had found it. Now you have confirmed that he did not, and I thank God and all his saints for it, for this is my priority now. I will find my brother's killer, but finding that letter comes first."

"What do you propose to do with it?"

"Take it to the empress, of course."

Trust no-one, Janna reminded herself. Bernard had done his best to keep the message safe, might well have given his life for it. He'd taken it on trust that the message was meant for the empress. And so, it seemed, did his brother. She remembered the conversation she'd had with Bernard. Right from the start, he'd planned to hand the letter over to Walter who, he said, would arrange its delivery to the empress. Janna had been given no reason to doubt Walter's sincerity, or his loyalty to the empress. And bringing the bishop's message to the attention of the empress's half-brother had become a matter of the greatest urgency. Walter had a fast horse, he could travel far more quickly than ever she could. He was the very man to take the message – if she could believe him. Could he be trusted? Did he really not know to whom the message was addressed?

Janna was in an agony of doubt. Walter waited impatiently for her answer. She glanced around, and met the curious gaze of both Ulf and Faldo. They were still too far away to overhear her conversation with Walter and she wanted to keep it that way. Not for anything would she let Ulf know that the letter was found. She gave them a quick nod and a reassuring smile, and turned back to Walter.

"What if I told you the letter was addressed to King Stephen, not the empress?" she asked warily.

Walter stiffened. "Why would the bishop write to the king? Unless…" His expression softened. "He is the king's brother, after all. He might bid him to be of good cheer. I suppose he might also have promised to intercede with the empress for leniency, for the empress has ordered his jailers to keep the king in chains." His shrewd eyes bored into Janna's. "How do you know the message is addressed to the king and not the empress?"

Should she admit that she had read it? Janna was awash in a sea of doubts and confusion. "Do you support the empress's bid for the crown?" she asked instead. "Or are you a servant of the king?"

"No, nor ever have been!" Walter said sharply. "I have the honor of serving my lady, and I will do all in my power to help her gain the throne that is rightfully hers."

"Even if that was not, after all, her father's wish?"

"Who told you that?"

"I heard some travelers discussing it," Janna said, not wanting to have to explain Ralph to Walter. "I heard that one of the barons, who was at the king's bedside when he died, reported that the king had changed his mind about the succession, and that Stephen's claim was perfectly legitimate."

"That's down to Hugh Bigod, the traitor!" Walter said angrily. "It was a lie, concocted in the belief that Stephen would reward him for it, not that it ever did him much good. But the barons wanted to believe him, because it relieved their own conscience for breaking their oath to the old king. They said then that they had been forced to make the oath, which was also a lie. It was Stephen who first put his hand to the oath – not once, but twice – when King Henry asked it. And they all followed willingly behind him. But the barons believed they'd serve their own interests far better under the rule of a weak and easygoing king like Stephen, who has ever tried to buy their loyalty. It is to their eternal shame that they broke their oath and supported Stephen, and brought down this calamity on us all."

He stopped to draw breath, while Janna looked at him in amazement. Not safe to have an opinion indeed! This man was almost spitting with rage, and Janna found herself liking him the more for it. Trust no-one? She looked searchingly at Walter, his sad eyes and open, honest face. "Your loyalty is to the empress?" she asked.

"Forever." He clasped a hand to his heart, his expression solemn. He fumbled in his scrip then, and produced a sheet of parchment, folded small. "I have this from the empress as a guarantee of my safe passage through her realm," he said. "She gave it to me after my mother arrived with news of Bernard's death and the missing message. The empress sent me out to find you, and to locate it, for we believe it contains vital information and was the reason my brother died. I knew where Bernard would have hidden it, but we weren't sure if his killer had found it or not. Now that I know the message is safe, I must take it to the empress without delay." He handed the parchment to Janna. "Look at the seal. Perhaps that will convince you of my good intentions?"

Janna inspected it. There was a Latin inscription around its edge: MATHILDIS DEI GRATIA ROMANORUM REGINA, with the seated figure of a woman in the center. She wore a crown, and held some sort of staff in her right hand. Mathildis? Matilda? It seemed possible. She unfolded the parchment and tried to read what it said, but the Latin defeated her. She scanned the page, and her eyes fixed on some writing underneath the Latin script. This, she could understand. It was written in Norman French, and asked that the bearer be given safe passage. It was signed with Matilda's name, just as Walter had said.

"You speak the truth." Janna folded up the parchment and handed it back to him.

"You've read what it says?" Walter sounded surprised.

"Yes." Janna had made up her mind. "What about you? Do you know how to read?"

"Of course."

"Then you'd better look at this." She turned her back on the jongleurs and cautiously unscrewed the handle of her staff. She took out the small packet and palmed it to Walter. "Read this as soon as you may, but don't let anyone see you looking at it now," she warned. But her warning was unnecessary, for the message had been quickly slipped out of sight.

"Even though you say it's addressed to the king, I shall take it to the empress," Bernard assured her.

"No!" Janna was in a panic that she'd done the wrong thing. "No, this is a matter of life and death! You must take it to Robert, Earl of Gloucestre, in Winchestre. Now, *today*, for I fear he has walked into a trap of the bishop's making."

"A trap? What are you talking about? The bishop is our ally!" Walter eyed Janna warily, perhaps thinking her wits had gone wandering.

She had trusted him so far, she must trust him now. Janna reasoned that soon enough he would read the message for himself, but she must convince him not to delay in delivering it.

"The letter is addressed to the king, and you are right. It is to urge him to be of good cheer, but not for the reason you think. Instead, the bishop takes credit for counseling the queen and her troops to lay siege against the empress on the eve of her coronation, so proving to the Londoners that the empress was powerless to protect them. The bishop says he intends to oppose and thwart her at every turn, and snare her if he can, with the intention of exchanging her life for that of the king. It is quite clear from the letter that he has never supported the empress; that he has been working against her from the start, in fact."

"*What?*" Walter paled as Janna unfolded the full extent of the bishop's treachery. "I must go to the empress at once, and warn her," he said breathlessly.

"Surely it is more important to warn the earl?" Janna said, and proceeded to put forward the argument that she'd used to convince herself that this was the correct course of action.

"I must first read this letter for myself." Walter looked worried and uncertain. Janna realized he didn't believe her.

"You will see the truth of my words once you do, but you must take it to the earl without delay," she urged him.

"I understand." His glance raked the group of jongleurs, and settled briefly on Ulf. He turned to Janna. "My mother told me that Ulf and Ralph de Otreburne joined the pilgrim band along the journey. I see Ulf still travels in your company." His glance hardened. "Where is Ralph?"

"Ralph? He travels with us to Winchestre. It is his horse that cast a shoe. He had to take it to the blacksmith back at that hamlet we just passed through."

"Red tunic, long fair hair, beard and mustache?" Janna nodded. "I saw him with the blacksmith." Walter scowled at the memory. "I understand he told you that he was a pilgrim. Why, then, has he not traveled to Oxeneford with the other pilgrims? Did you think to ask him that?"

"He's coming to Winchestre with me to help me find my father." Janna had no intention of sharing her suspicions with Walter, but it was safe to admit that much. Yet it seemed that was not enough to convince him. The disbelief on his face was easily read. "He thinks he knows who my father is whereas I…I do not." Shamed by the admission, she tilted her chin in defiance and looked him square in the eye.

"Is that all there is between you?"

Janna glared at him. "If Ralph knows aught of the bishop's letter, he still does not know that it's been found," she said. "And if you leave us now, he will never know there was anything to find, or that I had anything to give you."

"But he is not the only one from the pilgrim band who still accompanies you. What about the relic seller, Ulf. Why is he still in your company?"

Janna couldn't help feeling relieved that Walter's focus had shifted to Ulf. All her suspicions came flooding back. Ulf was a rogue, yes, she knew that much about him. But was he also a killer?

"Ulf knows about the letter," Walter prompted her. "My mother tells me she confided in him in her grief. Why is he following you?"

Janna took a quick breath. "To protect me. That's what he said, although I'm not sure I believe him. And I certainly don't need looking after!" She tossed her head, flushing angrily as she noted the sudden glint of amusement in Walter's eyes. "He really does sell relics," she said. "He's had a very profitable journey so far, and hopes to do even better in Winchestre."

"I'm sure he does," Walter said dryly. "I will speak to him before I go." He turned away, then stepped back with a final warning, his words a strange echo of his brother's last words to Janna. "Promise me you'll say nothing of this letter to anyone. Trust no-one." His expression hardened. "Both our lives will be in danger if word of this gets out."

He waited for Janna to make the promise then, to her relief, he left her. After a brief exchange with Ulf, he mounted his horse and set off at a gallop for Winchestre, with a broad smile and a cheerful wave giving the appearance that he had not a care in the world.

Janna watched him go, feeling a great burden lift from her shoulders as his figure dwindled in the distance.

"What was that all about, Janna?" Master Thomas strode over to her, closely followed by Faldo and the rest of the troupe.

Janna hastily collected her scattered wits together. "Master Walter is an old friend of my family. They...they gave him a message for me, just...just in case our paths crossed along his journey."

Master Thomas nodded, apparently satisfied, but his wife poked her nose in Janna's direction. "He seemed in a great hurry to be gone." It was clear from her tone that Walter had not observed the courtesies so far as Elanor was concerned, and that she took it as a personal affront.

"He...has urgent business in Winchestre." It was the truth after all.

But Mistress Elanor was still not satisfied. "And what is his business that it's so urgent?"

"He's a – a merchant."

"A merchant? Where then are his goods?"

Janna heaved an exasperated sigh. Really, the woman was cursed with even more curiosity than she was! "He was robbed. There are no goods left to steal!" she said firmly.

Elanor raised a disbelieving eyebrow.

"So what were you arguing about?" Faldo asked.

"We weren't arguing. He's angry about the theft, that's all. And he is in haste to report it." Janna felt herself coloring under their combined gaze. She walked away and flung herself down in a patch of shade, eager to avoid any more questions. Ulf followed her, and sat down beside her.

"That was Bernard's brother," he said quietly. Janna nodded, and closed her eyes. She was afraid to talk about him lest she give something away. She was even more afraid of what might happen if she did.

"He questioned me about Ralph." Janna pressed her lips together, refusing to take the bait. "He also asked why I had stayed in your company."

"And what did you answer?"

"I said Dame Juliana had asked me to look after you."

Janna gave an impatient exclamation, her annoyance clearly on show.

"Faldo was right, wasn't he?" Ulf persevered. "You were arguing. What about? What's happened?"

"Nothing that need concern you." Janna turned away. She was tired of being questioned, tired of having her word doubted, tired of being involved in the treachery swirling around the empress and her bid for the throne. She'd handed over the bishop's letter. She'd done what she could and all she wanted now was to be left in peace!

To be certain of it, she pretended she was falling asleep. But her brain continued to spin like a waterwheel. The letter was out of her hands now, but she knew that its safe delivery was only part of Walter's quest. Sooner or later, he would look for his brother's killer and extract vengeance. On Ulf? Or did he suspect Ralph? Stricken, her hand flew up to her heart. "It was Adam," she whispered to herself. "Adam!" Or was it Ulf? Or Ralph? Her uneasiness grew as her thoughts became darker; a black fog swirled around her, thick as the mist at the henge, sucking her into the void.

She only realized that she'd fallen asleep when Master Thomas's voice roused her. "We can go soon," he called out to everyone. "Here comes Master Ralph. It looks as if his visit to the blacksmith has met with success."

"I saw Walter hand you a letter to look at. Was that what you were arguing about?" Ulf came to her side as soon as he saw that she was awake.

"No! It was a message from my family, that's all." Janna picked up Bernard's staff and rose to her feet, desperate to discourage any further questions. But Ulf would not be put off. He laid his hand on her arm to keep her attention.

"I promised Dame Juliana that I would keep you safe, and I will honor that promise," he said seriously. "Dame Juliana foresaw the death of her son, and she told me that death stalks you too. Be careful, Janna. Please, be careful."

Janna shrugged him off. "How do I know I can trust you, Ulf?" she said, fear making her brutal in her honesty. "How do I know I can trust anybody?"

Ulf's eyes narrowed. "You can trust *me*," he said, and walked away.

Janna watched him go. She was sure her face bore witness to her distress and confusion. She dreaded seeing Ralph, having to meet his bright and knowing gaze. She walked over to Faldo, thinking neither Ralph nor Ulf could provoke her into revealing secrets if she kept always in the company of others.

"If you're training to be a jongleur like your father, can you recite something to me?" she asked, hoping Faldo wouldn't be able to resist showing off his knowledge.

Faldo brightened at the chance to perform in front of an appreciative audience. "Something from *The Song of Roland*?" he asked. "It's the most popular. The nobles like stories about Charlemagne the Great. So do the common folk."

"Common folk like me?" Janna teased.

Faldo grinned at her. "Common folk in the marketplace and at the fairs. Wait till you see St Giles Fair at Winchestre, mistress. We come every year for it. It's the biggest and the best! You wouldn't believe there were so many people in the whole world as come up on the hill where the fair is held. It's like a town up there, with every animal and bird you've ever seen for sale, and some you never have. And an array of goods to take your very breath away! We always do well there, for the people love to hear our songs and stories, and dance to our music." His face split into a wide grin, and he clapped his hands together in remembered joy.

Janna watched Ralph dismount, and her heart quivered with fear. Keep Faldo talking, she thought. "*The Song of Roland* will do nicely." Her nerves were strung taut. She was acutely aware of Ralph's presence. "Or you could teach me another song?"

Faldo gazed at her in astonishment – he knew how reluctant a singer she was. "There's a sweet song about love that was taught to me by a jongleur from across the water," he said, adding doubtfully, "It's a little...rude." He began to walk on, following his father and mother and the rest of the pilgrim band. Janna kept pace beside him.

"That'll do," she said.

"And you'll sing it with me?"

Janna sighed. But she was desperate. "Yes," she promised.

"*I still remember one morning when we put an end to our quarrel,*

And when she gave me such a great gift: her love and her ring.

May God let me live until I may have my hands under her cloak!"
Faldo's voice quavered on the last few words. He glanced quickly at
Janna, who gave him an encouraging smile. She'd expected something
far worse.

"I know some others, but they're all much longer," Faldo
said anxiously.

"No, I like that one. Sing it for me again." She closed her eyes as
he sang, trying to memorize the simple tune.

"Tell me the words again," she said, after Faldo had gone through
it a third time.

"And now it's your turn, Janna," he told her, when it became
obvious that by now she must know both the words and the tune.

"Sing it with me?" she asked anxiously, and Faldo nodded.

Ralph clapped them roundly as the song came to an end. "Bravo!"

"Again," Janna demanded. "Let's sing it again."

"I thought you didn't like singing, Janna? Or are you trying to send
me a message?"

"No message, my lord," Janna retorted. "I'm finding my voice." It
was the first excuse that came into her head. That it was true brought
a jolt of surprise. And a gleeful smile of triumph.

"*I still remember one morning,*" she began, this time singing on
her own. Her voice was not nearly so sweet and true as Faldo's
voice, but it was her voice and hers alone. To be able to sing with
joy gave her a great deal of pleasure, and some measure of pride.
"*When we put an end to our quarrel,*" she continued, turning aside
from Ralph so she wouldn't see his expression as the song became
more bawdy.

"Is everything all right, Janna?" he asked at the song's end. "You
seem nervous. On edge."

"All's well." But Janna didn't dare meet his keen gaze. She kept
her eyes on the track as they walked along in silence. She could find

nothing to say, for everything that came into her mind led to what she was so desperate to keep a secret. Eventually Ralph gave up trying to engage her in conversation, and walked on ahead in search of better company.

The words of the song stayed with Janna. She sang softly to herself as she followed the jongleurs along the track. It was all very well for women to think of romance and love, she thought, but it was quite clear from the song that the man had something quite different in mind. Was that the way of all men when an opportunity to bed a woman presented itself? She recalled how Ralph had almost seduced her. Was it for the age-old reason, or was he planning to investigate her purse instead? Ralph was now deep in conversation with Master Thomas. She wondered if they were discussing her, for he kept flicking glances her way.

Janna was ashamed of her suspicions. Ralph had given up his pilgrimage to Oxeneford to come with her to Winchestre to find her father, and yet she had lied and lied again to him. Could she not trust him with the truth? No, for the truth was not hers to tell. There was too much at stake now to risk even one word that might spread and spread like ripples in a pond, and come to the wrong ears as a result. She sighed. As soon as this is over, she thought, as soon as I know that the message is safely delivered to Earl Robert, I will admit what I have done, and find out just where Ralph's interests really lie.

She gave him a self-conscious grin as he dropped back to keep pace with her. "I believe you had some company while I was gone," he observed lightly. "Why didn't you tell me about Master Walter? I hear he paid you a great deal of attention."

"He's an old friend of my family." Janna launched automatically into the lie, but stopped abruptly. Ralph, more than anyone, knew that she had no family. "I knew him when I was a child, but he went away and I never saw him again until this day."

"And yet he brought a message to you from your family?" Ralph's mild tone belied the frosty blue of his eyes.

"No, not really. I knew him from Berford. My mother made up a…a potion for his cough." Janna did her best to retrieve the situation. "By happy chance he recognized me as he rode past."

"He spent a long time talking to you," Ralph probed.

"Perhaps he was enjoying my company?" Janna looked at him, sure that he could read the deceit in her eyes. This is intolerable, she thought, tempted after all to break her promise to Walter. She was conscious that she was doing nothing to help her own cause. If Ralph suspected that she was lying to him, he might well regret his decision to help her. Yet Bernard had probably died for the message he carried. And Walter had warned that her own life, as well as his, would be in danger if anyone knew what she'd found.

"What did you give Master Walter?" Ralph's voice broke into her thoughts. In an agony of indecision, Janna was about to plead ignorance but Ralph's grim expression checked her. "Master Thomas saw you," he said, adding softly, "What did you give him, Janna, that has taken him off at such a fast gallop to Winchestre?"

She stared at Ralph in panic. She couldn't deny what the jongleur had seen, nor could she tell him the truth, for the truth had the power to kill. Nor could she say that she'd given Walter a favor to carry, for if Ralph thought she was interested in Walter, or he in her, it would mean the end of their liaison and the end of any help he might give her. Should she rather say she'd given Walter a message to deliver? But what message? And to whom?

Her numb brain couldn't think of anything that might convince Ralph other than the truth, for he knew she had no kin there. Should she tell him the truth, and put him to the test?

"A message, perhaps?" Ralph asked coldly. Janna heard the anger in his voice. After what felt like a lifetime of indecision, she inclined her head.

"You gave him a message?"

Sensing danger, Janna took a quick step backward. "Yes," she whispered. "He told me where I might find my father, and I gave him a message to take to him."

"But you don't even know who your father is." Ralph moved closer. She read his anger in the taut stillness of his body. His hands clenched, his long fingers curved into claws like the talons of a bird of prey. Shuddering, she dragged her gaze away from them. She looked into his face, dreading what she might see there.

"You're lying to me! I believe you gave him the message that Master Bernard found on the dead man's body. I believe you've had it all along!"

"No. I – I didn't know I had it. I've only just found it."

"Yet you gave it away to a stranger? Why didn't you keep it to show me?"

Because I don't trust you. Janna realized that had been true all along. She'd wanted to believe in love; wanted to believe his only thought was to help her achieve her quest. She'd been lying to herself as well as to him.

"I...didn't know you were interested in the message we'd found," she said instead. "You told me you were looking for your cousin – and I knew for sure that the dead man we discovered was not him."

"You've lied to me! You've been lying ever since I met you. Why didn't you trust me with the truth?"

"Because you were also lying to me, my lord." Janna's heart was beating so hard she thought it might explode in her chest, might shatter into a million tiny shards of pain. His cold, blue eyes held her transfixed. It was like looking into the face of a stranger.

"I thought we were friends," he said softly. "In fact, I was hoping we were a lot more than just friends."

It was what Janna had once longed to hear him say. But not anymore.

He grasped her wrist so hard that he hurt her, but she didn't pull away. She couldn't. Everything she had hoped for was standing here in front of her. Her dreams for the future, finding her father, finding love…It was all an illusion, for now she knew who and what he really was, and where his true interest lay. She was on the brink of losing everything, and she didn't know how to save herself other than to keep silent about the contents of the letter.

"God help you for a fool," he said tonelessly. "You cannot know the harm you'll cause unless I can intercept your so-called friend." He turned on his heel and tugged on the leading rein to bring his palfrey to his side.

"No!" Janna cried. "Please, wait!" For she knew, with terrible certainty, what Ralph was capable of, and what he intended to do. But his foot was in the stirrup, and even as she cried out, he vaulted up into the saddle and dug his heels into the horse's side.

"You're too late!" she shouted desperately. Ralph didn't check or turn around, but instead spurred his mount to a gallop. Stricken and despairing, she watched as he rode out of her life, taking with him her shattered hopes and dreams, and placing in jeopardy the future of the empress and the safety of her envoy.

Chapter 12

"Don't cry, lass. He's no loss. I never trusted him anyway." Ulf's voice jerked Janna back to her surroundings.

"Neither did I," Faldo echoed loyally.

Janna shook her head in abject misery. The ache in her heart had spread throughout her body. She felt completely undone. Silently, she cursed the misfortune that had brought her and Bernard to the dead man's side. Bernard had died for it, and now her dreams had died along with him.

She tried to rally herself with the thought that it was as well she'd realized Ralph's true worth before he could truly break her heart, for it was clear now that he knew what was in the letter, and had been sent by the Bishop of Winchestre to track it down – and no wonder, for the bishop's treachery was plain to read in every line. Indignation stiffened Janna's spine and helped to dry her tears as she recalled how Ralph had tried to woo her, seduce her into revealing what she knew, making false promises and kindling her hope of finding her father in the process. Her rage and horror intensified as the vision of Bernard's slain body came into her mind. It was her fault he'd died, for it was she who'd let slip what they'd found.

"*Stupid!*" Janna berated herself. "Stupid, stupid, *stupid*!" How naïve, how gullible she was to be taken in by Ralph's charm and his lies. Janna's anger with herself, and with Ralph, ran like a thread of bright fire through her misery. She'd been stupid, yes. She'd told lies, but her lies were the sins of omission. She'd concealed from Ralph what she'd believed was none of his concern. But he had lied and lied again to her. He'd led her on with kisses and flattery, and with promises that he would help her find her father, when all along his goal was either to find the letter or delay matters until such time that it was rendered harmless. Who was the faithless one now? Ralph had played her as Elanor played her harp, plucking her trust and devotion with his lying words and promises. She'd thought he cared about her, thought he cared enough to break his journey to help her find her father in Winchestre. Now that she knew the truth behind his real interest in her, she was devastated.

All too clearly she remembered the henge, and the disfigured boy's careless words that had prompted Bernard to take action, and Ralph to retaliate. He must have searched for the message from the start, while knowing there was no urgency to find it while the pilgrims were still on the road. But he was with Bernard when the boy had mentioned the difference of opinion between the bishop and the empress. He'd understood Bernard's resolve to delay no longer, and must have determined at that moment to prevent him. Janna could only imagine how angry and frustrated Ralph must have felt when, with Bernard dead and all the time in the world to search through his belongings, he had still been unable to find the bishop's letter.

She closed her eyes against the pain of understanding what came next. Ralph had turned his attention to her, questioning her about the contents of her purse, and trying to win her trust by pretending to know how to find her father. He must have believed she knew where Bernard had hidden the message and that she'd found it during her search of his body and belongings. And so he had followed her, and kept her on side with his promises.

Ralph's promises were bitter gall. She could hardly believe how she'd misread him when the evidence seemed so obvious now that she was looking at it from a different angle. His interest in her and her opinion of the empress. His interest in the contents of her purse – and the steps he'd taken to try to examine it. Janna shook her head in disbelief. Her failure rang like a litany through her brain. *Stupid, stupid, stupid!*

She remembered Juliana, and the old woman's prophecy. "*Death follows you*," she'd said. Had she known all along that her son would die because of what Janna would reveal to Ralph? No wonder the old woman had begged her to leave the pilgrim group. But it was already too late by then, Janna thought, and wondered if Juliana had known that too. She scrunched up her face and squeezed her eyes tight, desperate to blot out the guilt she felt, and her remorse. If only she'd kept her mouth shut. If only...

But it was too late now for "If only." Too late for her, but not for the empress. A thin sinew of pride helped to strengthen her. Ralph had known from the start what he was about and, yes, she had been gulled by him. But in the end, and by the greatest good fortune, she had managed to outwit him. The letter was safe and on its way to the earl, just as Bernard had intended. But Ralph had gone in pursuit. If he caught up with Walter along the way, he would slaughter him as he had slaughtered Walter's brother! Janna put a hand to her heart. She could feel it beating hard beneath her fingers, urgent as the beat of a horse's hooves galloping on to Winchestre.

"Janna?" Ulf touched her elbow. She swung to face him, hardly able to talk or even breathe, so great was her misery. "Janna," he said again, and grasped her arms. He gave her a little shake, trying to bring her back to the present, to reality.

"It's all right," he said gently. "I'm here, lass. You can trust me. Just tell me what to do, and I'll help you."

Trust? Janna clasped her arms around her body and rocked to and fro. Tears, scalding as liquid fire, ran down her cheeks. She had to get to Winchestre without delay – but how? She didn't know which way to turn. She didn't know who she could trust. Trust no-one. That was the edict her mother lived by, but it had led to disaster. Trust no-one, Walter had told her, and so had Bernard. Janna wiped her eyes on her sleeve, no longer caring if the moisture stained the delicate fabric. She peered at Ulf, wanting to believe in him but afraid to trust anyone now.

"Why should you want to help me?" she asked gruffly.

"Because you've helped me in the past," Ulf answered readily enough. "You kept quiet when the guard might have arrested me for stealing the hand of St James. And you patched me up when those drunken idiots broke my nose." He raised his hand to his face, wincing at the memory. "You also found the means to cure my rheum. You have a kind heart, Janna. I haven't forgotten that."

Janna looked at him. She wanted to believe him. But Ralph's betrayal had shattered her confidence in her own judgment. Trust nobody, she thought again. It was safer, after all. She folded her arms against him, and kept silent.

Ulf sighed. "Perhaps there's something I should share with you. Faldo, could you leave us alone, please?" His words were an order rather than a request. The boy looked from Ulf to Janna, clearly reluctant to miss a moment of a story that promised to be even more dramatic than the doom of King Arthur. But Ulf jerked his head, his intention unmistakable. Reluctantly, Faldo walked away.

"I expect you're wondering why I've been following you around?" Ulf said quietly. "You may even have cast me as the villain in all this, for I know you thought the world of Ralph."

Janna felt a wave of desolation wash over her at the mention of Ralph's name. It was mixed with a feeling of shame that Ulf had read her mind so clearly.

"Let me tell you something," he said now. "It's true that Dame Juliana asked me to watch over you. She knew it would make no difference to me whether I traveled on to Oxeneford or went somewhere else instead. But I had my own reasons for wanting to protect you. You see..." He rubbed a hand across his mouth as he searched for the words he wanted. All trace of his customary gaiety was gone now. Janna found she was looking into the face of a man who was familiar with sorrow and despair. "I had a daughter once."

Janna pricked up her ears. Ulf had told her that he had no home and no family. So what, then, was this?

"My wife died shortly after she was born, but my daughter thrived. Mildryth, her name was. She grew up bright and bonny as a butterfly. She would have been about your age now, if she had lived." He stopped to draw in a shaky breath.

"What happened to her?" Janna prompted gently.

"She drowned when she was but five summers old. She was my responsibility, the love of my life. And I let her drown. I should have been watching out for her, but instead I was drinking at an alehouse with friends. By the time I realized she was missing, it was too late. She was gone." There was a glint of tears in Ulf's eyes as he struggled to collect himself. "I couldn't save her, and I have lived with that regret every day of my life since. When Juliana asked me to watch over you, I said that I would. In some measure it goes toward making up for my neglect of my own daughter."

Janna bowed her head, feeling mortified that she could ever have doubted Ulf's good faith. She tried to find the words to frame an apology.

"I haven't always lived on the road," Ulf continued, perhaps misunderstanding her silence. "I left my home up north after Mildryth drowned. I turned my back on everything and took to the road and to the drink. My life was down in the gutter until, one day,

I met a relic seller. We talked, and for the first time I found myself unburdening my guilt over my daughter's death. Of the goodness of his heart, he gave me what he said was the toe of St Peter. And he advised me to forgive myself. Here, let me show you." He fumbled in the purse slung around his neck. He pulled out a small cloth-wrapped bundle and unrolled it for Janna's inspection. "I'll never part with this, for it turned my life around, I can tell you."

Janna peered dubiously at the small bone. Ulf swiftly rolled it up and put it away again. "I decided then that I would also become a relic seller, because we all need hope, we cannot live without it," he said. "I went on a pilgrimage to the tomb of St James to pray for my daughter and to give thanks that I had found a new purpose in life. And I believe now that my way was made clear when I decided to continue my journey with the pilgrims and came to meet you, lass. I couldn't save my own daughter, but perhaps I can atone for it by helping you now. If there's owt I can do for you, you have only to ask. I have no other motive than wanting to make things right for you. But I can swear my good faith on a sliver of the true cross of Christ if it'll make you feel any better?"

"I thought you'd sold – given – that particular relic to Juliana?" Janna was somewhat reassured that at least her thoughts were ordered enough to remember the occasion.

"I have another. But I'll swear on something else, if you prefer?" In spite of the sadness of his memories and the gravity of the situation, a challenging twinkle glinted in Ulf's eyes.

Janna found herself responding to it with some relief. "The eyelash of St Edith? The quill with which St Paul wrote his letters?"

"That would be worth having," Ulf said wistfully. Janna gave an impatient exclamation. Ulf smiled at her, and put his hand on his heart. "I swear I will do all in my power to help you. I swear it on the toe of St Peter." There was no doubting the sincerity in his voice.

"First tell me one thing. Who do you support in this battle for the crown, the king or the empress?" Janna needed to know for, up until now, Ulf had always refused to be drawn on the subject.

"I have always found it better, safer, not to take sides. I told you that before."

"But you must tell me the truth now. I need to know."

Ulf pulled a face. "The empress. I suppose it's safe to admit as much to you, for Dame Juliana made her feelings plain to me after Bernard's death. As you didn't speak out at the time, I'm assuming you shared their regard for the empress."

"Yes, I do."

"Very well, then. We are in agreement, it seems. Besides..." Ulf glanced sideways at Janna. "Stephen has proved not fit to govern, while the Empress Matilda may yet bring peace to our land. So I would help her, if I could."

Janna weighed up her options. His support might not be quite as wholehearted as she would have liked, but it would have to do. "I have to get to Winchestre. Fast," she said.

Ulf nodded. "I thought so." He was silent for a moment as he contemplated possibilities.

"If only your dog was a little bigger, I could ride him," Janna ventured.

Ulf gave a quick snort of amusement. "Winchestre isn't all that far from here," he said. "When I talked to our hosts last night they mentioned it is but ten miles away and we've covered part of that already. If we set off now, if we walk without stopping, we should reach the gates of Winchestre some time this evening."

"But we won't get there in time to warn – " Janna gulped, and looked hard at Ulf.

He stared back at her, grave and unsmiling once again. Beside him, Brutus quivered, and thumped his tail. Ulf dropped his hand to scratch the dog's head and Brutus's tail wagged harder. There was no mistaking the bond between the two, the trust and love between them. It helped Janna to make up her mind.

"I have to warn Master Walter." Janna drew a deep, shuddering sigh. "I've found the letter that Bernard was killed for. It was hidden in his staff. It's a letter from the bishop to his brother, the king. It reveals that the bishop has always supported his brother, and that he plans to trap the empress if he can. Walter has taken it to Earl Robert, to warn him that the bishop is a traitor. But Ralph knows what's in the letter and that Walter has it. He's gone after Walter, and I know that he will stop him if he can, even kill him if he must. Ralph…" Tears burned Janna's eyes, blurring her vision. "Ralph is the bishop's agent."

"Christ's bones!" Ulf pursed his lips in a long, silent whistle.

"I'm sorry I didn't trust you," Janna said wretchedly. "If I'd confided in you sooner, we might have found some way to avoid raising Ralph's suspicions."

"I doubt it would have made any difference in the end." Ulf put his head on one side, considering the matter. "We cannot catch up with either Ralph or Walter, not without mounts of our own. But take heart, Janna." He took his hand from the dog's head and rubbed Janna's arm instead. She found the gesture strangely reassuring. "Master Walter knows his brother was killed for the letter he carried. He knows its importance, while Master Bernard did not. And so he'll guard himself as well as the letter. He won't make the same mistake his brother made."

"He also knows what Ralph looks like," Janna said, slightly cheered as she recalled that Walter had seen him at the smithy. "But he doesn't know that Ralph is after him!"

"Then we'll follow them, Janna. We must warn Walter if we can." He looked over her shoulder and gave a sudden loud whistle. "Hoy!" he shouted.

Janna swung around to see what he was about. Several riders were approaching, merchants judging by the packs that hung from either side of their saddles. At Ulf's whistle, they slowed down and surveyed the jongleurs with cautious expressions, ready to gallop away at the slightest hint of trouble.

"Can you offer us a ride to Winchestre, my friend?" Ulf called out to the leader. The man surveyed them with a stony expression. Janna held her breath as she waited for his reply.

"For the young lass here." Ulf gestured toward Janna, perhaps hoping to disarm the man's suspicion. The merchant's expression changed to a greedy awareness. His tongue flickered across his lips and he smiled.

Janna felt a twinge of misgiving. It seemed that Ulf was also having second thoughts. "And a ride for me too," he said, glancing at the other two merchants who had stopped alongside their partner.

The leader's eyes moved from Janna to Ulf, and back again. "No," he said curtly. "You'll hold us back. Only the girl."

Janna shrank back against Ulf. "I don't go anywhere unless...unless my uncle comes with me."

"Suit yourself." The merchant jerked on the reins, and the horse moved on. One of the merchant's companions gave a rueful shrug, and they both trotted after him.

"Stupid idea. My pardon, lass," Ulf said, once they were out of hearing. "I was thinking of the fastest way to get you to Winchestre. I didn't stop to think you might be in even more danger if you went with 'em."

"I was glad to see them go," Janna admitted. She regretted the lost ride, but understood well from the men's expressions what might have happened to her along the way if she'd accompanied them. In fact, she might never have reached her destination at all. She shivered at the thought, and jerked her head in the direction that the merchants had taken.

"Let's say our goodbyes and walk on," she said urgently, yanking on Ulf's arm to drag him with her toward the leader of the jongleurs.

"I hope I did no harm in telling Ralph de Otreburne about your meeting with Master Walter?" Master Thomas greeted Janna. "I had no idea he'd leave us like that, without even saying farewell."

"Do not fret, Master Thomas. I know Ralph to be skilled at asking questions and getting answers." Janna gave the jongleur the reassurance he wanted, for the harm was already done and there was no undoing it. Nor did she want to waste time debating it. She was consumed with impatience to reach Winchestre." We must also leave you now," she said. "We need to hurry on to Winchestre."

"You're going after him?" Thomas asked, not specifying who they were following, although Janna was fairly sure he meant Ralph. She ducked her head in agreement. It was almost the truth. So far as she was concerned, she never wanted to see Ralph again. But she was certainly following him, if only to do her best to keep Walter safe.

Saying goodbye to Faldo was more difficult, for she'd grown fond of the boy and was grateful to him for having the patience to teach her how to sing.

"But there's no need to say goodbye. I'll see you when we arrive at Winchestre," he pointed out matter-of-factly. "You're going to stay on there, aren't you? And so are we."

"I'll look out for you there, then," Janna promised, with a cheerful smile she didn't feel. "Come on, Ulf." The drumming of the horse's hooves still sounded in her ears and beat hard in her heart. She was desperate to be gone.

Chapter 13

Janna's feet were blistered and her legs were aching by the time they came to the town walls, which loomed dark and bulky against the night sky. They had walked through the long twilight, with only the light of the moon to guide their steps for the last mile. But Ulf had led the way, his sure strides bringing them ever closer to their destination.

"Have you been here before, Ulf?" she asked.

"Aye, several times. To St Giles Fair. It's held every September, and it's one of the biggest in the land. Those merchants who passed us? This is where they were coming, and why." He scowled. "Low-life scum!" He spat into a nearby pond, his spittle disturbing the stagnant water so that the shine of moonlight fragmented and shivered for a moment. Judging from the smell, there was vegetable matter decomposing there and possibly even a dead animal or two. Janna wrinkled her nose and tried to breathe through her mouth.

Ulf stopped walking and looked at the small settlement that had leaked outside the town walls. All was now in darkness. "I'm afraid we're too late to gain entrance through the town gates, but there's a small church adjoining the West Gate. St Mary in the Ditch, it's called. We may find shelter there for the night."

"How far is it?" Janna was so weary she just wanted to lie down and sleep, although she'd rather put some distance between her and the noisome pond before she did so.

"Not much further. That's the West Gate ahead, see?" Ulf pointed. Janna could just make out the extra height of the gate tower in the dark, higher than the earthen ramparts packed against the walls on either side. "The royal castle is there, on our right," Ulf continued, "and St Mary's is just along here." He flung his arms wide in triumph as the stone bulk of a small church took shape in the darkness. The flickering light of a torch illuminated its entrance, shedding light also on a rope beside the door, which Ulf wasted no time in pulling. But no-one came out to answer their summons, nor could they hear any sound of a bell ringing inside.

"Perhaps they untie the bell once it gets late?" Ulf hammered on the door with his knuckles. When even a loud shout produced no response, Janna decided it was time to make another plan. She remembered a grove of trees they had passed. It was not too far away and the trees would provide shelter should it rain.

"Let's just stay out in the open for the night," she said, and turned to walk back in the direction from which they'd come.

"I can't make you out, Janna," Ulf said, as he followed her. "I must say, you're very accommodating for a highborn lady."

"That's because I'm not highborn," Janna said with a chuckle, and proceeded to tell Ulf something of her background as they walked along. He'd trusted her with the truth of his situation, and now it was her turn. She hoped her trust was not misplaced, and that she wasn't about to put herself in jeopardy. But, after what Ulf had told her of his daughter, Janna felt reasonably sure she would not come to harm in his care.

She glanced at him as they trudged back along the track. So far as relics were concerned, she certainly didn't believe everything he said. But on everything else, everything that mattered, she thought he'd prove reliable.

The grove loomed ahead, myriad dark shapes against the star-spattered sky. With a sigh of relief, Janna hastened toward it. She subsided onto the ground, and propped her back against a lofty elm for comfort. She was so tired she was ready to go to sleep sitting up. Beside her, Ulf unrolled his cloak from his pack and spread it out. He put down his pack for use as a pillow. "You should be comfortable enough here, Janna," he said, leaning over to heave Brutus out of the way, for the dog had immediately sprawled out over the cloak and was feigning sleep.

"No. It's your cloak. You sleep there." Janna was embarrassed by Ulf's gesture, and somewhat shy. Ulf laughed, and walked away. "Go on," he said, and gave the dog a gentle nudge with his foot. "Brutus will protect your honor."

The dog wagged its tail, but didn't budge. Janna wondered if it had fleas, and reassured herself that at least the creature's body would provide some warmth. She glanced over at Ulf. He'd found himself a grassy spot and, as Janna watched, he stretched out, pillowing his cheek on his arm. "Sleep well, lass," he called.

"Good night, Ulf. And thank you." Janna hesitated. "For everything." She lay down on the cloak, feeling the warmth emanating from the animal beside her, but also smelling the pungent aroma of his coat. Perhaps this wasn't such a good idea after all! She turned her back on the dog so her nose wasn't quite so close to the source of the smell, and closed her eyes. But her mind would not shut down, for at once she found herself replaying that final heart-wrenching scene with Ralph. She shifted uncomfortably, feeling weighed down with sorrow and guilt. Ralph had wooed and won her with only one purpose on his mind: to find the bishop's letter. Bernard had died because of her. So, too, might Walter die unless they could find him in time to warn him.

Restless and agitated, Janna turned over, breathed in a lungful of dog stink, and hastily turned away again. She had given Ralph her love in the belief that he cared about her. Worse, she had trusted him to help her find her father. And in that, too, he had betrayed her. It was this betrayal that cut deepest. That she could have been so stupid, so gullible as to think he'd set aside important business of his own – and on that, too, he had lied – to go chasing rainbows on her behalf? Janna shook her head in wonder at her naïvety. She was furious with Ralph, and furious with herself. And yet she was sure she hadn't misread his surprise when she'd shown him her father's ring. There'd been a flash of recognition. That, too, had led her to believe that his interest was genuine, and his offer to find her father heartfelt in its sincerity. But that was over now, all over.

Her thoughts turned to Bernard, and her rage against Ralph returned in full force. She felt a deep and bitter regret for the part she had played in Bernard's death, but Bernard wasn't the only victim. There was also Adam, sitting now in the dungeon in Sarisberie and about to come to trial for a murder he didn't commit.

My fault, Janna thought wretchedly, wishing there was something – anything – she could do to put things right. But there wasn't. She would just have to live with the knowledge of her own stupidity, and its consequences.

*

She awoke to the sounds of birdsong. It took her a few moments to remember where she was, and why she was here. At once a crushing sorrow rushed back, swamping her in its depths. She sat up and scrubbed her eyes, trying to find the courage to face the day. Beside her, Brutus stirred. He opened one eye and looked at her. To Janna's surprise, his tail twitched in greeting, but whether for her or for the sunrise, she wasn't quite sure. She remembered the first time she'd tried to make friends with him, and had almost had her hand bitten off. "You old rascal," she said softly, and held out her hand to him.

His tail lifted and waved like a feathery flag. Now that they'd slept together, she'd definitely become a friend!

"Are you talking to me?" Ulf asked sleepily, with his eyes still shut.

"Yes." Janna felt cheered enough by this unexpected show of friendliness from the big dog to tease Ulf. "A rascal and a lazy-bones." She was suddenly consumed with anxiety, by the need to be gone. She sprang to her feet, and stood over Ulf. "I have to go. I have to find Walter and the earl."

At once Ulf opened his eyes. "I'll come with you." He jumped up, pulled his cloak out from under the heavy weight of his hound and rolled it up, prior to stashing it away in his pack. Janna hesitated, pleased by his offer but not wanting him to follow her just yet.

"I'm going to find some bushes first," she said and walked off, trusting him not to come after her. But Brutus did, crashing ahead into the undergrowth. Janna followed in his wake, hoping he'd frighten off any biting creatures and destroy all clinging spider webs in his headlong charge.

She came back to Ulf, now feeling hungry and thirsty. Wordlessly, he handed her a hunk of hard bread. He himself was already chewing. He took a swig of ale to wash down the mouthful, and held the leather bottle out to Janna. She smiled her thanks and took a few gulps. Where did Ulf come across these provisions? She looked at his bulging pack for the answer. Everything he owned must be in that pack. No wonder it was so large! Like a tortoise, he traveled with his home on his back. And yet, he'd carried it without complaint on their forced march yesterday, setting the fast pace that had brought them to Winchestre.

Ulf threw a few scraps of bread to Brutus. The dog swallowed them greedily, then put his nose to the ground and began to sniff around for something more promising. As they began the walk back along the road to Winchestre, the dog ran ahead of them. They came to a stagnant pond. Janna recognized the smell, and realized that this was where they'd briefly halted the night before. "Brutus!" Ulf yelled. But he was too late, for the dog had already plunged into the scummy water and was lapping it up with enjoyment. The water reached up to his stomach, staining his pale coat dark with dirt and mud.

With his thirst quenched, the dog began sniffing at the various objects mired in the shallows before selecting something that looked like a decaying animal. Sickened, Janna turned aside and kept on walking.

"He'll catch up with us when he's done," Ulf said cheerfully. Janna pulled her mouth down in disgust. "He'd rather eat than starve," Ulf said more seriously. "That's something you learn along the road, Janna. There isn't always a coin to pay for pies and ale and you can't always depend on charity either."

"I know." And Janna did. Even though she now carried some coins in her purse, she had known hunger in her life. But never hunger great enough to take her into a stinking pond, she acknowledged.

A massive earthen rampart loomed ahead. It was fronted by a wide ditch, which curved to their right around the castle walls. Another rampart and ditch protected the town wall to their left, the wall fortified with projecting towers at intervals for added security. The town was almost impregnable. Ulf gave a loud whistle. She glanced back to see Brutus coming up at a fast gallop. He skidded to a stop beside them and shook himself, sending a shower of filthy droplets their way.

"I hate how he does that," said Ulf, taking a quick step backward and dragging Janna out of the way as he did so, but he was too late. Janna looked down ruefully at her pretty gown. It was stained with the dust of her journey, and now bore an additional decoration of splatters of black mud. "I'm so sorry, lass," Ulf apologized, as he noted the full extent of the damage.

"I'll sponge it down; I'm sure the worst of it will come off." In spite of her reassuring words, Janna was certain she would ruin the delicate fabric if she tried. But there were other, more urgent matters to occupy her mind right now. "You know the town, Ulf. Where should we start our search for the earl, and Walter?"

"There are two, maybe three places we might try. The castle over there." He flipped a thumb to his right. "Or we can go on and through the West Gate and down the High Street. There's an old palace halfway along, close to the cathedral. I don't know if that's worth a visit." He scratched his nose, looking thoughtful. "The bishop's main palace is called Wolvesey; it's beside the river Itchen," he continued. "That's on the other side of the town. We're on Wude Street now, and there's a road leading off from here that will take us right to the Great Gate of the castle. I think it best to start our search there, for it's where the earl's most likely to be. But first, we must make a plan. What excuse shall we use to gain access to the castle?"

"I don't know." Janna stared at Ulf in dismay. "This is where we need the jongleurs!" she exclaimed. "Or could you offer to sell – I mean, show them your relics?"

Ulf brightened at the thought. "It's worth a try."

"But you won't, will you? Unpack your bag, I mean. We mustn't waste time!"

Ulf's face fell.

"We just need to find out if Robert of Gloucestre is in residence," Janna said, making sure he understood her meaning. "If he is, then you can show everyone what you've got in your pack. You can take as long as you like while I try to find the earl."

"Let's hope he's in residence then." Ulf shouldered his pack and, together, they followed the road to the drawbridge and gatehouse that formed the entrance to the castle. There they were met by a burly guard who, it seemed, took himself and his duties very seriously. Some fast talking on Ulf's part soon captured the guard's interest, though, and within moments Ulf had his pack off his back and was busy opening it.

"We are here to enquire after Robert of Gloucestre," Janna said, with a stern glance at Ulf. "Is he within?"

"Yes, but it's early yet. The earl will still be abed." The guard looked up at Janna in surprise. It seemed he'd hardly noticed her presence. Now that he had, his look turned to one of guarded suspicion. "What business do you have with him?"

"Private business."

The guard looked down his nose at Janna. "The earl does not receive *ladies* uninvited." The emphasis on the word left Janna in no doubt as to what the guard was thinking. She felt a surge of anger, but a moment's thought cooled her indignation. Let the guard think what he liked, so long as her purpose was served.

"And how do you know I am uninvited?" she asked, forcing a coquettish smile and a waggle of her hips to bolster her disguise. "He will not thank you for keeping him waiting."

The guard stared at her. Janna wondered if she'd managed to convince him.

"Very well." He gave a grudging nod. "Go to the royal apartments and state your business there." He turned to peer into the open pack in front of him.

Janna tilted her head at Ulf, for she needed him to accompany her. Reluctantly, he closed his pack. "I'll show you my treasures on the way out," he promised the guard.

There was a massive motte at each end of the bailey. The northern motte, close to the West Gate, was topped by a high stone keep that dominated its surrounds. Backing onto the wall, and close to the gate through which they'd just entered, were numerous buildings, including barns, sheds, stables and a smithy. Ahead, Janna saw a chapel along with what looked like a royal hall and apartments. Ulf steered Janna toward them. This time he had a small box ready in his hand as they approached the entrance.

"Here's something that may interest you," he told the doorkeeper. As Janna whisked through behind him and kept on going, she heard Ulf expanding on how the man's love life would improve if only he had St Valentine's tooth to intervene on his behalf.

"St Valentine is the patron saint of lovers," Ulf explained, with a hearty nudge into the man's ribs to emphasize his point. Valentine? Janna couldn't help wondering if Ulf made up the names of the saints as well as the merits of their so-called relics.

She squared her shoulders and walked into the hall with a confident air, hoping that everyone would assume she had every right to be inside the castle, although she wasn't quite sure what to say if questioned. Servant? Wife? Hostage? Harlot? She grinned to herself, thinking it fortunate that the castle's occupants seemed more concerned with breaking their fast than asking her business. Servants scuttled about, busy with chores, but they paid her no mind and Janna did her best not to attract their notice. She had no idea where she was going, but thought that if this castle was anything like the castle at Sarisberie, she would probably find the earl upstairs in a private chamber. She looked about for a staircase and, finding it, ran up it as fast as she could.

The stairs opened into a solar, comfortably furnished with table, stools and a couple of chests. Dishes, food and a jug of ale were set out on the table ready for the lord to break his fast. The walls were painted with decorative scenes. Embroidered tapestries, placed to keep out the worst of the drafts, added their own bright splashes of color. The solar was empty. Janna crept forward and cautiously peered into the room beyond. There seemed no-one there either and so she stepped inside, curious to see what a lord's bedchamber looked like.

"You! What are you doing in here?" A man dropped the straw pallets he was busy stacking and sprang out in front of her, barring her way. "How dare you enter the earl's private quarters."

"I beg your pardon, sire." Janna answered him in Norman French, as befitted the occasion. She dropped a meek curtsy, all the while staring at the huge bed that dominated the room. She gave an envious sigh as she noted the luxurious hangings that partly shrouded the feather bolster at its head, the puffed mattress, the fine white linen sheets and blue- and red-dyed coverings. Truly, one would sleep soundly every night in such a bed!

"Go on, get out of here!" The earl's manservant grasped her arm and gave her a push. But Janna gathered her scattered wits together.

"I have urgent news for my lord, the Earl of Gloucestre," she said, resisting the manservant's efforts to get rid of her. "I must talk to him without delay."

"I don't know how you gained entrance to my lord's chamber." The manservant still had Janna's arm in his hard grasp. "But you can get out again right now."

"Oh, leave the young woman be, Joss." The voice came from a side opening in the wall. A man stepped out of the garderobe, adjusting the elaborately embroidered cuffs on his sleeves. Like his half-sister, his hair was dark and Janna noted that he also had the same dark brown eyes as he surveyed her with a quizzical expression. Robert, Earl of Gloucestre, half-brother of the Empress Matilda. He was alive, unharmed, and free.

Janna felt a great relief as she sank deep into another curtsy. She waited for the earl to give her permission to rise. His eyes had widened at the sight of her, but he said nothing, merely stuck out a hose-clad foot. His manservant hastily produced a pair of leather shoes with pointed toes and knelt before him. The earl continued to scrutinize Janna as his shoes were strapped to his feet and fastened at his ankles with silver buckles. Janna began to feel increasingly uncomfortable under his gaze. She was deeply conscious of her travel-stained, mud-spattered gown, and suspected she was only moments away from eviction.

"My name is Janna, my lord," she said quickly, anxious to explain her presence in the earl's chambers. "Johanna," she amended, thinking her proper name more impressive. She stood up, frightened that she'd overbalance and fall over if she stayed in a curtsy for too much longer.

"And you have urgent news for me?" There was an expression of disbelief on the earl's face as he continued to inspect her closely. "Who are you?" he demanded unexpectedly.

"Johanna, my lord." Janna's heart sank. If the earl was so witless he couldn't even remember her name from one instant to the next, what chance did she have of convincing him of the bishop's treachery? "I am nobody important," she hurried on, "but I was traveling with a group of pilgrims recently. We came across a dead man in possession of a message written by the Bishop of Winchestre."

The earl's disbelief was replaced by an expression of utter incredulity. "Yes?" he said cautiously.

"The man had met his death through an accident, no more than that. But the message was addressed to the bishop's brother. The king."

"You may leave us, Joss." The earl waited until they were alone before gesturing to Janna to continue. She couldn't tell whether or not he believed what she was telling him as she hurried through her explanation. She could only trust that he wasn't too stupid to understand that the bishop had been against the empress right from the start and that he would know what to do about it.

But the earl surprised her with his grasp of the situation. "I already know the contents of the letter," he said, after she expressed her fear that it hadn't yet reached him. "Walter brought it to my chamber last evening past."

Janna sagged with relief, releasing tense muscles she hadn't realized were strained so tight. Walter had reached the earl first in spite of Ralph's pursuit! But the danger was by no means over. Once Ralph told the bishop what had happened, he would know then that his treachery was betrayed and that he must act to protect himself.

She must warn the earl, and Walter too, that the bishop's plot was uncovered and his agent on their trail.

Not brave enough to interrupt the earl, she forced herself to patience as he continued. "Walter told me he'd ridden hard to bring the message to me without delay and to beat the curfew, but he did not say where he'd come from, or who had given him the message. So I thank you, Johanna, for coming to see me yourself. Tell me, how do you know what Bishop Henry said in his letter?"

Janna gulped. She had no idea what the punishment was for reading a letter not intended for her eyes, even though she'd done it with the best of intentions. "Er..." She scratched around for a likely excuse. "Er..."

To her relief, the earl didn't wait for her answer. "And why should you suspect that something might have happened to Walter along the way to prevent him from bringing it to me?"

A sudden understanding of what she'd unleashed fell on Janna's shoulders with a force that almost crushed her. She lifted her chin and tried to summon up the courage to answer him truthfully. She hadn't given enough thought to the consequences of speaking so freely, and now she was trapped for, if she told the earl what he wanted to know, she would at the same time condemn to death the traitor who had promised to help her find her father.

"A stranger joined our pilgrim group some time after we encountered the dead man and found the message. The stranger told us he was a pilgrim and he traveled with us thereafter," she began, wishing that she did not have to go on. But the earl was waiting for an explanation. If she did not give it, he and Walter might fall into a trap and meet their deaths because of it.

"His name is Ralph de Otreburne," she continued reluctantly. The earl gave a slight nod. It seemed he'd heard the name before. "Walter questioned if I knew of him. I suspect he believes that his brother may have died at Ralph's hand."

"Has this Ralph de Otreburne come in pursuit of Walter? Is that why you feared something might have happened to Walter along the way?"

"Yes, my lord." Janna would have given just about anything not to have to answer the earl's questions.

"And how does he know that Walter has the message?"

"He – he found out." Janna flushed with angry shame. "As soon as he realized that I'd given Master Walter the message and that he was bound for Winchestre, he set off in pursuit."

"Then we must warn Walter that the bishop's agent is looking for him," the earl agreed.

"Yes, but there is also danger to yourself, sire," Janna pointed out.

"Yes, indeed." The earl nodded thoughtfully, his eyes never leaving Janna's face. She shifted her weight from one foot to another, not sure if she should go now or wait to be dismissed. Or did the earl want to interrogate her further?

He summoned his manservant then, who at once fumbled in his purse and drew out several silver coins. Janna put her hands behind her back and stepped away. She didn't expect to be rewarded, and was embarrassed that the earl could think that was the reason behind her warning.

"Take it," the earl advised. "You've earned it. And have no fear, mistress. I haven't been idle since learning of the bishop's treachery. I had intended to visit him today and force him to sign a public declaration of support for my sister, so buying time while I return to Oxeneford to muster our troops. After what you've told me, I must rethink this situation. But you need have no concern for Walter. He will be warned of the peril he faces from this Ralph de Otreburne. The bishop's agent will be found and brought to trial for treason, as well as for the murder of Walter's brother. Tell me, has Walter met this man? Can he identify him for me?"

"Master Walter has seen him only once, sire. I don't know if he would recognize him again." Janna knew she should volunteer to help look for Ralph, but every instinct screamed against it. Although angry at Ralph's betrayal, she quailed at the thought of him in chains, facing torture and death.

"But you must know the bishop's agent well, for you say he traveled with you for a time. So I would ask you to keep company with Walter, and ensure his safety until he leaves Winchestre. Come with me." Without waiting for a reply, the earl set off toward the stairs, snatching the coins from his manservant as he passed. These he thrust directly into Janna's hand. Not daring to defy him, she slipped them up her sleeve for safekeeping. Thirty pieces of silver, she thought, hating what the earl had asked her to do. With all her heart she wished that she could find a way out of it.

"Where is your home, Johanna?" the earl asked, as he led the way down the stairs to find Walter.

"I come from Berford, near the Forest of Gravelinges, sire. My mother was a *wortwyf* there. A herb wife," Janna amended, in case the earl didn't understand the language of the Saxons.

"And who is your father?"

Janna blushed scarlet, ashamed to tell him the truth. Yet she wasn't brave enough to lie to an earl. "I know not, sire," she admitted, shame-faced.

He swung to face her. She could read the questions in his eyes. He seemed about to say something, then checked himself and shrugged. He walked on, with Janna following him. She wanted to ask him what action he would take against the bishop, but dared not. It was with difficulty that she held her tongue.

"Walter!" The earl's bellow brought everyone in the hall instantly to attention. Janna looked about but could not see Walter among the crowd. She was relieved to note that most of the hall's occupants were soldiers all still breaking their fast. It seemed that the earl had brought with him a sizeable guard.

"Walter!" the earl bellowed again, when no-one came forward in answer to his summons. He began to move between the soldiers, peering about for the missing man. "He was here last night," he said over his shoulder to Janna.

Was Walter hiding for some reason? She felt sick as she suddenly recalled Juliana's anxious foreboding. Where was Walter, if not already dead, and by Ralph's hand?

"Get yourselves ready and wait for my instructions," the earl commanded. "And you!" He beckoned one of the soldiers forward. "Raise the cry after one Ralph de Otreburne, for he is guilty of murder and must pay the price for it. What does he look like?" He swung around to confront Janna.

Janna had thought she felt as bad as it was possible to feel. But she was wrong. This was much, much worse. She had to choose between condemning a man to death, a man whom she'd thought she might love, and who might lead her to her father, or ensuring the safety of the empress, the earl, and the future of the kingdom. And yes, also avenging the death of Bernard. Whatever choice she made, she would have to live with the consequences. Yet she knew that the choice had already been made, and that the consequences would tear her apart and bring to ruin all her hopes for the future.

Janna wanted to run away and pretend that none of this was happening. She struggled to control her emotions. Ralph had betrayed her and now she, in turn, was about to betray him. She was under no illusion about what she was being asked to do: give the earl's men a description so that they could hunt Ralph down, try him and kill him. It took all of her strength to speak, to force the words of betrayal from a throat gone dry and aching with grief.

"He wears a dark green cloak, my lord, and a red linen tunic with embroidery here, here and there." She indicated her neck, sleeves and hem. "He wears fitted breeches and fine leather boots. His hair is long and fair, and his eyes are blue. He has a mustache." She raised her hand to stroke her upper lip, indicating its shape and size. "And a short beard."

"I see you know him well," the earl said dryly, twisting the knife deeper into Janna's heart. The soldiers smirked as they looked at her. She wished, suddenly and desperately, that it was within her power to click her fingers and just disappear.

The earl turned back to his men, who instantly stiffened to attention under his steely gaze. "Get out and look for Ralph de Otreburne," he barked. "If he couldn't reach the bishop last night, it may be that we can still intercept him. Also watch out for Walter, and warn him that he was followed to Winchestre. He'll know what to do. Be ready to wait on me at noon, when I myself will call on the bishop. We'll leave Winchestre straight afterward."

He turned and jerked his head, indicating to Janna that she should precede him from the hall. "I will also send the castle servants out to look for Walter," he told her, not troubling to disguise his concern. "May I suggest that you accompany them, mistress?"

"I will gladly go in search of Master Walter, my lord," Janna agreed, "but please, will you give me leave to go straightaway? Every moment's delay is a moment wasted." Should she look for Ralph as well as Walter? She felt sickened by what she'd just done. But if she saw him, what then? Could she warn him that the cry had been raised against him? Her stomach churned, her heart and mind were twisted with indecision.

"Very well, you may go."

The earl was about to stride away when Janna's concern for his safety got the better of her.

"My lord," she said impulsively, and then stopped, overcome by the enormity of her folly. He paused, and gave her an enquiring look. Janna had no option but to brazen it out. "The bishop. You cannot trust him, my lord! Once he finds out that his treachery is known, you'll be in the gravest danger, for he won't change sides, no matter what he might tell you. If you call on him this noon, you run the risk that he'll act against you, for he'll have nothing to lose and everything to gain if he can take you prisoner."

"Do you think I'm too stupid to have worked that out for myself?" The earl's face darkened into fury. Yet something stopped him from berating her for her unwanted advice. Janna watched as his eyes narrowed into careful scrutiny once more. "Who are you?" he asked again.

"Johanna, sire." Janna was getting a little tired of this.

"You remind me…"

Janna waited for him to say the empress's name, and had her explanation ready on her lips.

"Of my father," the earl said unexpectedly.

"My lord?" Janna lifted one eyebrow, hardly feeling flattered to be compared to a man, even if he was a king!

The earl grinned. "A trick of the light," he said. "You are exceedingly impertinent, Johanna, but you interest me greatly. And you haven't yet told me how you know what the bishop said in his letter."

Janna groaned inwardly. "I read it, sire," she confessed.

"You can read?" The earl stared at her. Janna wanted to run, to escape the wrath she was sure was to fall on her head. She took a deep breath, and stood her ground. "I spent a year in an abbey, sire. Wiltune Abbey." She'd already said too much, so she might as well go all the way. "I saw your half-sister there, sire," she said. "The Empress Matilda. I was thought to resemble her as well." That would teach him to compare her to the old king!

"By God, so you do," he said softly, and stepped closer.

"I admire her greatly, sire, and I would do anything to help her onto the throne." Janna was sure now that she had gone too far, and that the earl's fury would blow her away. But he stood silent for a moment, still watching her.

"We may well call on you to honor that promise, one day," he said quietly. "But for now I have other things on my mind, including your warning about the bishop. I shall see what he has to say for himself. And I shall call him to account, you may be sure of it. But I shall also have my soldiers at my back to guard me while I do so."

With a curt farewell, he strode off, leaving Janna to find her own way out of the castle. She almost flew out of the hall, so great was her relief at escaping unscathed. Agitation mingled with exhilaration. She had stood up to an earl, and had lived to tell the tale! She couldn't wait to tell Ulf what she'd done.

But what *had* she done? Condemned Ralph to be hunted like an animal, hunted and put to death. Crushing guilt and sorrow returned like a dead weight. Her shoulders slumped under the burden of her distress.

Chapter 14

Ulf came to meet her, obviously hoping to show off his relics within. His face fell when she insisted that he turn around and leave with her. "We have to find Walter and warn him about Ralph," she said, after she'd told him of her meeting with Rober of Gloucestre. "You can come back with your relics some other time."

To her relief, Ulf didn't argue. "You've got a nerve talking to an earl like that," he said admiringly, as they skirted a well and continued across the bailey.

Janna felt a momentary pride, but the sick feeling came back as the urgency of their search pushed all other considerations from her mind. "I've told them about Ralph," she confessed miserably. "They've gone in search of him. They'll try him and kill him, Ulf, and it's all my fault."

"How in the name of the good Lord God do you work that one out?"

"I had to describe him to the earl's men."

"Good," Ulf said briskly. "That'll be one less piece of vermin on the street!"

Janna gasped in shock. Ulf shrugged. "It was Ralph's choice to involve himself in the bishop's affairs. And it was his choice to lie and cheat and kill to achieve his ends – yes, even sweet-talking you to help his cause. You've done nowt, lass, except call him to account for his actions. He's murdered a good and innocent man, remember, and may kill another if we don't get to Walter first. So don't torment yourself, for he's not worth a whit of your care."

"Bernard's only dead because I told Ralph about the letter in the first place," Janna admitted in a small voice.

Ulf glanced sideways at her, but made no comment.

"Not everything about the letter; I just let slip that there was one." Janna knew there was no excuse for it, none at all. Ulf continued to watch her.

"If I hadn't said anything, Bernard would still be alive." It was like worrying a sore tooth – she couldn't stop thinking about it.

Ulf sighed. "Don't take too much of the blame on yourself, Janna. Just think on this: Ralph must have heard about the death of the bishop's messenger, and would have taken care to view his body at Wiltune and also search it. He knew the letter had gone and that you and Bernard were first on the scene. That was why he followed us. Really, there's no mystery about it. He would have known that one or other of us had the message. You just made it a bit easier for him to find out who, that's all. He would have worked it out soon enough for himself."

Janna was silent as she considered Ulf's words. They eased the ache in her heart, but only slightly. She was still silent as they came to the gatehouse that would take them directly into the town.

"You can't pass here." A guard stepped into their path, blocking their way.

"I am a relic seller." Ulf was about to pull open his pack, but the guard's upthrust arm made him pause.

"A relic seller? Then you will pass through the West Gate like everyone else, and pay your dues just the same as any other trader."

"I could show you wonders..." Ulf began, eager not to have to retrace their steps, but even more eager to ingratiate himself with the guards of the castle.

"Get on your way!" The man flicked his hand in a dismissive gesture, as if sweeping muck off the streets.

Ulf looked at him. The guard stared back. Ulf was the first to look away. "Come, Janna," he said curtly. "We're wasting our time here." He turned and stomped off, muttering something under his breath that sounded as if he believed the guard's mother had consorted with a pig.

Smothering a grin, Janna followed him. Once at the gate through which they'd first entered, Ulf wasted no time in hefting his pack off his back and opening it.

"No!" Janna swatted it closed with an impatient hand.

"Hoy! You said you'd show me something special," the guard said indignantly, as she dragged the reluctant Ulf through the gate.

"I'll be back!" Ulf shouted. Janna had no doubt that he would.

They followed the line of the ditch, the high walls and earthen ramparts that guarded the town until they came to the mighty gate that served as a portal for all roads from the west and north. Janna left the talking to Ulf, who had been to Winchestre before and who greeted the surly gatekeeper like a long-lost friend. It seemed the man resented being dragged from his bed upstairs to open the gate every morning. Even the presentation of a tin scallop shell "from the tomb of St James of Compostela" failed to curb his grumbling, although it did serve to take the place of a toll. Janna was a little taken aback when the gatekeeper mistook them for father and daughter, but Ulf made no effort to correct his mistake.

"So," she said, as they passed through the gate and looked down at the town spread before them. "You know Winchestre, or so you say. Where should we start our search for Master Walter?"

Ulf pointed down the street on which they were standing, which sloped toward the center of the town. It was paved with flints, but narrow. A gutter ran along its length, a repository for animal bones, scraps of rotten vegetables and other bits of detritus. A couple of mangy dogs scavenged about. They growled when they noticed Brutus, but quickly retreated when the huge dog began to chase them.

Ulf whistled the alaunt back to his side." We can cover more distance if we search separately," he said, and gestured down the length of the street. "This is the High Street, and it runs right through the town to the East Gate on the other side. Why don't I take one side of the street and you the other?"

"What if Walter's already dead? What if we're too late?" Janna gave voice to what she most dreaded.

"I doubt anything's happened to him," Ulf comforted her. "Not yet, any road. He obviously came straight to the earl, and it sounds as if the earl expected him still to be within the castle."

"Why, then, do you think he left without asking the earl's permission?"

Ulf shrugged. "He may have wanted to get back to his family in Oxeneford. Or take a message back to the empress that the bishop's letter has been found. Or go to Sarisberie to be with his mother while Adam is interrogated."

"Adam!" Janna had forgotten all about him in her anxiety over Ralph and Walter. "He's innocent of Bernard's death. We have to let them know at Sarisberie!"

"Aye. Adam is innocent of this crime at least." Ulf patted Janna's arm, seeking to allay her anxiety. "Walter will know what to do. If we can't find him, then I'll go back to Sarisberie myself. I'll talk to the constable and to Dame Juliana. They can decide what's to be done with Adam."

Janna could take no comfort from Ulf's promise. She was tense and anxious. A dreadful foreboding clouded her mind, a dark shadow that she could not banish. "Death follows you," Juliana had told her.

And so it had. First the courier, although his death had been an accident. Bernard, too, had died. Was Juliana now going to lose another son because of her? She trembled at the thought that she was to blame, and that she might already be too late. As for Ralph, he was now a hunted man. He, too, would die because of her.

"Janna." Ulf took her arm, concern creasing his forehead. "Watch out for Ralph. Take care not to cross his path. If you see him you must hide, for he knows that you also have knowledge of the letter. That makes you dangerous to him."

Stricken, Janna stared at Ulf. He was right to warn her, she knew that. But it was hard, so hard to reconcile what she now knew of Ralph with the man she'd once thought him to be. She was filled with anguish as she remembered the kisses they'd shared, and the love in his voice when he spoke of his family. Nor could she forget his promise to help her solve the mystery of her father. A worthless promise? Or could it have been truly meant, even if at the same time he was making use of her?

Ulf padded across the street and was soon lost to view. Unsure what to do or where to start looking, Janna began to stroll slowly along, hoping for a clue. The town was becoming more crowded now. Pedlars walked about with packs on their backs, singing out their wares, pursued by housewives and servants with noses a-sniff for an early bargain. Shutters opened one by one and goods were put out to tempt the passers-by. She averted her eyes from the bloody carcasses on display in the butchers' stalls, and strolled on, keeping careful watch about her for signs of either Walter or Ralph. Her mind thrashed in turmoil; she could not decide what to do. What if she saw Ralph? He had betrayed her, and now he was a hunted man. Should she take Ulf's advice and hide if she saw him? Should she raise the cry against him?

No! She felt bereft just thinking about it. She'd done enough. It was up to the earl's men to find him – if they could. Uppermost in

Janna's mind was the thought that Ralph might hold the key to her father's identity. If she saw him, she must take the chance to ask him what he knew. A plan began to form. Something given for something in return? If Ralph told her what he knew of her father, she would warn him that he was a hunted man. Surely there could be no danger in that. Not to Walter, for she would tell Ralph that the earl had received the message and the bishop's treachery was already known. She could persuade Ralph that it was up to him now to save himself. Perhaps he could flee Winchestre in disguise?

No, she thought. Set against her own interests was the fact that Ralph was the bishop's agent, and a killer. He must not be left free to kill again. Ulf had warned her to be careful, and Ulf was probably right. An image of Bernard's bloody corpse lying across the stone altar flashed through her mind. If she warned Ralph to escape, Walter and his mother would be denied justice for Bernard's death, and that she couldn't condone.

With the decision made, Janna walked on. Might as well hunt for a pip in a cornfield, she thought despairingly, as she peered into shops and searched the faces of the people she passed. What if Walter had already left Winchestre and gone to Sarisberie? But what if he was indoors somewhere, perhaps visiting one of the houses close by? She could hardly knock on doors and ask for him on the slight chance he might be inside.

She wondered what Ulf was doing, whether he'd had any luck. If he found Walter, he had no way of letting her know, for they'd made no arrangement to meet later on. She clicked her tongue in exasperation, and looked about in case she could spy him. The stocky figure of a man hurrying ahead of her caught her attention. She squinted up her eyes to see him better. Walter? She began to run after him, but the man had disappeared. Telling herself that her eyes were playing tricks on her, conjuring up what she wished to see rather than what was really there, she slowed down to catch her breath.

There was a high stone wall on her right. Janna recalled that Ulf had mentioned an old palace and thought this must be where it was situated. Small stalls abutted the wall along its length, with an array of wares set out under their sloping roofs. Set into the wall was an iron grille with a stout wooden door beyond. There was no-one about. Was the palace abandoned? Obviously the earl was staying in the castle rather than with the bishop, while Ulf had told her that the bishop had a palace close to the river. Clearly, this was not it.

Janna stopped for a moment to think, while her gaze automatically sifted the passers-by, searching for anyone who looked familiar. What would Ralph do, once he realized he was too late to intercept Walter? If he had any sense he'd go to the bishop at Wolvesey Palace, for only the bishop's protection could keep him safe now. But if Ralph had reached the bishop, the bishop would know that his treachery was uncovered and thus the earl and his men would lose the advantage of surprise. On the other hand, if Ralph wasn't at Wolvesey, it meant he was probably still hunting for Walter. Janna's steps quickened. She would never forgive herself if something happened to Walter, if she was too late to save his life.

Filled with a new sense of urgency, she hurried on, giving churches, alehouses, a mint, and a wool store each a cursory inspection. A high spire and towers loomed into view on her right, dwarfing the buildings between them and the street where Janna stood. Perhaps the bishop was in his cathedral, and his agent with him? On reflection, Janna thought it more likely he'd be sitting in his palace like a spider in its web, weaving plots with his agents and his courtiers about him.

Her footsteps took her on past a mill. She heard the rushing of the water wheel, the rattle of grain being fed down the chute, the grinding roar of the millstones. Beyond the mill was another length of stone wall. The bishop's palace?

"That's the Nunnaminster," said a passer-by, in answer to Janna's question. "The convent of St Mary." Certainly no chance of finding Walter there, or Ralph either.

Here, close to the East Gate, canals ran down the sides of the streets, the water scummy with refuse and tainted with the stink from the labors of tanners and dyers. Janna wrinkled up her nose, recognizing the smell. A man was busy untethering his horse from a post at the far side of the gate. Janna watched as he mounted. She was almost sure, but took a moment to scrutinize him more carefully. Walter! He raised a hand in farewell to the guard. He seemed in a hurry to be gone.

"Walter!" Janna shouted, and began to run. He checked and looked behind him. Janna was sure he'd seen her but, to her amazement, he didn't stop. Instead, he kicked his horse into a gallop, dodging carts and horsemen with an agility that spoke of long years in the saddle. Even though she knew it was futile, Janna ran after him through the gate, across the river and on down the road, shouting his name. But Walter's horse was fast and he was quickly lost to sight.

She stopped, exhausted, and bent over to ease the pain in her side. *Aelfshot*, the Saxons called it, believing that bodily pain was caused by small darts or arrows shot by elves. Janna, however, knew that she only suffered pain like this when she'd run too far and too fast. She also knew that all the prayers and chants, the herbs, precious stones and other cures her mother had taught her counted for nothing. The pain would wear off all by itself once she had rested.

She took comfort from the fact that Walter was alive and was probably out of danger now that he had left Winchestre, but she couldn't help feeling annoyed that he hadn't stopped to heed her warning or even hear her reminder about Adam's innocence in Bernard's death. Surely he owed her that courtesy, at least.

When the pain in her side had lessened, she turned back to the town and walked slowly along the road until she came to the bridge across the river. The river was much broader than the narrow race that fed the mill, but it too bore traces of the tanners' and dyers' trade. It was deep in parts, and lined on either side with drooping willows that trailed green fronds into the swiftly flowing water. Now that there was no longer an urgent need to find Walter, Janna's thoughts returned to Ralph. Had he confessed to the bishop that the earl had received the letter intended for the king? Would he be punished for his failure to intercept it? Would he know, by now, that the cry had gone out for his arrest?

Ulf had warned her to stay away from Ralph, but Janna was still desperate to find out what she could about her father. The thought of the lies Ralph had told her, and his betrayal, cut her heart to shreds. He was a cold-blooded killer, she knew that. But in all his dealings with her he had been kind, at least until the end. And even then, with so much at stake, he had not raised his hand against her. Surely it wouldn't hurt just to look for him? If she found him, she could decide then what to say to him. But where was the bishop's palace, and how was she to gain entry?

Ulf had said that Wolvesey was beside the river. She glanced up and down the river's length to see if she could sight it. Tall stone towers rose high above the trees downriver. She thought that might be it, but it wasn't obvious whether the palace was situated within or outside the city walls. She debated going back through the East Gate, but she'd be trapped there if the entrance to the palace, like that of the castle, was outside the town walls. Besides, the small track winding down beside the river looked shady and inviting, and she was thirsty. Making up her mind, and feeling somewhat happier now she had a plan of action, she crossed the bridge and hurried down the steps to the river path.

A pair of swans paddled into the shallows. They stopped, and one of the swans bent its long neck. It stuck out a webbed foot for balance and began to groom itself, rubbing its beak along its snowy feathers, nuzzling them into order. A family of ducks waddled down to the river's edge. They launched themselves into the rushing water, quacking their contentment. So had swans and ducks lived here for centuries past, raising their families and hunting for food, not knowing or caring about the affairs of men and the misery they caused. Janna sought consolation in the thought that in time, her misery, too, would pass. One day she would look back and wonder why Ralph's betrayal had hurt her so badly, and why the battle between king and cousin had seemed so vitally important. One day perhaps – but not now.

The sound of rippling water accompanied her passage, as did the small family of ducks, spinning downward with the current and using their webbed feet to slow their headlong rush toward the mill that Janna could see in the distance. The river ran very shallow in parts. Colored pebbles lay like jewels along its bed, visible even in the cloudy water but shrouded sometimes by long green strands of cress that waved and coiled with the river's rapid flow. Black moorhens flicked their white tails and poked red beaks into the vegetation along the river's edge. A flash of blue caught Janna's eye. A kingfisher hovered over the water for a moment, then dived to capture a small fish. Laden, it hastened back to its perch where it beat the fingerling against a branch before swallowing it head first. Janna craned her neck to watch it as she walked along, admiring the jeweled flashes of blue and green as its feathers caught the sunlight.

The gurgle of the river as it sped toward the mill reminded Janna that she was thirsty, and hungry too, for she'd had little to eat bar a scrap of dry bread and a mouthful of ale. She knelt beside the river and, hoping that it was safe enough to drink, scooped handfuls of water into her mouth, relishing the liquid as it slipped down her dry throat. Catching sight of her gown as she knelt, she edged closer so that she was close enough to dip the worst of the muddy spots into the water. She would need to look respectable if she was to gain access to the bishop's palace, and so she rubbed the fabric between her fingers to loosen the dirt. The water might well stain her gown but at least it would be clean. Unlike her! Janna ducked her head, lifted her elbow, and surreptitiously sniffed her armpit. And blinked hard a few times. The sweat of the journey, particularly the fast march to Winchestre, had left its mark. She cast a quick glance up and down the length of the river. Was it lonely and private enough to strip off her gown and join the ducks in the river for a quick splash?

The sight of a man reclining under a willow tree some distance away gave her a jolt. She hadn't noticed him before, he lay so still. Regretfully she stood up, abandoning her plans. She continued to walk, planning to tiptoe around him without disturbing him. He was so quiet, she thought he must be asleep.

As she came closer, she saw that he lay sprawled over a low-lying rock. Janna jerked to a stop. Her body reacted to the sight even before her mind could accept the truth in front of her. She began to shake, her whole body quivering with reaction. But she could not move, could not run. Her limbs felt leaden, her brain too numb to command action. All she could do was feel what she could see, even while her mind refused to comprehend it.

She crossed her arms and clutched her fists to her chest, and fought to regain control. Hot tears blinded her. She dashed them away so that she could look again, even though she didn't want to see. Nor did she want to believe. His face, so familiar, was turned up so that he gazed into the green fountain of weeping willow fronds. He wore a red tunic, dark red at its center and fading to a lighter red elsewhere. He lay still, unmoving. He was no phantom of her imagination. He was real. And he was dead.

Janna pushed aside the trailing fronds of willow. She forced herself to take a step forward, and then another, and another, until she came close enough to look down, to see, and finally, to understand.

Ralph lay before her, a gaping wound at his throat. Blood stained the front of his tunic a darker hue. Blood had also spilled from the wound and over the stone to soak into the earth below. For a moment Ralph's face blurred and Janna saw Bernard stretched out and bleeding over the stone altar and the ground below. She blinked, and Ralph's features came clear into her vision once more. His eyes stared into hers, blinded by death. He wore an expression of faint surprise. Had he recognized his killer? Had he understood that justice was about to be done?

She knelt beside him. Reaching out a shaking hand, she closed his eyes, needing to escape the gaze that had so transfixed her in life. After a moment's hesitation, she touched his cheek. "*Requiescat in pace,*" she whispered. It was more than Ralph deserved, yet he had died unshriven. At the end, she cared enough about him to wish that he might find redemption for his soul.

And then the full extent of her loss burst upon her, and she began to weep without restraint. Weep for the death of a man she'd once imagined as a husband and lover, and who had betrayed all her hopes and her dreams. She knelt beside him, and bitterly reproached herself. Why, oh why, hadn't she insisted right from the start that he tell her all he knew about her father? Instead, she had let herself be gulled by him, flattered and charmed into believing that he genuinely cared for her.

A sudden thought stifled Janna's weeping. Had Ralph courted her because he hoped to advantage his situation through her father? She thought back to the time when she'd shown him her father's ring. It was certainly possible. True, he'd treated her with courtesy from the start, but had doubled his attentions after that. So what did that tell her about Ralph? More important, what did it tell her about her father?

She searched Ralph's face for answers, but he still wore the same expression of surprise that told her nothing. Instinctively, she looked for his belt and scrip. He wore them still. His assassin had wanted revenge for a brother's death. He'd not had theft in mind when he killed Ralph.

Janna sucked in a quick breath and then, before she had time to think about it, she quickly unfastened Ralph's scrip and groped inside. Her searching fingers touched a small leather pouch. She pulled it out and stared at it. It took a few moments to recognize what she held: Winifred's purse! At once she opened it, although she could already tell that it was empty. The hand had gone. Given to the bishop to compensate for the lost letter? Janna wondered if Bishop Henry considered such a prize a fair exchange for having his treachery known to all.

But how had Ralph come by Winifred's purse? She remembered then the scene in the alehouse, the drunken sot who had lurched into their table and almost fallen into her lap. Ralph must have seized on the diversion to cut the purse from Winifred's girdle. But why? He couldn't have known about the hand because she'd warned Winifred not to tell him, not to tell anyone.

Janna cast her mind back, trying to remember if anything had been said to alert Ralph to the fact that Winifred might own something precious. She remembered that Winifred had mentioned their "unfinished business," and had gestured toward her purse at the same time. A giveaway sign for anyone with a suspicious mind. Had Ralph offered to accompany Winifred in her search for Ulf in the hope that she might show him the letter he thought was concealed in her purse? Winifred had mentioned she'd had the devil's own task in shaking him off so that she could speak to Ulf in private. Janna nodded thoughtfully. Thwarted of his quarry, Ralph must then have cut off her purse to see for himself what it contained. What a surprise he must have had!

It was one mystery solved, although Janna greatly regretted that the bishop would profit from Winifred's wrongdoing. Suppressing a shudder, she felt about in Ralph's scrip to see if there was anything else of interest. Her fingers touched something, a scrap of parchment, judging from the feel of it. Had the bishop written another letter, and was Ralph on his way to deliver it when he was killed? If so, it would certainly be worth reading!

Janna drew it out and unfolded it. Only a few words were penned on it and she read them without difficulty. "John fitz Henry, Alwarene Street."

John. The name leaped to her eye. Ralph had known several men with the name of John, so he'd told her. Was this one of his friends? Or was this her father's name, and the name of the street where he lived?

Janna stared down at the parchment in her hand. She'd begun to shake again, but this time with excitement and hope. Could it be? Had Ralph kept his promise to her, in this at least? Or was she chasing after shadows, wanting to believe the best of a man who had shown himself capable of deceit and betrayal, theft and murder? John fitz Henry! Her father?

Her stomach was roiling; she thought she was going to be sick. She clutched the parchment tight and held it close.

A sudden commotion startled her. A huge pale dog had launched itself into the river in hot pursuit of the ducks. They scattered in alarm, quacking their terror. The dog surged through the water, barking and snapping after them. His barking stopped as he crunched down into feathers. Brutus. Several swans sailed regally past, favoring the dog and its prey with a sidelong sneer before lifting their heads and extending their long necks as proof of their superiority.

Janna looked about for the dog's owner. Ulf was hurrying along the river bank, his pack bouncing on his shoulders as he rushed to call his dog to heel. He was carrying something in his hand. He hadn't seen her. Having learned to stay well away from Brutus while he was wet, Janna stood up and waited while Ulf whistled Brutus to his side. She watched as the dog shook itself, showering its master in a waterfall of drops. That done, it lay down and began to devour the duckling, feathers and all.

Knowing she was safe for the moment, Janna called out to Ulf.

His steps faltered as he caught sight of Ralph. His face paled as he realized what had happened and who it was lying so still beside her. Then he hurried forward and put his arms around her. She leaned into him and cried all over again for the man who had wooed her, who had betrayed her trust, and who had died such a horrible death. And she cried also for what she had done that had brought about such a bloody conclusion. Juliana had been right; death had followed her from the start. If she could undo anything in the world, it would be her careless words to Ralph that had spelled Bernard's doom and, ultimately, Ralph's too.

"Walter's doing?" Ulf said quietly.

Janna nodded.

"And he is?"

"Gone." Janna jerked a thumb in the direction of the East Gate.

Ulf pursed his mouth. "I'll wager he'll be finding his way back to Sarisberie. He'll want to tell his mother that he has avenged Bernard's death."

"And Adam will be exonerated – of that murder, at least." Janna gave a mournful sniff, and wiped her red eyes on her sleeve.

"I'm sorry, lass." Ulf patted her hand, trying to bring comfort. "I know you cared for Ralph. If it's any consolation, I think he cared for you too. It was only time and circumstances that..." He lifted his shoulders in a shrug.

Janna wanted to believe him. If Ralph had cared for her as much as Ulf thought, he might well have taken the time to ask questions about her father, and to write down what he'd found out. Wordlessly, she unclenched her hand and showed Ulf the scrap of parchment.

"I can't read," Ulf confessed. "What does it say?"

"John fitz Henry. Alwarene Street." Janna's heart gave a sudden kick of excitement. Suddenly her father seemed very close.

"Is it important?"

"I came to Winchestre to see if I could find my unknown father. I showed Ralph his ring. It has a crest on it and I think Ralph recognized what it meant. He promised to help me look for him." Janna's voice faltered. She had to swallow hard before she could continue. "I found the parchment in his scrip, along with this." She held out Winifred's purse.

Ulf's eyes widened. He began to laugh. "I suppose it's empty?"

Janna nodded.

"Poor Winifred. Her loss is the bishop's gain, I suspect?"

Janna nodded again.

"But Ralph thought Winifred might have the letter. That's why he cut her purse?"

"Yes."

"Bastard!"

Ulf, Janna reflected, was a man and so he wouldn't have been as susceptible to Ralph's charms as she had been. He would not have been taken in, as she was. And Ulf was right. There was nothing good to be said about Ralph's character, nothing at all.

Perhaps regretting his judgment, or at least his means of expressing it, Ulf held out to her what he'd been carrying. It was a swan's feather, white and downy soft. "Thank you, Ulf." Janna was touched by his kindness.

"A feather from the wing of the archangel Gabriel," he said solemnly.

Janna didn't know whether to laugh or be reverent. She looked at the twinkle in his eyes, and took the risk of smiling.

"It'll bring you comfort."

Janna raised a questioning eyebrow.

"It will also bring you luck, if you believe in it," Ulf assured her.

"Then I'll believe in it," Janna told him, reflecting that if he spent some time along the river bank, he'd probably find enough angel feathers for an entire fluffy wing.

Her thoughts were echoed when Ulf said, with a glimmer of a smile, "If the good bishop is a collector of relics, I should pay him a visit."

Janna held out the feather, but Ulf brushed it away. "No," he said. "That's yours." He looked at the parchment in Janna's hand. "Alwarene Street," he said. "I know where that is. Do you want to go there?"

"What, now?" Janna's hands felt clammy. She suddenly found it hard to catch her breath. "But what about...?" She gestured toward Ralph's body.

"Leave it be. There's nowt you can do for him, and we don't want to be caught up in the hue and cry after his killer, do we now? So we'll just pretend we've seen nowt and know nowt, and we'll go looking for your father instead. Come on." Ulf hooked his arm through hers and, not giving her any chance to come up with an excuse, he began to hurry back along the river bank in the direction of the East Gate, whistling to Brutus as they went.

"No! Wait!" Janna wanted a moment's privacy before facing the crowds along Chepe Street. "I have my father's ring here in my purse." She touched the small bulge through the fabric of her gown. "It might help us to find him."

Ulf nodded, and turned his back while she hurried between the sheltering fronds of a willow tree.

"May I see it?" he asked when she came back to him, clutching the ring tight in one hand and the swan's feather in the other.

His eyes widened as she handed it to him. "Are you sure this belongs to your father?"

"Yes! Well, no. I'm not sure. But I think so. I found it along with a letter to my mother." Janna was puzzled by the glint in Ulf's eyes and the dawning excitement on his face. "See, here?" She traced the J of the swan. "My father's name is John, so it seems likely that this is his ring. Doesn't it?"

"Christ's bones!" Ulf let out an incredulous whistle. "Do you know what this is?" he asked, touching the crown at the side of the swan.

"It means that my father was loyal to the king. Not King Stephen," she added quickly, lest Ulf mistake her. "He only came to the throne after my father gave this ring to my mother."

"No. What it means is that your father was probably a bastard."

"What?" Anger flared bright. Janna swung her hand back to strike Ulf. How dare he compare her father with Ralph!

Ulf pushed her hand away. "That's not a reflection on his character, not this time," he said, with a wry smile. "What I'm saying is that your father was illegitimate. His name says that he is John, son of Henry, and so does his ring. He's one of the old king's bastards."

"But...but – " Janna was having trouble understanding what Ulf was trying to tell her. "What does that mean?"

Ulf smiled. "It means," he said gravely, "that you are the granddaughter of a king!"

Chapter 15

Janna was hardly conscious of the crowds thronging the High Street as Ulf pushed his way through, dragging her along in his wake. She was still fighting to come to grips with what he'd told her and what it meant for her future. What was most on her mind was the realization of Ralph's final betrayal: that he must have recognized the insignia on the ring right from the start and determined to use her to better his own position. No wonder he'd treated her with such respect! He didn't love her at all, it was her connection to the crown that he coveted.

This confirmation of his final betrayal was shattering. But Janna knew she could not dwell on it, for they were on their way to meet her father and she must focus, now, on the ordeal that lay ahead. She was the granddaughter of a king! She was the illegitimate daughter of an illegitimate son of the king! There was a small warmth in thinking that, if her father's birth was also in question, he must surely look more kindly on her birth, on the fact of her existence.

Questions tumbled through her mind. Did Eadgyth know who she was bedding when she went off with John? Did she know she was consorting with royalty? If so, why didn't she go to the old king and demand his help once she realized she was with child? Was she too ashamed? Or was she afraid that if she found the king she might also find her lover, married and living happily with someone else? Not having read John's letter, she didn't know how much he'd loved her and that he planned to return.

Yes, Janna thought, as she walked along with Ulf. Her mother's fear of encountering her lover no doubt kept her as far from the old king as possible. And now she, her daughter, was about to meet John for the very first time! Would her father be at home? What would he look like, how would he greet her? Would he be glad to see her, this reminder of his past, or would he send her on her way? What if he was wed? What if his wife was home and sent Janna away before she had the chance to meet her father? One moment Janna felt her spirits lift in excitement and hope, and the next she was cast down in despair.

Ulf kept glancing sideways at her as they walked along, but he did not speak. Perhaps he sensed her turmoil and realized she needed time to get used to her new, strange circumstances. Janna was grateful for his silence. He turned to the right, and then stopped so suddenly that Janna bumped into him.

"It's quite a long street," he said." There'll be several estates along it, I'll be bound. How shall we know which is the right one?"

Janna surveyed the warehouses and shopfronts that lined the street, and realized that locating her father might not be quite so easy as she'd hoped. "If my father is the king's son, would he own a shop?" she asked.

"I don't know. I know nowt of how royal families conduct themselves." Ulf scratched his head. "Why don't we ask someone?"

Sighting two men in conversation outside one of the shops, they crossed over to speak to them. "Can you tell us where we might find John fitz Henry?" Janna asked, holding out the ring to them.

"That's Sire John to you, mistress," one of the men reproved her. The other studied the ring in silence, then gestured in the direction of the town walls. "His manor's up near the North Gate."

Janna started walking, anxious to get there as fast as she could, to outpace her growing fear. All she wanted was for her father to love her and to welcome her, and make her part of his family, if he had one. That was what she most desired. But first, she had to find the courage to see this through. She walked ahead of Ulf, her quick strides betraying her nervousness.

Ulf tugged on her sleeve to slow her down. "Have you thought what you're going to say to your father when we get there?"

Janna shook her head. "I'm too frightened to think," she admitted breathlessly. "Oh, Ulf, you don't know how I've longed for this moment. I was never sure I'd succeed in finding my father. And now…" She smiled at him, full of wonder at the moment.

"Whatever happens, I'm here and I'll help you," he promised.

Janna was grateful for his reassuring presence for they had to ask several times before they were finally directed to an imposing door set within a tall wall. A bell attached to a rope invited their attention, and Ulf gave it a hearty tug before Janna could stop him. Now that the time had come, she was sweating with terror. She needed a few moments to compose herself. But their arrival was announced and she must deal with the situation as best she could.

The door opened and a short, fat man peered out. Was this her father? Surely she should feel something, some stirring of recognition, some calling of the blood? But Janna felt nothing other than fear.

"Yes?" His glance raked first Ulf and then Janna. It was clear from his expression that he was not impressed by what he saw. His mouth turned into a tight bud of disapproval when he looked down at Brutus, who now sported a ruff of bloodied feathers around his muzzle.

"We seek Sire John, if you please," Janna announced, having learned her lesson. The man bobbed his head, showing a round bald spot at his crown fringed by a rim of greying hair.

"What is your business here?"

"I have his ring." Janna showed it to him.

The man's eyes widened, and he visibly gulped. "I'll fetch the steward straightaway," he said, as he opened the door wider. He beckoned them to follow him through a large hall to a room at the back of the imposing townhouse.

"Please wait here in the scriptorium. Make yourselves comfortable, I pray you," he said, gesturing toward several stools. Without waiting for their reply, he vanished once more. Janna had noticed a flight of stairs which led to rooms above the scriptorium. From the time she'd spent at Hugh's manor, she suspected they might be her father's solar and living chambers. Soon now, he would come to her.

She walked over and peered up, wondering why the steward had to be fetched when it was her father she wanted to see. Was he up there now, in his private chambers? Would he, by some chance, sense who was waiting downstairs for him, waiting to come into his life? Would he see something of Eadgyth in her daughter? Was he, even now, on his way down the stairs to maybe greet her with a kiss and a warm embrace? Janna was tense with anticipation and fear.

But no-one came, and time wore on. Seeking distraction, she moved over to a table and picked up some pages of parchment. They were scribed with notes and numbers which seemed to be names of properties and descriptions of goods to be sold or traded. Janna looked at the writing, wondering if this was her father's script and these were his accounts. "Do you think that man's forgotten us?"

"The steward's obviously in no hurry to see us." Ulf looked at Janna. "It might be as well," he suggested, "if while we wait, you tell me everything you know about your father just in case this steward proves obstructive and needs persuading. I know you went to the abbey at Ambresberie to question the nuns. What did you find out? Why did your mother tell you so little about him? And why are you so anxious to find him now?"

The last was a question that Janna wouldn't answer. The true cause of her mother's death and her reason for finding her father were best kept secret. But she told him everything else, including her mother's belief that her father had abandoned them.

"Come with me." The fat servant's reappearance took Janna by surprise, so lost was she in recounting the past. He bustled them out of the house, panting after his exertions. "The steward's in the orchard," he said, by way of explanation. "I didn't know where to find him."

Janna chafed with impatience. She didn't want to waste time talking to the steward if her father was upstairs in his solar. But it seemed they had no choice but to follow their guide. She looked about her, drinking in every detail as they passed a storeroom crammed with bales of wool and a long workroom thrumming with industry.

A sunny garden now spread in front of them, with a well at its center. Janna gazed wide-eyed at rows of vegetables, flowers and herbs, growing tall and lush in the summer sunshine. There was ample here to feed her father – and his family, if he had one – plus a whole retinue of servants. Janna looked behind her in a vain effort to see through the windows of the floor above the scriptorium. Was that a shadow moving there? Was her father, even now, looking down upon them and wondering who they were?

The doorkeeper had veered off to one side of the garden, which was screened by trees. Janna turned to follow him into the orchard. It was densely planted with trees of varying size and shape. Janna recognized apple and pear trees; the fruits were still green and hard, but they would swell and ripen in autumn. She became aware that her jaw was clenched tight. Her heart leaped about, crazy as a grasshopper in a field of wheat. She took a long, slow breath and made a conscious effort to relax.

Their guide hurried up to a man who was sitting at ease beneath an apple tree. "Here they are," he said, and bustled off again without further explanation.

"My name is Warin, steward to Sire John." He didn't trouble to rise and greet them. He was bent and wizened, and had a wary expression on his wrinkled old face. Janna was at once sure that, no matter what she said, or what proofs she might offer, he would neither believe nor help her. She looked at Ulf, expecting him to say something. But Ulf shook his head slightly, making it clear that it was up to her to convince the steward to take them to her father.

"Yes? What do you want?" he asked, sounding annoyed at having his afternoon disturbed in this way. Janna wondered if he'd been asleep under the apple tree when roused by the doorkeeper.

"My name is Johanna." Janna took a deep breath to summon her courage and give her the strength to continue. "I am the daughter of Sister Emanuelle, whom your lord knew a long time ago."

The steward blinked in surprise. He clambered to his feet, the better to survey her. Clearly, he doubted her word. A sudden bark drew his attention, and his brows knotted together in a thunderous frown. "Kindly control your hound!" he ordered.

Janna followed his gaze and saw, to her horror, that Brutus had launched himself into a fine patch of lavender and was busy squashing the bushes flat in pursuit of some small creature. Ulf whistled, but Brutus ignored him.

"Unless you put that dog on a lead, you'll have to leave!" The steward sounded delighted to have an excuse to get rid of them. But Ulf merely grinned at him, rooted around in his pack for a moment, and hauled out a length of twine. He walked over and grabbed Brutus, who hung his head, knowing what was to come. The steward scowled at the pair. He seemed determined to ignore Janna. But she hadn't come so far to be thwarted now by his insolence.

"I am here to see my father," she said, demanding his attention. "I am here to see Sire John."

Warin blinked again. He turned to look at her, a closer inspection. A slow smile tugged the corner of his mouth, but his eyes stayed hooded and cold. "Sire John does not live here," he said. "He is in Normandy, with his wife and his family."

Time stood still. Reality seemed suspended while Janna struggled to absorb what the steward had said. *Normandy. Wife. Family.* Her numbed brain struggled to comprehend the calamitous news. She couldn't believe she'd come all this way for nothing. And yet it was what she'd feared all along. Her father was wed. He had a wife and a family. Even Ralph had warned her that her father might be in Normandy. Was that why he wouldn't tell her at once what he suspected? Had he wanted to check on her father's whereabouts first, and prepare them both for a more gentle introduction?

The fleeting warmth brought by the hope of Ralph's regard quickly gave way to icy numbness once more. "Does...does my father ever visit his property here?" she asked.

"No." The steward smiled spitefully.

"Then it's time he did," Ulf said, coming to Janna's rescue. "You knew Mistress Johanna's mother, did you not?"

Janna noticed his new formality with her name. She hoped it would be sufficient to impress the steward. She was grateful that Ulf had interceded on her behalf. Nothing like a persistent relic seller and a large dog to get to the bottom of things, she thought, as a faint spark of hope rekindled.

The steward didn't answer. Ulf took a purposeful step forward. Beside him, Brutus growled. Warin quickly skipped back, keeping a nervous eye on Brutus as he did so.

"Were you in your lord's employ when he brought Sister Emanuelle away from Ambresberie to live here?" Ulf tried again.

The steward stared at his feet and said nothing.

"Show him the ring, mistress," Ulf encouraged Janna.

In her confusion, she held out the swan's feather to Warin, then quickly snatched it away and proffered her other hand. The steward's gaze fixed on the ring. He raised his eyes to Janna, and she read there a grudging respect.

"So you must send for your master as a matter of urgency," Ulf said, taking another threatening step toward Warin. "I am sure you send messages on a regular basis, accounting for your management of his estates, and so on?" Warin gave a reluctant nod. "Then you must send him a message now. Tell your master that he has a daughter, Johanna, and that she awaits him here in Winchestre."

The steward looked from Ulf to Janna. She thought he was about to refuse, and spoke up quickly. "Let me have writing materials," she ordered, sending a silent message of thanks to Sister Ursel, who had given her the means to make contact with her father. "I shall write him a letter myself, and in it give proof enough to convince him that I am no impostor."

The steward hesitated. Janna knew that he would defy her if he could. She wondered if she was wasting her time, and if her message would even be sent.

"It is in your interest to send the message to Sire John immediately," Ulf said, with a gentle tug on Brutus's lead so that the hound lifted its head and bared its teeth at Warin. "How long will we have to wait, think you, before he comes over to England?"

"I cannot say!" Warin nervously licked his lips. "He may have to attend to more urgent business which may delay his journey, or even prevent it."

Ulf gave another gentle tug. Brutus gave a deep growl. Warin took several hasty steps backward. "Nothing can be so urgent as a meeting with his daughter," Ulf said slowly, making sure that his message was clear to the steward. "How long, think you?"

"Two or three weeks, maybe less?" Warin thought a moment. "It depends on how soon he can find passage on a ship, and also if the tides and winds are favorable."

"Then we shall return next week. And the week after that. And every day thereafter, until such time as your lord arrives. And we shall hold you accountable if he does not come. Please be quite clear about this."

Both Warin and Janna looked at Ulf with new respect. Janna wished she could utter commands so convincingly, then remembered how she had demanded that the steward provide her with writing materials. She'd made a start at least!

Warin gave a resigned shrug. "This way, if you please," he said. With his displeasure apparent in every disapproving line on his wrinkled old face, he stumped out of the orchard and through the garden to the scriptorium from which they'd come. Once inside, he gestured at a small table set beside a window so that it could catch the light. With an expression that showed he begrudged every courtesy he was forced to show Janna, he fetched a sheet of parchment for her use, and some sharpened goose quills. An inkhorn stood close by.

Janna looked at the closely written accounts she'd perused earlier, and swallowed nervously. She knew that her script could never match the steward's skillful lettering, knew that she would be judged and found wanting. Nevertheless, this was her first chance to communicate directly with her father, and she was determined to make the most of it. She sat down and picked up a quill. She hadn't had nearly so long as the steward to practice her writing, so she should keep her letter short. She didn't want to shame herself more than necessary in the eyes of her father.

And now the first challenge awaited her: How to address him? She recalled the letter written by the bishop to his brother, the king. What was good for the king would surely do for her father. She dipped the quill into the inkhorn.

"*To my honored lord and father, greetings,*" she wrote. It was a good start, she thought, marred only by a blotch where she'd paused too long and the ink had run. "*I am your daughter, Johanna, named after you by my mother, Eadgyth, who was once infirmarian at the abbey at Ambresberie. You will have known her as Sister Emanuelle. I have a letter written by you to my mother.*" Should she tell him that her mother had never read the letter, that she didn't know how to read?

No. Explanations could wait until later. Janna dipped the quill into the inkhorn once more.

"*I also have a ring with your crest, and a brooch with 'Amor vincit omnia' inscribed thereon,*" she continued. Would this be proof enough to convince her father that she really was his daughter?

"*To my great grief, my mother has died. But I am now in Winchestre and I hope that we may meet here very soon.*" Janna paused, and chewed thoughtfully on the end of the quill before recollecting what it was. She hastily spat out the splintered fragments. Should she say anything else? No, that was enough for now. How, then, should she sign herself?

"*Your loving daughter, Johanna,*" she wrote. Her father might think her presumptuous, but it was no more than the truth.

"Send this to your master without delay," she commanded Warin, taking her cue from Ulf.

The steward bobbed his head, and held out his hand for the letter. "I shall send it this noon," he said. "Pray, let me show you out, mistress." He shot a nervous glance at Brutus as he ushered them through the hall. Janna looked at the huge dog, which trotted close to the steward's side, almost shepherding him to the door. She smothered a grin. If anything could persuade Warin to do as he promised, it would be the close attention of Brutus. The thought was almost enough to make up for the disappointment of not finding her father at home.

"And so we wait," Ulf said, when they were out on the street once more.

"We need to find shelter while we do so," said Janna, her mind coming down to more practical matters.

"I can take shelter wheresoever I might find it, but what will you do, mistress?"

"Janna, Ulf. My name is Janna. That's who I am!" She was uncomfortable, had thought Ulf was putting on airs for the steward's sake. She hadn't realized he would continue to humble himself afterward.

"Janna," Ulf repeated solemnly. He jerked his thumb back in the direction of the gate. "Why don't you stay there? It's your father's home. There's no reason why you can't – "

"There's every reason why I can't," Janna contradicted firmly. "They don't believe in me; they've shown me no courtesy at all. No, I'd rather ask the sisters at the Nunnaminster to take me in. It's a convent, I believe. I walked past it on the High Street."

"Good idea!" Ulf nodded in approval. "Why don't we go there now? I'll escort you – that's if you wish me to accompany you?"

"Of course I do!" Janna was sorry the relic seller seemed to think she wanted nothing more to do with him. "I will still see you after today, won't I?" she asked anxiously. "Because I'd really like you to come with me when I visit that steward again. I'm so afraid my father won't come in person, that he won't want to abandon his own family. But if he sends a message instead, I doubt Warin will tell me anything – unless Brutus is there to persuade him!"

Ulf grinned, back to his former cheerful self. "If you wish it, then of course I'll stay in contact with you. Try to keep me away! I've never brushed so close against royalty before!"

"Royalty?" Janna gave a self-deprecating laugh. And yet it was true, she realized, stunned by the prospects suddenly opening before her. She had come so far since the dark time of her mother's death, further than she had ever dreamed possible. But there was still a long way to go before she could return home to seek justice against the lord who had brought about her mother's death. First, she had to find her father and persuade him of the rightness of her cause. But that wasn't the end. When she went home she would also have to face Hugh and Godric, and their wives and families, if by then they were wed. She shook her head, struggling to throw off the burden of memories and regret.

She must not think of them now. Nor should she dwell on the many mistakes and misjudgments she'd made in the past, for there was no turning back time to put them right. Instead, she must learn from what had happened. Learn caution, learn to guard her heart and her quick tongue. More importantly, she must learn who it was safe to trust, and who not. Her mother had been wrong to trust no-one. Ulf had shown her that. And not only Ulf. Others, too, had given her their help and their friendship when she'd most needed them. Since starting her journey she had learned much, including the wisdom to judge that there was still much for her to learn. And now she must look toward the future, and guard herself against errors of judgment and action, lest she jeopardize the success of her cause.

She looked down at the feather still clutched tight in her hand. "*It'll bring you luck, if you believe in it,*" Ulf had told her.

She would believe. And the feather would surely bring her luck, and her father with it.

Glossary

Aelfshot: A belief that illness or a sudden pain (such as rheumatism, arthritis or a "stitch" in the side) was caused by elves who shot humans or livestock with darts.

Alehouse: Ale was a common drink in the middle ages. Housewives brewed their own for domestic use, while alewives brewed the ale served in alehouses and taverns. A bush tied to a pole was the recognized symbol of an alehouse, at a time when most of the population could not read.

Amor vincit omnia: Love conquers all.

Baron: A noble of high rank, a tenant-in-chief who holds his lands from the king.

Breeches: Trousers held up by a cord running through the hem at the waist.

Carol: A song or music played for dancing.

Chansons de geste: Songs of heroic deeds.

Cresset: A primitive light made from a wick floating in a bowl of oil or animal fat.

Currency: While large sums of money could be reckoned in pounds or marks, the actual currency for trading was silver pennies.

There were twelve to a shilling and twenty shillings to a pound. A penny could also be cut into half, called a "ha'penny," or a quarter, called a "farthing."

Dorter: Dormitory.

Dowry: A sum of money paid for a woman, either as a marriage settlement or to secure her place in an abbey.

Feudal system: A political, social and economic system based on the relationship of lord to vassal, in which land was held on condition of homage and service. Following the Norman conquest, William I distributed land once owned by Saxon "ealdormen" (chief men) to his own barons, who in turn distributed land and manors to sub-tenants in return for fees, knight service and, in the case of the villeins, work in the fields. The Abbess of Wilton held an entire barony from the king and owed the service of five knights in return.

Garderobe: A small chamber for storing clothes; a latrine; privy.

Gong-fermors: Their job was to clean out cesspits and spread the waste over the fields.

Henricus dei gratia wintoniensis episcopus: Henry, by the Grace of God, Bishop of Winchester.

Hue and cry: With no practicing police force other than a town sergeant to enforce the law, anyone discovering a crime was expected to "raise a hue and cry" – shouting aloud to alert the community to the fact that a crime had been committed, after which all those within earshot must commence the pursuit of the criminal.

Infirmarian: Takes care of the sick in the infirmary (abbey hospital).

Lais: Narrative poems

Mathildis dei gratia Romanorum regina: Matilda, by the Grace of God, Queen of the Romans.

Moneyer: A moneyer (or coiner) was responsible for minting the coins of the realm.

Motte and bailey castle: Earth mound with wooden or stone keep (tower) on top, plus an enclosure or courtyard, all of it surrounded and protected by a ditch and palisade (fence).

Pilgrim: Anyone who makes a journey to a sacred place.

Postulant: Anyone who enters the abbey with the intention of becoming a nun.

Pottage: A vegetable soup or stew.

Requiescat in pace: Latin for "rest in peace." The letters RIP are still engraved on headstones today.

Sacristan: Looks after the sacred relics and treasures of the abbey.

Scrip: A small bag.

Scriptorium: A room in a monastery (or abbey) where monks (or nuns) wrote, copied and illuminated manuscripts. In a private home it served as the office of the estate.

Solar: A private room where the lord could retire with his family or entertain his friends.

Steward: Appointed by a baron to manage an estate.

Theod herepath: The people's way.

Tiring woman: A female attendant on a lady of high birth and importance.

Villein: Peasant or serf tied to a manor and to an overlord, and given land in return for labor and a fee – either money or produce.

Wortwyf: A herb wife, a wise woman and healer.

Faldo's Song (Chapter 10):

Stella maris, semper clara	Star of the sea, ever bright
Rosa munde, res Miranda	Spotless rose, most admirable
Misterium mirabile	Wondrous mystery

Author's Note

The Janna Chronicles are set in the 1140s, at a turbulent time in England's history. After Henry I's son, William, drowned in the White Ship disaster, Henry was left with only one legitimate heir, his daughter Matilda (sometimes known as Maude). She was married at an early age to the German emperor, but for political reasons and despite Matilda's vehement protests, Henry brought her back to England after her husband died, and insisted that she marry Count Geoffrey of Anjou, a boy some ten years her junior. They married in 1128, and the first of their three sons, Henry (later to become Henry II of England) was born in 1133.

Henry I announced Matilda his heir and twice demanded that his barons, including her cousin, Stephen of Blois, all swear an oath of allegiance to her. This they did, but when Henry died, Stephen rushed to London and was crowned king. Furious at his treachery, Matilda gathered her own supporters, including her illegitimate half-brother, Robert of Gloucester, who became her commander in chief. In 1139 she landed at Arundel Castle in England, prepared to fight for her crown.

Civil war ravaged England for nineteen years, creating such hardship and misery that the *Peterborough Chronicle* reported: "Never before had there been greater wretchedness in the country...They said openly that Christ slept, and his saints." The civil war mostly comprised a series of battles and skirmishes as the principal players fought for supremacy, while the barons took advantage of the general lawlessness to go on the rampage and claim whatever land and castles they could, some of them changing sides several times in the hope of advantage.

The year 1141 marked a turning point in Matilda's fortunes. Two brothers, the Earl of Chester and William de Roumare, seized and occupied Lincoln Castle by first tricking the guards into admitting their wives. The Earl of Chester subsequently changed sides to support the Empress Matilda – a welcome move, as the Earl of Chester's daughter was married to the son of Matilda's chief supporter, Robert, Earl of Gloucester. After some negotiation, Stephen eventually mustered his troops and went to reclaim Lincoln on an ill-fated expedition. According to the chronicle of Henry of Huntingdon, when Stephen heard Mass and, following the custom, offered a candle to Bishop Alexander, it broke in his hands. Henry wrote: "This was a warning to the king that he would be crushed. In the bishop's presence, too, the pyx above the altar, which contained the Lord's Body, fell, its chain having snapped off. This was a sign of the king's downfall." And so it came to pass. The king was defeated and imprisoned in Bristol Castle. The empress met with the papal legate, Bishop Henry of Blois (Stephen's brother), who promised his support, along with several other bishops and archbishops. There was also a meeting between Matilda and Archbishop Theobald in Wiltune shortly before Easter, at which time the archbishop held off promising allegiance until he had spoken to the king and sought his permission to "act as the difficulties of the time required" (to which Stephen actually agreed!) Matilda then made her way to London for her coronation.

A note about the hand of St James the Apostle. This relic was given to Matilda by her husband, the German Emperor, on their marriage. After his death, and to the dismay of the German people, Matilda brought the relic back to England. It was given to Radinges (Reading) Abbey by her father, Henry I, who was also buried there. I felt some indignation on Matilda's behalf (the hand was given to her, not to her father!) so I took the liberty of moving the hand to Wiltune (where Matilda's own mother had spent her childhood) on the grounds of safe-keeping, as Radinges was a hotly contested site throughout the civil war. According to the records, Matilda was at Radinges in March 1141, just before Easter and before she went to Wiltune, so it seemed a reasonable flight of fancy. I subsequently read Marjorie Chibnall's *The Empress Matilda* and the statement that, although the hand was meant to be at Radinges Abbey, "Henry of Blois somehow carried it off into his private treasury early in Stephen's reign" – so it seems that I have solved the mystery!

While King Stephen was incarcerated in the castle of Bristou (Bristol) after being taken prisoner at the Battle of Lincoln, the Empress Matilda prepared herself to take Stephen's place, supposedly with Bishop Henry's support. Shortly before her coronation in June, she was chased out of London by the queen's troops and the Londoners who had turned against her. She fled to Oxeneford, and spent July there, rallying forces and making promises to the barons, giving gifts of land and titles in return for their support. She had alienated many of them with her high-handed ways, including Bishop Henry, and when Robert of Gloucestre visited Henry in Winchestre in mid-July to settle their differences, he achieved little. He finally returned to Oxeneford to muster the empress's army.

In my novel, the letter gives evidence of Henry's treachery. A chronicle from the time, the *Gesta Stephani*, suggests that the bishop might well have been behind the London uprising. The same account also suggests that he may never have supported Matilda's bid for the throne at all. Other accounts date their falling-out from the time Matilda refused to honor her promise not to meddle in ecclesiastic affairs when she insisted on appointing William Cumin as the new bishop of Durham against Henry's wishes. But the real sticking point in her relationship with Bishop Henry was her refusal to confirm the Honor of Boulogne, held by the king, upon the king's son, Eustace. She may even have promised the title and lands to others.

Records show that the king received messages while incarcerated at Bristou: it seems fair to suggest that his own brother might have kept in touch with him (but perhaps not quite so indiscreetly!)

An early "history" of Stonehenge comes from Geoffrey of Monmouth's *History of the Kings of Britain* (written around 1136 and dedicated to Robert, Earl of Gloucester.) Geoffrey was also the first to write a coherent narrative of the reign of "King Arthur," the wellspring for all subsequent versions of the legend. These are the "new stories" related by Faldo to Janna. Geoffrey credits Merlin with moving the stones from Ireland to Salisbury Plain, the site of Stonehenge. He also refers to the healing properties of the stones: "They washed the stones and poured the water into baths, whereby those who were sick were cured. Moreover, they mixed confections of herbs with the water, whereby those who were wounded were healed, for not a stone is there that is wanting in virtue or leechcraft."

I've kept to the place names listed in the Domesday Book compiled by William the Conqueror in 1086, but the contemporary names of some of the sites are: Barford St Martin (Berford), Baverstock (Babestoche), Salisbury (Sarisberie or Sarum), Amesbury (Ambresberie), Oxford (Oxeneford), Winchester (Winchestre), Reading (Radinges) and

Bristol (Bristou). Wilton (Wiltune) was the ancient capital of Wessex, and the abbey was established in Saxon times.

Some of the most important accounts I have used while researching The Janna Mysteries include *Gesta Stephani* (The Life of Stephen), William of Malmesbury's *Historia Novella*, *The Empress Matilda* by Marjorie Chibnall *The Reign of King Stephan 1135-1154* by David Crouch, and *King Stephen* by R.H.C. Davis. For those interested in learning more about the civil war between Stephen and Matilda, Sharon Penman's *When Christ and His Saints Slept* is an excellent "factional" account of that history. On a lighter note, I have also read, and much enjoyed, the Brother Cadfael Chronicles by Ellis Peters, which are set during this period. While Janna's loyalty lies in a different direction, her skill with herbs was inspired by these wonderful stories of the herbalist at Shrewsbury Abbey.

While writing The Janna Chronicles, I have been fortunate in the support and encouragement I've received from so many people both in Australia and in the UK. In particular, my thanks to Dr Gillian Polack for her advice and assistance in all matters medieval. Thanks also to all at Momentum for their thought, care and expertise, and for enabling me to introduce the Janna Chronicles to a whole new audience.

www.ingramcontent.com/pod-product-compliance
Lightning Source LLC
Chambersburg PA
CBHW020818260626
47169CB00003B/727